# Girl

in a

# Pink Hat

*Nanzie McLeod*

First published in the United Kingdom by
Nanzie McLeod, Glasgow

The author has asserted her moral rights.

British Library Cataloguing-in Publication Data.
A catalogue record for this book is available from
the British Library.

ISBN 0 9529527 4 2

Origination by Robographics, Glasgow
Printed by Bell & Bain Limited, Glasgow

# Girl

## in a

# Pink Hat

Best wishes to Maureen
from Nanyie

We well hope for some good
business!

*Also by*

Nanzie McLeod

TALES
*of the*
ARLINGTON

✧◆✧

TALES
*of the*
EAST NEUK

✧◆✧

PITTENWEEM
SOJOURN

✧◆✧

I NEVER COULD DO
CROSSWORDS
A BOOK OF VERSE

# Contents

# INTRODUCTION

I started to write short stories when I became a grand-mother, nearly twenty years ago. Perhaps I felt I might now retire from my maternal, caring duties as my children were now producing a new generation? Of course that was not quite the case. Or perhaps I felt that I too should produce something and there is a strong maternal and protective feeling towards a story that one has written. Whatever the motive and however late in life, I started to write.

I have always been a late starter. For instance, I did not speak a word until I was two years old, using only mime to communicate. I am assured that when I finally started to speak, my pronunciation was perfect and I spoke in sentences (whether complex or not is unrecorded). Allowances should be made for the memory of a fond mother.

Perhaps my problem has been procrastination, the eighth deadly sin according to one of my stories. Perhaps I was just too busy doing the other things that had to be done in life. There were plenty of those. I was certainly gaining experience, if that is a prerequisite of the author. I have used that experience in some of the stories and relied on imagination in others.

I know that I read fiction for entertainment and relaxation, rather than education, and I tend to avoid those novels described as 'well-researched'. It might have been better if I had done more research, for, I have recently learned of inaccuracies in the story 'Toil'. I think it is now too late for corrections and if well-informed readers spot the mistakes, please accept them as poetic licence. Toil is a strange story anyway, with echoes of science fiction, that genre which was so enjoyable, a sort of fairy story, until 1969 when man landed on the moon. It is probably one of the first stories that I wrote down

I wrote 'Problem Solved' at the turn of the century. The starting point of that story is the Millennium Dome, which was then a hot topic. The Dome's design, size, cost and future use were constantly under critical discussion in the media. Comedians cruelly found it a hilarious subject to kick around. I realise that as the Dome has faded from public attention, my story has become dated and lost some of its immediacy. Should a copy of this book resurface in an Oxfam bookshop in forty years' time, I suppose that, just as quite trivial memories of life during the second world war are now so fascinating, this story might have some historical interest and might even be accepted as fact!

Sometimes the story that I think I am going to write does not materialise. I often lie in bed to consider all aspects of the subject, follow it well into the plot, describe characters to myself, imagine conversations, *then an entirely different scenario appears on my laptop screen!* It might be the same people in a different plot or even another group altogether. Sometimes it starts off in all the detail that I had worked out so carefully, then towards the end of the story, I realise that the development has taken me far from the original idea. This often happens to me and I suspect to other writers as well. It is difficult, if not impossible, to wrest the power back into your own hands. Probably best just to accept. I know I do.

The title story is an instance of this phenomenon. The cover is a self-portrait that I painted in my mid-twenties. I thought I would like to use it as homage to my lost youth. Surely it would not be too difficult to write a story to match the picture. That was where I was very wrong. I thought and thought, and each time I tried to realise those thoughts some other story appeared on the screen. Certainly I had three new stories but not one had any reference to a pink hat or even a to stern looking young woman in her twenties. Eventually I did produce a story. I am not particularly pleased with it, but into the book it had to go, as that was the title I had decided on. You can see from my portrait that I like to stick to a decision, once it is made.

'Cruise' is another story that would not get itself written. A few years ago I treated myself to a cruise. While it was not the most successful holiday of my life, it brought much grist to my mill, not all of which is yet ground up. I wanted to write a tale of mystery because there was a mysterious Mrs Wilson on board. My steward often spoke of her wealth and her sea-

sickness. I never saw her or heard a sound from her cabin. My
steward was very interesting and we had long conversations,
but sometimes he would leave me hurriedly, saying,

"Excuse me, I must just see how Mrs Wilson is."

I was intrigued by her possibilities, but I never quite
worked out the plot. I considered her as a successful lady
criminal, or a murdered corpse, even just a figment of the
steward's imagination, perhaps an excuse to leave me when he
felt that he had no more to talk about. He was a bit of a
blether, though interesting. I made several attempts to concoct
a thrilling but believable plot, but Mrs Wilson remained out-
with the scenario and eventually I allowed her to fade away.
Once she was discarded, I made six attempts to create my tale,
some of which stumbled and fell at an early stage. On looking
them over, I thought that some readers might perhaps enjoy
seeing the process as well as the product. It has become the
fashion for a work of art to require a considerable piece of
text to explain the artist's concept and development of the
theme and I have extended the idea to literature. Several
friends have advised against this, but then it is *my book*. Read
only number four if you like, for I consider it finished.

Arranging stories in some sort of order is almost as difficult as writing them in the first place and less fun. Here are
short stories, long ones, realistic, fantastic, set in foreign
locales, how can one decide? I tried. I wrote each title and its
category on a small square of paper and shuffled them about
in infinite permutations. It seemed impossible to make any
choice at all. However I do not myself always read a book of
short stories consecutively, so you, dear reader, must just pick
and choose.

# SPACE

It was three days after Robert's funeral that Sybil started to dance. Late at night after the sad-faced visitors had left, she had been kneeling on the rug in the sitting room. Her hands were clasped about her upper arms as though she were cold and she wept as she listened to the slow quiet music which seemed to express the sadness of the world. Without any conscious effort, she found her arms creating patterns in the air around her body, then she stood and developed the movement as much as possible in the restricted space. She was filled with astonishment. It was bizarre that she should dance in the middle of such grief. She felt ashamed. Surely dance was usually associated with joy, though perhaps in more primitive societies it was acceptable to express a sense of loss in this way. She had no idea, but dancing had certainly helped her at that moment.

She was pretty sure that she could not have stopped herself from dancing there on the Persian rug.

Of course Sybil had always danced. Sybil was born to dance. As a little girl she had, along with most of her classmates, attended ballet class for several years. She had gained excellent marks in exams and had been given solos in the annual displays. Sybil seemed able to marry her movement to the music in a way that even other mothers were, reluctantly, forced to admire. Later she had attended several workshops in London and delighted in the less restricted and more athletic movements of modern dance. But of course, when she became a wife and mother, she had stopped all her classes. It was Robert's suggestion that the extreme exercise might tire her too much and although she had not quite understood his reasoning, she had agreed to stop, in order to please him.

For three weeks after the funeral there was a procession of visiting friends and relatives, not one of whom realised how much Sybil longed for their departure. Their leave-taking shared a ritualistic similarity. In spite of her sadness, Sybil saw the comic side of this repeated ritual. The words were always delivered with a slightly tilted head and raised eyebrows above an unblinking and sincere gaze and were almost always exactly the same.

"Well, I think I'll just get away now, Sybil dear, if that's all right. And I think you should just go to bed now. My goodness it's nearly eleven o'clock. You'll be fine, won't you and if you want anything, just *anything at all,* ring me. Now ring me *any time.* I mean that, dear. Remember now."

And when she answered, they immediately straightened their heads, looking alert and on the qui vive to do her slightest bidding. They often bit their lower lip to convey their shared distress.

But Sybil needed no help, for what could anyone do?

As soon as the front door was locked behind the last visitor, Sybil would hurry to the sitting room and after pushing the furniture back as much as possible, she would dance.

As the days passed, her choice of music changed and her dance changed with the music. Shostakovitch replaced Schumann, Rachmaninoff replaced Chopin because slow and beautiful music was no longer sufficient. As well as the sense of loss there was considerable anger which required expression.

Although she had loved him so dearly, Robert had often made her angry in the fourteen years that they had been married. He was a man who had a strong sense of his own infallibility, a man who was determined to make all decisions for himself and for everyone connected with him, a man who always 'knew best'. There was much more than a flavour of the Victorian pater familias in his attitude. It was just unfortunate that his decision-making was so often at fault. Many times Sybil found herself in the position of dealing with the consequences of Robert's determined but impulsive decision-making. This time the consequences had been fatal.

She could picture so clearly the small crowded room in the Highland hotel. Twenty people from various parts of Britain, who were all hopeful of climbing the local mountain on the following day, were sitting in the antler-bedecked bar. The local policeman had come along specially to speak to them about the weather conditions. Sybil could remember his voice with its slow careful articulation, as he glared from below shaggy grey eyebrows at each individual in the room.

"Good-evening, ladies and chentlemen," Sybil was enraptured by his pronunciation of gentlemen. Just like Para Handy.

"I am here tonight to point out the dangers of climbing in this area when the weather conditions are unpredictable. Although I expect that all of you ladies and chentlemen, *unlike some people*," here he paused to great effect, sweeping his eyes around the faces in the room like the beam from a lighthouse, "all of you will have the correct apparel and suitable footgear for the mountain-climbing, but it is a hazardous business in the best of weather and I am sorry to inform you that the forecast for tomorrow is not a propitious one. I would remind you that, should you decide to ignore my advice, it is not chust your own life which you are putting at risk. In the case of accident there are others who will be involved in rescue work. And I would bring to your attention the three sad accidents which have already occurred this winter."

Sybil thought the policeman wonderful, however a sideways glance at her husband showed that he did not share her admiration. With a shiver she realised that, no matter what anyone said, Robert intended to climb on the following day and Robert became the fourth in the fatal accident statistics for that winter.

Once more and for the last time, Sybil had to deal with the consequences of Robert's unilateral decision-making. Yes, Sybil was angry as well as sad.

With the change in emotion, her dance required more space. She moved the smaller items to other parts of the flat. It was a large turn-of-the-century flat situated on a corner and the sitting-room was particularly spacious with a five-windowed bay and another large window. The floor was sanded and varnished and the room, apart from the bulky three-piece suite, made a very fair dance space. Robert had bought the suite as a surprise for Sybil and at the time she had enthused prettily as was expected of her. Robert liked to surprise her with additions to the household and though it was not the sort of furniture that she would ever have chosen to live with, she had accepted it as a fait accompli.

Two weeks after the funeral the small ads in the local paper offered,

*Smart 3pce suite for sale.*
*Bargain price for quick sale. Hardly used.*

The suite was sold and uplifted in two days. That night Sybil experienced a type of rapture on entering the large bare room and she danced on the golden boards until three.

It was now necessary to usher her sympathetic guests straight into the kitchen.

"It's so much cosier in here and we can sit at the kitchen table to drink our coffee. Would you like me to make you a pancake?"

And in spite of their remonstrances she would bake something and murmur about 'how therapeutic' she found it. The extra effort assuaged her guilt and made it unnecessary to consider moving to the sitting-room.

She knew she was being devious, but she was unable to give an explanation of her dismantling of the room to anyone. She knew that the truth would seem incredible to her loved ones. They might think that it was a fabrication to hide some complex motive. They might think that her sorrow had unbalanced her. She was particularly worried about how her conventional mother would react. The TV in the kitchen seemed reasonable enough and the rugs in the hall looked good but she knew she could not hide the bare room for ever.

Sybil's sons were immediately aware of the changes, of course. On the day that the suite went, Andrew, who was four, immediately fetched his tricycle and rode it round and round the empty room. The delighted expression on his face plainly showed that Andrew thought the lack of furniture a superb idea. Using magazines and cushions strewn on the floor, Sybil laid out a slalom course for the little boy and for an hour he concentrated on achieving a 'clear round'.

When the two older boys, Graham and Donald, returned from school Graham immediately removed his boots and started practising his cartwheels and hand-stands in the new-found space.

"Mum, could I have a mat for somersaults and straight back-leg rolls?" Graham was a dedicated gymnast.

Donald, after gazing at the room for a few minutes, went to his bedroom without making any comment. Sybil felt disappointed. She also worried that the destruction of the familiar environment might be really bad for such a sensitive eight-year-old. On the other hand, she realised that it was the first time that she had heard Graham and Andrew laughing since the accident.

The weeks passed and although there was a quiet sadness about many things that they did, there was no doubt that in a funny way life was easier than it had been for Sybil when Robert was alive. She was lucky that insurance and pensions would cover her financial situation for the next few years until she could return to teaching. Sybil now had to deal with all the accounts and though they did not have a lot of money, they had enough. She enjoyed planning their lives and their day-to-day routine was calm and happy.

Almost immediately after the accident, their schedule had changed. Breakfast now started much earlier, for one thing. Robert had never been at his best in the morning and had insisted that the children should not be fed before eight o'clock. But Sybil's midnight dancing seem to generate energy and she was happy to start breakfast at seven or even earlier, just as soon as the boys first wakened. She found them most forthcoming at that early hour. While Robert had always insisted on listening to the radio at breakfast, Sybil found it very easy to miss out on news of world-wide strife and disasters. It was far more fascinating to hear of the pleasures and fears of her boys. She learned many things about school that had puzzled her. Little Andrew was more anxious to display his declamatory skills than at any other time of the day and his repertoire of songs and riddles made for general hilarity. The evening meal, too, was eaten earlier and eaten with relish and with much conversation. The boys enjoyed tales of Sybil's own schooldays and even with the table-banging and the laughter, there seemed to be less cutlery falling to the floor and less milk spilt than formerly.

Nevertheless Sybil did not discuss her dancing with her sons. She felt that those hours of music and graceful, sometimes strenuous, movement were her secret.

As a child, one of her favourite stories had been that of the Twelve Dancing Princesses. The secret trapdoor in the bedroom, the woods with their leaves of gold and silver, the dark lake with the twelve handsome princes waiting in the twelve boats to row them to the lighted halls where they would dance all night, these scenes were the epitome of romance to the little girl who loved to dance. Imagining herself as part of the story gave her delicious happiness. She even liked to think of the tattered slippers lying beside the bed in the morning.

Now she had her own secret night dancing and she treasured it.

The boys knew that she danced, of course.

Donald wakened one midnight soon after the sitting-room was completely emptied and whispered,

"Graham. Are you sleeping, Graham? What's that music?"

After a long pause, Graham replied,

"Just Mum, listening to music, I expect. Go to sleep."

"But there's something else," Donald insisted. "what is it?"

His senses, sharp and alert as a young rabbit's, were aware of the gentle vibrations of Sybil's light leaping as they travelled through the joists and floorboards.

"Perhaps she's moving furniture again?" suggested Graham doubtfully.

"There's none left to move!"

The two boys lay and listened and each found a mysterious pleasure and comfort in the partly-heard music and the occasional and almost imperceptible tremor of their beds. As sleep started to overcome them, a small clear voice came from the cot,

"That's my Mummy dancing, again."

One Friday evening after dinner, Donald asked,

"Mum, can I take some chairs into the sitting-room?"

Sybil was so dismayed that she forgot to demand the obligatory "please". It was just as she had feared. Donald, unlike his brothers, had seldom entered the empty room, although he would often stand in the doorway gazing around at the floor and walls with a sad expression. She had deprived him of a normal home just when Fate had deprived him of a father. And now the poor child was about to try and recreate the lost environment.

"And could I have some blankets too. Please. I want to make a den for us."

"Oh, of course, darling. What a good idea." she tried to hide the relief in her voice. "I'd like you to bring everything back out again before bedtime though."

"No probs."

While Graham performed ten cartwheels around the room and a last few somersaults on his new mat before it became an integral part of the den, Sybil and Donald collected kitchen chairs, a stool, the coffee table, some large cardboard boxes and several blankets. Then, quickly and confidently, Donald started to construct an incredibly complex den. His brothers were delighted and immediately crawled inside, although Donald himself seemed inclined to stand and admire his handiwork.

"Did you know how you were going to make it before you started, Donald?" Sybil asked because she was most impressed.

"Oh yes I've been thinking about this for a while. Ever since the room got empty, in fact."

As it was Friday, the boys played until nine o'clock with Andrew sleeping under the coffee table like a little dormouse for much of the time. Sybil was happy to help them to clear it away.

"That was great fun," said Graham, "we could do that every Friday night." Donald blushed at the unspoken compliment paid to his creation.

Eventually, of course, everyone became aware that the sitting room was empty. But no one mentioned it. It was discussed and puzzled over amongst her friends, but no one liked to say a word to Sybil. No one could offer any explanation. It was obvious that she was 'coping' well mentally, and it was known that she did not need money. She had always been such a conventional girl. What on earth were her reasons? Everyone was intrigued but remained tactfully silent.

Sybil was surprised and amused that no one had said anything. Not even her mother. Sybil felt that, should the subject be broached, she must have some justification for the bare room prepared. She imagined various surreal explanations and thought of saying that the empty room represented the empty place in her heart, but was immediately ashamed of herself, because that was patently untrue. Of course there was an empty place in her heart. She had adored Robert, lived for him you might say. But the room was nothing to do with Robert, nothing at all.

One night, at the end of a particularly strenuous dance, she threw herself on the wooden floor and lay looking upwards at the light-fitting above her head. The sight of it always generated a faint feeling of surprise, as she remembered how much freedom Robert had given her in choosing it. That was unusual as Robert felt very strongly about all the household fittings and furniture, and while Sybil's preference would be discussed, the final choice was nearly always Robert's. With sudden clarity she knew that the room, if it represented anything, stood for her own personality, for her own self that she was discovering and developing.

As she realised this fact, a great relaxation flowed through her muscles and she seemed to discard the last of those small nagging feelings of guilt.

The day arrived that Sybil's mother, sitting in the kitchen said, "Sybil, about your sitting-room, dear."

"Yes, what about it?" She felt that her voice sounded aggressive but vulnerable. What on earth was she going to tell her mother? She had no idea and the shell of her new-found strength was still too soft to withstand the probing of a loving mother's questions.

"I was wondering, I don't want to be a bother or anything you know, but would it be possible..." at any rate her mother was having as great a difficulty in asking as she would have in answering.

"Well you know, your sister asked me to make those patterned curtains for her dining room and they are just enormous and I'm not at all keen but I thought if... I wondered if I could just lay the fabric out in your sitting-room and I could match up the patterns more exactly. Would that be all right, dear?"

Sybil smiled broadly.

"Of course, Mum, as long as it is all cleared away by the evening and there are no pins left lying around." and she hugged her mother's thin shoulders to take away the severity of her proviso.

# PASS THE SALT, PLEASE

He had asked her twice to pass the salt and both times she had ignored him. The three of them were seated at Sunday breakfast. They shared the house, more or less amicably.

Of course there were a few spats and disagreements, occasional jealousies and foolish misunderstandings, but they were genuinely fond of each other. Fred, Craig and Dora, two guys and a girl.

It seemed to work most of the time.

Fred smirked to himself. He believed it was called a *menage a trois*.

"What's that little secret smile about, Fred?" Dora asked in her softest, friendliest voice.

"Best not to ask!" said Craig, looking sideways and making one of his strange faces with the eyebrows up high and the mouth pushed out.

Fred asked for the salt again but instead of passing it, Dora asked him if he were enjoying his scrambled eggs.

Fred refused to answer. It was a stupid question, as she could see that he was eating them.

She was a girl of course and sometimes idiotic

"I haven't made them for weeks and I think I stirred them too hard."

Her tone was apologetic, but Craig was enthusiastic.

Overly so, Fred considered.

"I think they're just absolutely perfect, Dora." Craig leaned towards her as he spoke, "Really tasty and very filling! It's a treat! Just what I need to give me strength today when I have to work. What a *bitch* that job is! Working on a Sunday!"

Fred thought the eggs would certainly have tasted better with more salt.

Craig had added salt.

In fact it was Craig that had put the two little acrylic grinders of salt and pepper on the table, for Dora never added salt to food on her plate.

"I cook things with just the right amount of seasoning." she would assert, "Any more salt is bad for your arteries."

"To hell with my arteries. I'm too young to worry about that sort of thing" Craig would laugh and set the condiments on the table, then add them both generously to everything that he ate, grinding them gleefully over his food.

Dora did not smile at those times but looked down at her plate, as though measuring the salt content and her mouth was smaller and thinner than usual.

Normally Fred joined Craig in any laughter, but refrained if Dora might be offended. She was obviously never amused by the addition of salt to her cooking. Fred would frown slightly at the salt business to show how much he wanted to please her. Craig seemed to be so uncaring. It was a subtle method of gaining her approval, for Fred generally tried to avoid overt competition with the older, taller guy.

Besides, Dora did all the cooking and it would be a bad day if she decided to stop.

After forty two seconds, Fred's good intentions evaporated. His longing for salt grew to be too much. As his younger arteries were obviously in less danger than Craig's, he asked for the salt once more.

Dora turned her head and looked seriously and deeply into his eyes.

Fred felt faint, for she was a wonderful looking girl. Her hair was very smooth and dark in the shadows with bright sparkling bits where the sun caught it. Her mouth, when she was happy, was deep pink, full and shapely. As her blue eyes gazed meaningfully into his, he felt himself relaxing and relinquishing all desire for the salt. How well he knew that gentle curve of her cheek and the softness of the skin. How well he could imagine a sweet kiss from those lips. He was mesmerised.

Almost immediately she broke the spell by turning away to speak to Craig.

Fred's face darkened.

He hated when she did that.

It was so cruel.

It was as though she felt impelled to remind him that there was another man in her life.

She remarked brightly,

"I'll cut the grass today, Craig, if you have to go to the office. It's really long and I quite enjoy doing it."

That was another calculated insult. Why did she not ask him, Fred, to cut the grass? It was man's work.

He pushed some more scrambled egg into his mouth. Very tasteless!.

"I'll take those bottles and papers up to the re-cycling, too. Fred darling, you can help me, if you like."

Fred ignored this sop to his vanity.

He looked over at the salt.

He supposed it was foolish, but as well as the salty flavour, the grinder was something he yearned to handle. So many things were made of garish plastic these days, bright red, blue or yellow plastic. So cheap and nasty! You got tired of looking at those colours, but these chunky, clear acrylic grinders were very different. They were classic and pure, really well designed. Highlights sparkled all over those satis-fyingly smooth, crystalline twisting knobs, topped by silver screws. Inside the clear canisters, visible and tempting, were rough lumps of sea salt in one and multi-coloured pepper grains, really beautiful, like tiny beads, in the other. The simple mechanism was fascinating too. With a twist of the wrist, you could change the flavour of your food.

The desire to mill and scatter grains over his plate became an obsession and Fred asked with sudden irritation,

"Why the hell can't I have any salt?"

He felt better for swearing. Craig was always swearing.

Dora pushed her hair back and smiled vaguely at him, patting his hand.

"That's great, you've enjoyed that, now finish every bit and I won't have to do any washing-up!"

She often made that inane joke.

Fred looked quickly at Craig, who was spreading marmalade on an oatcake.

Craig had left a small pile of scrambled egg on his plate.

Why was he not adjured to finish every bit?

It was blatant favouritism.

An unbearable cocktail of injustice, frustration and jeal-ousy exploded in Fred's heart and, losing control completely, he shrieked,

   *"It's such a BITCH to be fourteen months old!"*

   Dora smiled as she popped the last piece of toast soldier into the wide open mouth, while Craig turned to the Sunday Observer sports page.

# Welcome Home Olive!

*Riverside Villa*
*Aberfeldy*
*5th September 2000*
*Dearest, darling Olive*

Jack and I were so thrilled to hear your voice on our answering machine when we got back from London last week. It was like a miracle! I could hardly believe it. All these years since we last heard a word, is it three? Four? Five? Cannot work it out and we had no idea where you were. Some folk said Australia and I *believed* them. I could have asked your Mum of course but I didn't like to get in touch with her. To be perfectly honest I was rather afraid.

But how wonderful to know that you are home again and we *must* meet up just as soon as we possibly can. Jack agrees. Really soon. It will be so wonderful, we'll break out the best champagne and have a real old natter, just the three of us. I can hardly wait! You know and I know that it would just be *criminal* to let all those years of friendship go for nothing. The past is the past and it's no use crying over spilt milk. I'm sure you must feel the same as I do. I am longing for you to come out and visit us here in the country and you really must stay for a few days. It's rather a big house and takes quite a lot of looking after, though I do have domestic help of course, but I know you would enjoy the walks by the river and through the little forest. I can hardly wait!

Do you remember that snap of us as babies sitting on a tartan rug? Do you know? I still have that photo somewhere, faded and curled at the edges. You had your cute little straight fringe and I had my fat cheeks and blonde curls and our two mummies were looking at us so dotingly. That photo looks almost historical now with those big bright patterns on the dresses. I just cannot credit that I am in my thirties, can you? I remember our teens so clearly. I often think of those sweet little blue velvet shoes that I wore to our school dance.

It was so kind and so typical of you to offer to lend them to me. I suppose I took it for granted then, but I do appreciate it now. And I don't think I ever returned them, did I? Oh we must must meet up, very, very soon. I am just desperate to have a chat with you and hear all about your exciting years in Canada. I would have you out tomorrow if I could, but we do have various things to organise before we go off to our time share in Spain next month and I hardly feel able to face the tasks which must be done. London is so terribly exhausting and we saw six different shows in four days. Jack adores the theatre, but of course you know that. I wonder if you are as keen a theatre-goer as you were in the old days? I would really much rather go shopping myself but Jack insists, and I don't mind the musicals so much.

Cannot wait to see you and give you a great big hug,
*Lots of love and kisses,*
Sue.


*Riverside Villa*
*Aberfeldy*
*10th November 2000*
*Dearest Olive,*
Thank you for your little note. I'm sorry to be so slow in replying. I always take a lot of time to recover from Benidorm, what with the dogs to be collected from the kennels and all the bills to be seen to, and the washing and cleaning to do after a holiday like that. To be very honest, we do rather over-indulge ourselves in Spain, restaurants are so cheap, booze too, of course. After that sort of bingeing I usually go to Weight Watchers for a few weeks, but this year I took a long weekend at that wonderful health farm in the Borders. Absolute starvation and such hard workouts, but it does the trick. Obscenely expensive of course but *instant results*! Marvellous.

Then there was bonfire night last week, we always have quite a big 'do' on the fifth with neighbours in for wine and nibbles after the fireworks, but that's enough about me. Fancy you being in Canada all these years, in the Prairies too. That sounds just so exciting. What adventures you must have had. I believe it is just a winter wonderland of snow! I bet you were skiing in the mountains practically all the time. The summers must have been glorious too, with the Pacific waves breaking on those long golden beaches and you take such a lovely tan, so easily. Jack and I have to be terribly careful with our fair skin. Just masses of Ambre Solaire, factor twenty-two. Of course I toughen myself up on the tanning beds in Glasgow before we take our holidays. I like to be a nice pale brown for most of the year. Don't you?

*I just wonder what you got up to when you were in Winnipeg, you naughty girl!*

You don't say much about it in your letter but everything is so luxurious and affluent in Canada, I bet you had the greatest time and I'm just dying to hear all about it. I'll ask you so many questions! Did you make lots of money too? It must be so terrific to travel. Knowing that you have been away in such exciting places makes me feel a lot better about what happened before you left. You know what I am talking about, as if any of us could ever forget! It was a terribly emotional time for all of us and I suppose that I should apologise, but that would not change things, Olive, would it? Nothing I could say could explain how things happened. We were impulsive or perhaps it was just Fate. Jack said that there was nothing else he could have done at the time. I know your parents were furious and the other two bridesmaids and the best man have never spoken to us since. In fact, quite a lot of people have given us the cold shoulder, old friends too, which seems unfair because I had known Jack just as long as you had.

Anyway I'm sure that we will surmount any last, little vestiges of ill feelings when we meet again. After all those years that we have known each other and we were more like sisters than anything, weren't we, I'm sure we will just forgive and forget. I certainly hope so.

Now about your visit, and I want you to be sure to stay overnight when you do come to us, but unfortunately it cannot happen quite as soon as I had hoped. It is Jack's fault really, he has business to attend to and then Christmas is getting so near by the time we are free so I'm afraid we must postpone our reunion until January but let's make it really

early in that month. I'll write again after we have all recovered from the New Year orgy-porgy. That takes about a week I
find, don't you agree? Shocking I suppose.

Jack says he will explain all about the cash when you
come down here. He says it's really very simple.

Looking forward to our reunion so very, very much,
*Love from your old friend,*
*Sue.*


*Riverside Villa*
*Aberfeldy*
*16th February 2001*
*Dear Olive,*
I must say I was terribly surprised by your last letter. It has
taken me rather a long time to reply, as I felt so hurt at your
tone. How was I to know that you had such a horribly difficult time in Canada? I find it very hard to believe that there
are slums and broken down shanty towns there. I always had
the impression that everyone in Canada lived a very comfortable life. I'm not doubting your word of course. And there
was no need to be superior about my ignorance. Geography
was always a boring subject and how was I to know that the
prairies were flat and thousands of miles from the sea? I'm
sure there are lots of things I don't know and don't want to
know, but I am certain that I have read that Canada has a
beautiful, very sunny climate. Perhaps you'll tell me the book
was wrong. And I have always thought that snow is absolutely gorgeous and romantic and I don't see how you could
ever 'get sick' of it. And of course I am sorry that you had
such a bad time and that money was such a problem, though
I hardly see that as my fault. There were so many unfair
reproaches in your letter. Someone else did actually suggest
that that disastrous day, you know what I am talking about
and I wish to God it had never happened, was bad for your
Dad and caused his heart attack the next night, but I would
never have dreamed that you too would believe such an
outrageous thing. It is *very* unjust. After all he was an old
man of nearly sixty and we never know what is ahead of us,
do we. Everyone knew how upset your mum was about the

whole situation, too. She certainly complained for months to anyone that would listen. And I cannot understand why you are so troubled about our using the same holiday bookings for our honeymoon. It seems so trivial. After all, you had both been to the Seychelles before anyway and the tickets would have gone to waste otherwise. I thought you were the one that was so careful about money. A propos money, Jack does not agree at all about the amount you mention. There is surely some misunderstanding. He remembers clearly that your loan to him was an investment in his business and was far less than *quarter* the sum that you speak of. He will, in time, return everything that you are due of course. Unfortunately nearly everyone in business is finding it sticky going just now and he could not possibly realise such a sum in the foreseeable future. The business has not gone just as well as we had hoped and times are tough. Perhaps you will come out here for lunch some day and he will go into all the details and explain it to you properly, for it is very complicated. I know I'm hopeless at that sort of thing and I expect you are much the same. Maybe in a few months' time, it would be convenient for you if he could arrange small weekly repayments. I am sure there is absolutely no necessity for involving a lawyer. After all, we are all old friends, although I was terribly crushed by your letter.

As for the astonishing news that you have a child of three years old, I really do not know what to say! Yes, everyone knows that you and Jack were living together for years before the wedding was arranged, but honestly the fact that the little girl is very fair proves nothing. There must be many fair men in Canada and as I have said before, nobody knows what you got up to out there. It is extremely disruptive to suggest that this child belongs to my husband. It is nearly four years since you left the country and we certainly have not heard a word from you, not even a postcard.

I feel I cannot write any more just now. I am too upset.
*Sincerely, but very dismayed,*
*Sue.*

*Royal Hotel*
*Aberfeldy*
*1st March 2001*
*Olive,*
You are *terribly* mistaken to demand that my husband has a DNA test and I think that the letter which your lawyer has sent to Jack accusing him of embezzling funds is quite outrageous. I am sure that any papers which you may produce will be *completely unable* to prove that you gave Jack anything like that enormous sum of money.

Jack and I have been so upset by your behaviour since your return from Canada that we are living apart for the moment. I hope you are satisfied.

Your actions hardly seem to be those of a sane woman and I am afraid you must just accept the consequences of those actions. It is very regrettable, but our life-long friendship is now completely and utterly finished. Nothing that you could say will ever, ever change my mind.

*Sue Robertson.*

# AMANOHASHIDATE

We were standing on a high hill looking down at a calm grey sea below us. At our feet vivid splashes of what might have been rhododendron blossom, but was not, cascaded down the hillside. One misted mountain was close to us while others disappeared gradually into the ethereal distance. A fine cool rain was falling or rather seemed to hang in the caressing air. I felt relaxed and happy with memories of other similar scenes of exquisite, though damp, beauty on the West coast of Scotland. But though I felt so much at home, I was in Japan and gazing down on Amanohashidate or The Bridge to Heaven, one of the three major natural beauties of that country. If it seems strange that such a beautiful country as Japan should have only three designated beauty spots, it is necessary to understand how much ritual and how many small rules still govern life in that country on the other side of the world. Rules and ritual which the less-disciplined West has long discarded or perhaps never had. In my own lifetime I have seen many mores disappear, for instance my parents would have been horrified to be seen in the street without a hat and though too many rules and regulations can certainly be restrictive, sometimes it is as difficult to deal with too much freedom. But probably my Grandmother was saying the same thing when she was my age. And there is no doubt that things are also changing in Japan.

Amanohashidate is a large and ancient sand-bar which connects an island with the mainland. Created over the centuries by the action of the Sea of Japan, this two-mile long barrier now protects a large area of sheltered coastline where picturesque fishing villages line the shore, their houses built on stilts and their boats moored neatly underneath each house. The boats still have access to the open sea at either end of the sandbar, where modern swing bridges turn smoothly on their own axes, allowing visitors to walk the two miles from the mainland to the island through the ancient

pinewoods which clothe the 'bridge' and amongst which
shelter small temples, shrines and holy wells, with here and
there pretty wooden cafes which cater for the less spiritual
part of man. The inner, protected side of the 'bridge' is
buttressed with a strong stone wall while the outer or sea side
has a series of seven or eight graceful sandy bays reaching
from one side to the other. At regular intervals, lines of stout
wooden posts help the bays retain their symmetry. The bridge
is a perfect example of the Japanese genius for controlling
and gently redirecting Nature in an unobtrusive and aesthetic
way.

However these details were not yet apparent to me, as I
stood and looked downwards at the gracefully winding
Bridge to Heaven. I was with my friend Chihoko, a lady who,
married to a Scotsman, has lived her life equally in the East
and the West. She was the raison d'être of my visit to Japan
and with her indefatigability and enthusiasm, her instructive
knowledge, her amusing anecdote and her caring companionship, she was a guide such as few travellers can ever have
had, a courier beyond compare. We had made an excursion
that day from our hotel, travelling in a small clean train that
moved sedately through thick forest and mountain tunnels,
astonishing us at intervals with suddenly disclosed scenes of
small villages or farmhouses surrounded by watery fields
awaiting the planting of the rice crop. Chihoko talked of
happy memories of planting rice as a child although her
pinky still bore scars of harvesting the tough stalks. With
delicacy and understatement she described her family's
adventures towards the end of the war. Her father, a high-
ranking medical officer in the Japanese navy, feared for the
safety of his wife and five children as the end of the war
approached. He decided to move them from the city to some
remote property which his brother owned in the country.
Chihoko's mother a pale and sophisticated lady, no doubt
used to the conveniences of a town and adequate domestic
help, was forced to learn how to carry water, to cook outside,
to grow her own food, and to wash clothes in the river beside
the sun-burned peasants. It cannot have been easy for her,
although her daughter obviously had such good memories of
that time.

The city which they had left behind them was Hiroshima.

Finally the train left the delightful tunnel of pines, bamboo and blossom and we drifted across a vast plain surrounded by mountains until we reached the sea and the village of Amanohashidate. Chihoko had visited this beauty-spot before with some English students. On that occasion she had viewed the scene from the hillside on the island on the opposite side of the 'bridge'

"It was raining that time too!" she muttered ruefully as she put up her umbrella.

On leaving the neat little station we followed the directions to the 'Ropeway to the Viewpoint' or at least Chihoko did and I followed her. It is humbling and no doubt salutary for a person of my years and experience to find themselves unable to read directions or communicate with your fellow man. It gives one an insight into the outings of young children or dogs. One follows obediently and unquestioningly to an unknown destination, while underneath there are regular moments of panic in case one should lose sight of the leader.

The rain had stopped by the time we reached the entrance to the ropeway. Chihoko told me that there was a 'vehicle' to take us up the mountainside to the viewpoint. I suggested it might be a funicular. No, not a funicular. Perhaps the gondola type of ski-lift with which I was familiar in Europe and North America? Yes, perhaps. That is what it was on the other side where she had taken the students. Chihoko nodded. Perhaps, yes.

We bought our tickets for the 'ropeway' at a little kiosk with a brightly coloured banner above it, then ascending further, we turned a corner and my heart nearly stopped. We stood at the foot of an immensely steep hillside. A narrow gash had been cleared through the thick forest to a point far above us and, in a continuous shaking and unsafe paternoster procession, about one hundred brightly painted, little, dangling, tin seats ascended and descended the hill again, just like those famous soldiers of the Duke of York. As it was early in the summer they were all unoccupied and it seemed as though they travelled for no reason other than their own pleasure. As I stood there in a slight daze, an attendant appeared, grabbed a seat as it was still moving and wiped some of the dampness off with a piece of sackcloth and indicated that I should seat myself. Before I could question my own resolve, I stepped into the pathway of the chair and found myself swept off my feet and launched into the air. There was no safety belt and it was a very small seat and being taller than the average Japanese my thighs sloped downwards in an entirely unsafe way. I clutched the pole which suspended the chair from the moving chain above my head in my right hand and held my handbag convulsively in my left, that handbag which becomes so vital when you are far from home, with money and passport, airline tickets, travellers cheques, camera, notebook for telephone numbers of English-speaking friends in Japan, not to mention the miniature Swiss army knife which my daughter gave me, assuring me that it was a necessity when circumnavigating the world. Almost immediately the grassy incline was fifteen feet below my dangling sandals and as the ground continued to fall away from under my feet at a terrifying rate, I wondered who would be able to recover my bag, should I drop it.

As well as being petrified, I was also alarmed to hear shouting behind me and wondered if Chihoko were all right but, "Sauve qui peut", I could not have looked round at that moment if my life depended on it.

The shouting was in fact the attendant admonishing Chihoko to,

"Put up your umbrella! Put up your umbrella!" in that bossy way of public servants which is recognisable to any Glasgow citizen. Amazingly she did put up her umbrella, courageous creature that she is. Even if I had had one of those useful appurtenances, I should never have dared to unfurl it in those first precarious and panic-stricken moments.

However, as the whiteness faded from my knuckles and I relaxed and accepted the situation and realised that I was quite secure, I started to appreciate the unique quality of the experience. Firstly it was much quieter than most methods of travel, certainly travel through the air, although there were a few squeaks and groans as the chair passed each of the little supporting pylons. Secondly it was wonderful, indeed *magical* to be flying so gently and so slowly beside the tree tops at the edge of the clearing. Although I could not quite touch the foliage as we trundled upwards. I could observe and smell the aroma of a variety of beautiful and healthy trees. The perfumes were fragrant, aromatic or resinous and wafted past me as I drifted past. With the mist of rain and the music of the unseen birds in the forest, it was an exquisite and unique experience. I compared myself to Titania carried aloft on her throne by fairy cohorts and wished that it could last for hours.

Too soon we reached the summit, where another attendant grabbed my chair for a brief moment, allowing my feet to touch the ground on the exact spot indicated. A circle with two footprints was painted in bright yellow with an arrow pointing the direction that I should take in order not to be bowled over by the relentless procession of chairs. Or perhaps even more humiliating, to be picked up and brought down ignominiously to the foot of the hill once more. To make absolutely sure of my safety, I took hold of the attendant's arm like a long lost friend. When he had helped Chihoko to dismount, he furnished me with an umbrella. Many tourist attractions there have a supply of these articles, as rain is just as much a part of the Japanese life as it is of the British, although I do not think they complain about it as much as we do, as though it were some strange unexpected phenomenon.

And so we reach the point at which I began this story with the view spread before us, a view strongly reminiscent of excursions to sea and mountains on the other side of the world.

Not only is Amanohashidate designated as one of the three most beautiful views in Japan, there is a special way in which to view it.

Just as when in the tea house, one should at first admire the 'place of ornament', then seat yourself and eat the tiny dry cake which is served before the frothy green tea (whose strength will astonish you) which must be drunk in three and a half sips, the last sip being slurped with a little sound in order to indicate that you have finished. Just as these rules exist in the teahouse, so on the viewpoint, you must step up on to the viewing platform, turn your back to the view, then bend over and peer between your legs at the view for several moments. *Matanozoki* is the word for this inelegant position. There is a rail to hold as matanozoki will quickly bring on dizziness. Perhaps this very dizziness enhances the hallucination, because the sky becomes the sea and the sea becomes the sky and the sandbar bridges the gap between them. I have to say that my sail through the treetops had put me in the mood for all sorts of wizardry and I certainly thought it looked like the Bridge to Heaven.

After the first few minutes we were joined by other tourists, all Japanese. Husbands gallantly held umbrellas and assisted their ladies to mount the platforms and though some ladies had the handicap of a long skirt or voluminous trousers all obediently bent over and keeked between their legs while photographs were taken of them 'matanozoki'. But I am sorry to report that everyone came up smiling and shaking their head, They had not seen it as a Bridge to Heaven!

Sacrilege!

They should have lied.

Of course it looked like the Bridge to Heaven!

After enjoying the space and distance in front of us, I became aware that there was a fairground on the level part of the hill behind me. It was painted in beautiful subtle colours, quite unlike its garish western counterpart and the pretty Ferris wheel, roundabout, complicated helter-skelter and snack bar were quite charming, though closed at the moment. Why had I not noticed these bright playthings before? And who would use them? Surely no parent would trust their child to one of those little dangling metal seats without a safety belt? And the idea of carrying a small wriggling child on sloping thighs on that long slow ride made me shiver. There was no other approach that I could see. What a mystery!

We returned to the steep path which led back down to the travelling chairs, but the attendant waved his arms violently and motioned us back up the hill. I did not need language to understand his gestures and realised, almost before Chihoko did, that we were going down the 'up' pathway and *it was not allowed* although there was not one other tourist in sight just then. We turned and walked farther along to the correct exit, passing a charming terracotta statue of twin babies. A bib of red gingham was tied around the two little necks and in front of them were fresh flowers and some coins as offerings. It was all protected from the rain by an incongruous golf umbrella advertising a racing car.

"It's a shrine for 'lost babies'. Miscarriages and abortions." Chihoko explained to me.

At some point a P.A. system had started to play background music which I had hardly noticed. Music is everywhere in Japan. Neither Japanese music nor the irritating muzak of department stores is heard, but often classical Western music, which I found delightful. This was not classical however and I had paid little attention to it. At the moment that it first struck my consciousness, just before we started our descent, a popular song from my girlhood was being played, a sad and evocative tune of nearly fifty years ago. I expect all young people have special melodies which are forever entwined with a particular person. At the risk of sounding very corny, this piece of music conjured up for me the picture of the boy I met at my first ball, when I was seventeen. This young man, we shall call him S, was very tall, handsome and debonair and he drifted and danced in and out of my life for the next seven years, always seeming to be taller, more handsome and more debonair than the other young men in my life. I do not know when I had last heard that tune, but I knew it must be forty years since I had seen S as he had gone to London at that time and married someone else, much to my grief. There seemed to be a special glamour attached to outings with S and my mind was filled momentarily with brief subliminal pictures of the times we had spent together. I realised that just as important as his brown curls and charming smile, were the memories of myself as I was then. I remember a Sunday morning motorbike ride when I wore 'pedal-pushers' which were half-mast trousers and the *de rigeur* leisure wear for the Hollywood starlet of that era. Elizabeth Taylor was often to be seen lounging underneath a blossoming tree in those particular nether garments. Mine were tobacco brown and made of an expensive linen-like fabric called moygashel, which gave them an added status. Another trip with S was to the country, in his father's car and I was dressed in a favourite navy blue dress with an extravagantly long fluid skirt and the nicest little shoes of red suede,

punched with flower-shaped holes. Yes and it was with S that
I went to, what seemed to me the acme of sophistication, a
dinner dance at Foresthills Hotel which was situated on beautiful Loch Ard. I thought it an excitingly long drive from
Glasgow for an evening date. I wore yellow that night and
was so nervous that I could hardly lift the glass of sophisticated dry sherry to my lips without spilling it. It was S who
suggested, as my driving test approached, that I should prac-
tise a hill start with a match below my back wheel in order to
achieve absolute perfection and I still do make sure that that
necessary manoeuvre is perfectly accomplished. And yet there
was one fly in the ointment, one important lack in the attractions of this paragon. If I remember correctly, he disliked cats.
Profoundly disliked them. This one fact would have precluded
any future happiness for us as a couple, I fear. For forty years
my house has never been without at least one cat.

What narcissistic memories of that naive and untried
young woman. A girl with too many romantic dreams and
too much energy spent on what seemed to be *comme il faut*.
Strange to think of the complex and demanding life that lay
ahead of her.

And what of S? Had his life been rewarding? Successful?
Happy?

Forty years is a long time and it would be as wrong to say
that I had forgotten him completely as it would be to say that
he had never been out of my thoughts. No doubt on the rare
occasions that I heard our 'tune' I would think of him, as I did
now, fleetingly and then dismiss the memories. One night
about nine years ago, however, I dreamed about him. I was a
mature grandmother, earning her living, indulging her
hobbies of gardening and swimming, doting on the new baby
and I do not know what might have inspired the dreams but
they were very vivid and brought S to the forefront of my
mind. The dreams were so clear that the next morning I wrote
a poem. I had just started to write poetry, or rather verse, at
that time (a very therapeutic pastime) but I know that one of
my daughters thought it a sad and beautiful poem and
wondered about this part of her mother's past.

As the familiar melody on the P.A. system stopped, I
suddenly remembered a strange coincidence. While doing his

National Service in the navy, S had visited Japan! He was the
first person that I had ever known that had been there. He
had been enthusiastic about the country, saying it was very
beautiful and rather like Scotland. Surely he had awakened
my first interest in this distant country, all those years ago?

What a patched, darned and embroidered piece of fabric
is the mind, lying in its many folds and is it wise to shake it
free of dust too vigorously?

Shrugging off those powerful memories, I again experienced a slight shock of panic as I was swept off into space by
one of the indefatigable little chairs. But the downward
journey was even more delightful, as the beautiful view
slowly dropped out of sight. There was also more feeling of
unlimited air and space beneath one's feet.

Intoxicating!

As I descended, some Japanese tourists were ascending
and we passed each other, smiling broadly and bowing
dangerously from our precarious perches.

Next Chihoko and I walked over the Bridge to Heaven,
strolling through the pine forests, admiring the picturesque
shrines. I drank some water from a holy well, against
Chihoko's advice, I may say. We sat on one of the perfect
crescent beaches and I removed my sandals and dipped my
toes into the waters of the Sea of Japan, regretful that I was
not swimming, though it was fairly chill, but no colder than a
cool day at St Andrews, I judged.

My real regret of that day concerns a photograph. I took
some attractive shots but one was *not taken* and it is always
the one that was not taken that sticks in your mind. Beside a
small restaurant, which was closed, stood a six foot high
board with an oval hole cut out near the top. It was exactly
similar to those we see at English seaside resorts with a
skinny gent or a fat lady in antique swimwear depicted
beneath the aperture. This one had a wonderful samurai in
dramatic kabuki pose, flourishing his swords. Why oh why
did I not position myself and have Chihoko take a photograph
of me? What foolish shyness or inhibition stopped me
sticking my ugly mug through that hole and opening my
mouth wide in a Kabuki snarl? What a lost opportunity!

On returning to the station we found that we had an hour

to wait for our train. A television set at the coffee bar was showing Sumo wrestling. As we sipped our excellent coffee, Chihoko explained some of the finer points to me and I realised that, surprisingly for a serious-minded academic lady, she was an enthusiast and an expert, familiar with the names and careers of each contestant. Watching Sumo in a Japanese railway station seems much more fascinating than in a British sitting room and I was particularly entranced by the grace and ritual of the exquisitely attired referee.

Back in Scotland four weeks later, a very strange thing happened.

The previous year I had taken part in a BBC documentary about the Arlington Baths, the long-established Glasgow swimming club to which generations of my family have belonged. It was a very good programme and though its first showing had been only in Scotland, it was now to be shown nationally. One week after it went out, there was a message on my answering machine from S, that distant memory from my past! He had seen the programme in London, recognised me and found out my phone number from the club. Forty years ago he too had been a member of the Arlington, although at that time the sexes were strictly segregated and we had never met at the club.

Now I must return his call and shall I tell him of the poem of ten years ago? Or of that evocative tune on the hillside at Amanohashidate?

# PROBLEM SOLVED

There were long queues at each of the twelve entrances to the great white circular building and the crowd shuffled forward slowly in the gentle rain. Multicoloured umbrellas and waterproof coats glowed like massed blossoms in the laser lights which constantly played over the vast area. In spite of the dampness, the atmosphere was festive with smiles and vivacious talk. Sometimes a loud roar of laughter would ring out and others would turn with bright expressions, ready to share the joke. All corners of the British Isles were represented by the myriad accents. Soft western vowels jostled with flat northern ones and the general repressed mumble was here and there drowned out by a self-confident Oxford enunciation or by the loud uninhibited tones of those determined 'to make a night of it'.

A small rosy cheeked man with a military moustache and loose false teeth was declaring, in the clipped singsong of suburban Edinburgh,

"I certainly feel very lucky tonight, m'dear. Just you wait, I've got it all sewed up. Down to the last digit. Absolutely sewed up."

His wife, taller, younger and doleful, showed no reaction. She had listened to this assertion for six days. After a pause, she asked,

"How will we meet up afterwards if you do get picked for the electronic slates? How will I get back to the hotel, Jack? I wish I hadn't come at all. I could have visited Sheila in Twickenham."

"Nonsense, nonsense m'dear. Of course I'll get picked for the E.S. The odds are terrific. One in ten of all ticket holders here tonight will be picked and those are excellent, excellent odds m'dear. Believe you me, I'll be up on that platform at the end and they'll come and collect you to join me."

"How could they possibly find me in such a crowd, Jack."

"There'll be no problem finding you with the technology that they have at their command, m'dear."

"I do so hate being lost in crowds. It takes me back to..."

He interrupted her hurriedly, "I've explained it all to you before. Cheer up m'dear, and just trust me. And take a taxi if you get lost. Expense won't matter after tonight."

His hearty chuckle sounded empty as his wife turned her unsmiling face in the opposite direction.

Behind them stood three young women whose shrill Cockney speech rose above the general hubbub that enveloped the looming structure beside the river. Breathless after a bout of giggling, and communal pushing, the tallest of them demanded,

"And can you reelly count all them distant relatives? Even if you ain't never met 'em?"

"I bloomin well 'ope so. I'm dependin' on Uncle George and 'is bloody big family. Three wives! Imagine! Wotta godsend! I never would 'ave got it to work out otherwise."

This was a thin bespectacled girl in a spectacular water-proof, printed with blue roses.

"Was he divorced or are they...?"

"Ow, dead... they're all dead. Don't think divorce counts."

"Sure it counts. I don't see why it shouldn't. If you're goin' to drag in cousins from Australia, I think divorce should count."

This was a dark petite girl who spoke so defensively. She was the child of divorced parents. "Well I'm not sure about the Australian cousins, unless the rules have chinged."

"They're always chingin' the rules but as long as you 'ave the birth stifficate and a contact phone number, s'all right, ain'it? So's they can check the details tonight, y'know."

"Wot I don't understand," said the tall girl, "is wot is a squire root?"

The three girls screamed and leaned against each other in helpless raucous laughter.

"I'm serious! Is it to do with relatives? Goin' back to your roots, y'know? Is that whorrit's abaht?"

The dark girl spluttered,

"Lucky you ain't a contestant, Glad. I'll explain later, when we're drinkin' the bubbly."

Next in the queue, huddled under a large umbrella, stood a farmer and his wife from Yorkshire.

"Art sure we're at the right entrance, Peg?"

"Aye our tickets say E and look up there above us... high up, higher up you great gormless..." She slapped his shoulder affectionately, "What does it say? It says E! So we mun' be right."

"It's a terrible big buildin' this. I wunner why they made it roun'? Summat t'matter wi' a roun' buildin'. S'not sensible. How're ye to ken where front nor back is."

"Just you get the numbers to work out right, old dear. D'ye remember all the things we went over? An' doan't forget the tractor registration."

"Ah'm not like ta make a mistake after all they years o' bloody forms ta fill, God how I hate 'em."

The plump wife smiled fondly and squeezed her husband's arm.

"Perhaps after tonight we'll be givin' it all up."

"Naw, they doan't give the same big prizes they used to. They doan't hand out the millions no more."

"An' rightly so. There was awful things happenin' to the poor souls that won so much. Families splittin' up and suicides and there was a murder even..."

"Doan't you believe it. That's just a tale ta save the government money."

"Surely not, Ah read it in't papers. Anyway it's rare to be away from the farm for a night or two just us together. I've wanted a holiday for a long time. Ah liked comin' down t'river in that little boat."

They leaned their heads together and she kissed his cheek.

"Ah just hope the boys manage wi'out us."

"Course they will. They be men now, my dear, though you might not admit it. Just you be sure an' get picked for the slates."

Behind them stood a family party. A mother and two daughters were chattering excitedly to a handsome boy of eighteen, who frowned as his mother repeatedly smoothed his hair and twitched his tie and jacket.

The father, slightly apart, spoke furtively into his mobile phone.

"How is he? Oh... still compos mentis is he? And his breathing? No, no morphine... not yet. don't give it yet...

no... unless he is very distressed of course. Yes yes... in that case, naturally, I suppose... of course... but it does weaken and we only need another few hours."

The father turned back towards his family smiling heartily.

"Everything's fine in Norwich. Grandad's sitting up and had his supper and sends you his best wishes, my lad. He's sure that counting him will bring you luck tonight."

But the youth was too nervous at the ordeal ahead to consider his grandfather as other than a number.

It was now eighteen years since the government had launched the National Lottery and in a brilliant 'double whammy', a favourite political phrase, had solved two problems. The Lottery offered ordinary people the prospect of becoming very, very rich at a time when they were feeling particularly poor and as the people themselves provided the impressive sums which would bestow happiness on all, it was self-financing. Miraculously, as well as making a nice little pile for the businessmen who ran it, the lottery also gathered in a tremendous amount of money for hospitals, charities and cultural pursuits which the State could no longer afford to subsidise at that time. It was a heaven-sent gift for the financially strapped government and it was embraced with delighted enthusiasm by the British public, always so ready for a flutter. There were few folk who could appreciate the immense odds against winning, for with the advent of calculators and electronic tills the ordinary man in the street had lost much of his familiarity with numbers. The idea of millions of pounds was just too dazzling and it was simple and convenient to buy your ticket at supermarket or corner shop. Even the Post Office made it handy for pensioners, parents and the unemployed, who, when collecting their modest stipends, could invest in one of the flimsy numbered slips, which might well be the ticket to a financial heaven. Soon the lottery was held twice weekly and most conversation in pubs, discos, or at dinner parties, centred boringly around the spending possibilities of many millions.

Not everyone was happy of course. Bankruptcy stared Ladbrokes and Littlewoods in the face and they paid off thousands of workers. The Church, in spite of its own dependence on raffles and tombola, denounced gambling as sinful. Then some unfortunate winners came to grief with nervous breakdowns or sheer self-indulgence. When syndicates won, there were often nasty squabbles over exactly who had paid into them. That human sin of greed, always most obvious in the loving family circle, sometimes led to sensational headlines such as the two sons who tried to have their father committed as insane, because he wanted to spend five million in reforesting Wales. Then there was the man who felt it undesirable that a multimillionaire be burdened with a fat, grey-haired, fifty-year-old wife and discovered, expensively, that even a hundred thousand was not enough to make her disappear quietly. The tabloids loved it.

Many sensible folk pointed out that smaller prizes would be fairer and any ordinary person would be happy with fifty thousand. Only a millionaire really knew how to deal with several million. However the government insisted that the gambling instinct was only aroused when prizes were temptingly enormous.

Naturally the Opposition tut-tutted in the usual self-righteous way of oppositions and pointed out that the working man was pouring money into, "opera, ballet etc. effete things which he had always held in healthy disdain". However when the Opposition won the next election it retained the Lottery and its financial benefits, unaltered.

It was five years later, when takings from the Lottery were slowly but very definitely dropping, that the new government was forced to consider a change.

A think tank of distinguished psychologists, lawyers and advertising men received satisfyingly colossal fees to solve the problem of the wilting lottery. Unfortunately after six months of research and debate, they could not agree on the reason for the decline, nor on any way to avert it.

Then it was passed to the Scottish Parliament, who, apart from the fiasco of their new headquarters, had acquired the name of being clever with money. They had no more success than the think-tank.

Eventually a Scottish MP created a reputation for himself by bringing the government's attention to one of his constituents from the East End of Glasgow, a man called Jimmy Wheeler.

Jimmy was in his sixties and had worked all his life in the business of conning people and making them happy to part with their cash. In his youth he had travelled to fairgrounds around the country. settling in the city each winter for the Carnival. He had experience of all the gimcrack games that can squeeze money from the gullible. Starting with hoop-la stalls and moving to open-mouthed clowns and rolling pennies, he had graduated to rifle ranges, Houseyhousey and the Wheel of Fortune A particularly observant man, there was nothing that Jimmy Wheeler did not know about tempting the punter. Nowadays, Jimmy had a leathergoods stall in the Barras, that colourful Glasgow fleamarket, where you can buy anything from an ostrich feather fan to a motor bike, a battered saxophone to cut-price bed linen.

The shrewd MP brought Jimmy to London and prepared to act as his interpreter.

Jimmy Wheeler, in Buchanan tartan trousers and a bright blue leather jacket of unique cut, stood on the luxurious Downing Street carpet and self-confidently lectured the Prime Minister and his staff. Highly articulate, though uneducated, Jimmy needed no interpreter and he was not nervous. Talking was what he did best and he projected his rapid-fire speech at the PM and his aides just as naturally as he would have done had he been stationed at his ramshackle stall in the Barras, while trying to shift a new consignment of Spanish handbags to reluctant Glaswegians. Frequenters of the Gallowgate market had listened to him rehearse for this moment for forty years.

"Whit yur reelly needin' is mair jookery pokery in yur lottery. Aye, ye see ye've goat a' they wee ba's drappin' doon wi' the numbers oan thim an' the music blarin' an' some big show-biz bugger therr smilin' an' earnin a forchune but it's deed borin' fur the punter. Thur's naethin' fur'im tae dae an' then it's a' over, quicker'n a fart an' he disnae even see the winner guzzlin' his bubbly. Thur's nae reel excitement an' it looks cheap tae. Y'see in this day n'age ye're needin' mair technology. It disnae look tae me as though ye'd spent the cash. Big prizes right enuff, but ye need mair nor that, mair action, mair puzazz, mair usin' yer brains... studyin' form, like. Know whit Ah mean? Whin yur doin' the pools ye like tae choose yer favourite teams, don't ya an' ye like tae know the names o' the hoarses or the dugs at the track. I'nt that righ'?"

He smiled condescendingly to the Prime Minister, who seemed about to speak but was not quick enough.

"But nooadays the punter hisnae goat ony haund in it. It's nae fun whin ye're jist watchin' an' no' daein' nuthin'. Noo tak Housey-housey f'rinstance or Bingo if ye like, they hiv thur caird an' they've goat tae keep an eye oot an' listen noan-stoap fur tae mark thur cairds right... keeps thim busy, makes thim feel useful, lucky. An' mebbe if thur birthday or thur hoose number comes up or they use a lucky pencil, they'll win, see. Wee things like that keeps thim interested, makes thim feel "Hing oan noo. Try again!" ye know whit Ah mean?"

He punched the prime minister on the arm, not gently.

"D'y'unnerstaun' whit Ah'm gettin' at, mate? They need tae hiv mair tae wark oan thursels an' it needs tae be mair personal-like an' they need tae hiv mair o' a chancet o' winnin'. Big prizes is a' verra weel but we a' like tae *win* even if it's only a plastic rabbit or a hauf deed goldfish..."

"You think that personal involvement is really so important, Mr Wheeler." The PM, rather desperately interrupted, determined to regain some standing.

"Absotively *yes*, a thousand percent *yes*, and plenty flashin' lights too, they always go down a treat. Now if you would so like, Ah will draw you up a wee plan that A've been turnin' over fur dunkeys an' ye kin see if ye like it..."

Wheeler's plan, always referred to in Government circles as the 'jookery pokery lottery', was basically an arithmetical problem. A similar idea had been used in a popular TV game show of the last century called Countdown. Carol Vorderman, the mathematical lady who had demonstrated the puzzle all those years ago, was still attractive enough to be offered the plum job of checking that answers were correct in this new national competition. The game consisted of a pre-established number announced by the Government on Friday night. Each contestant, by mathematically manipulating their own

personal numbers which might be the number of children or
brothers and sisters or just bona fide relatives, birth-dates,
telephone or house numbers, car registration, National
Insurance or employee number, must be able to juggle all
these digits satisfactorily to reach that week's stated goal and
thus gain a prize. These numbers could be added, subtracted,
divided or multiplied to reach the particular number required
that week. Contestants must send their entry fee by Monday,
but only ten thousand would pass through the electronic 'net'
and be invited to travel to London and compete. The competition was held each Thursday. By Tuesday those who had
passed through the first 'net' would receive word to go to
London on Wednesday. Those lucky ones who were called,
were given hotel accommodation but paid for their own food.
They could bring guests, although guest tickets were very
expensive, but it was agreed that the spectacle and the excitement were well worth it.

The event was held each Thursday in the Millenium
Dome which had been constructed to celebrate the turn of
the century, but which had since become a derelict embarrassment to the Government. Hotels and transport firms were
able to offer special mid-week 'lottery deals'. Ten thousand
ticket- holders and their guests converged on London every
Wednesday and many arranged to stay longer in the hope
that they would have winnings to spend. A large part of the
tourist industry was drawn back from the brink of
bankruptcy by Jimmy Wheeler's jookery pokery lottery.

Of course there was the second 'net' to pass through, for
only one in ten lottery ticket-holders queuing at the twelve
entrances would be ushered to the 'electronic slates' in the
plastic Bubble of Silence. This enormous pressurised sphere
within the dome would house the lucky thousand final
contestants in a protected world, while they hopefully
covered their miniature computers with numbers. The nine
thousand losers, whether frustrated or relieved, must discard
their hopes and resign themselves to watching with the ordinary guests in the tiered seating which lined the vast
auditorium. Strangely, it was the friends of losers who
tended to petulance, even violence, in their disappointment.
The losers themselves often experienced a sense of relief, for

the stress of the occasion was overpowering. Normally, several contestants would faint, even before they took their place within the Bubble and there had been two heart attacks, neither fatal, fortunately.

The time allowed for calculation was twenty five minutes, uneccessarily long and seemingly interminable to the contestants, as each checked and re-checked.

The tension was almost unbearable in the tangible silence of the Bubble, each concentrating face of the lucky thousand illuminated by the flashing lights around their 'slate'.

While laser lights were playing over the sweating competitors, television cameras were swinging and dipping amongst the crouched figures. When the gigantic desperate face of a loved one appeared on the mammoth overhead screens, hysterical laughter and cheers were to be heard from different parts of the vast concourse. But the competitors, protected from noise in their plastic womb, continued to work out their sums as quickly and clearly as possible.

It was an experience that no one would ever forget.

When the shrill siren announced 'handing-in' time, the audience erupted into violent noisiness, screaming crazily and producing rattles, drums, trumpets and whistles which they used enthusiastically, if not musically. Some groups did bring more sophisticated instruments, saxophones, trombones and French horns were popular and there were usually several violins. In the incredible cacophony which followed the 'handing in', only snatches of jazz and Vivaldi were likely to separate themselves from the horrible noise and establish their identity in a miraculous way.

Inside the Bubble, most of the exhausted competitors produced balloons from their pockets and proceeded to blow them up. It had become accepted that this was the best therapy and would relieve the tension, while awaiting the result. Soon several thousand brightly coloured balloons floated upwards in the Bubble, adding to the carnival atmosphere.

Technology made it possible to check the results in less than twenty minutes and when the time arrived to announce the hundred winners, it was never more and never less than one hundred, a cathedral-like hush enveloped the entire audience.

The presentation was deliberately low-key. The lucky contestants were called and left the Bubble, while the unlucky others remained seated. Looking stiff and dazed and smiling uncomfortably, the winners were cheered as they tottered along a fifty metre red carpet towards an exit. They were then bundled into limousines, where they would find their elated friends and relatives awaiting them. All winners were then swiftly and adroitly removed from the area immediately surrounding the Millennium Dome. It was imperative that any unpleasant incidents be avoided.

The evening finished in an anti-climactic silence as the audience left the Dome.

The crowds who poured from the many exits of the surreal building were orderly and quiet, with few smiles. Even the lasers seemed slow and dim. The excitement was over and now there was the difficulty of getting home. This had always been the insoluble problem of the location. As usual, the last ferryboat had left, there was a dearth of taxis and there was no option but to join the long queues for train, bus or underground.

Later in the evening, many would relive some of the evening's excitement, for a few of the winners would be interviewed on TV, sitting awkwardly in their hotel bedroom, submitting themselves to the strange, but mandatory, custom of a sticky shower from a shaken bottle of Champagne.

There was one important long term result of the Jookery-pokery lottery, unlooked-for, yet highly acceptable. Without any directives from the government, Britain started to climb out of the educational pit into which it had fallen. Because it was necessary to be numerate in order to have any chance of winning the contest, the popularity of arithmetic soared amongst school children. Four-year-olds chanted their tables instead of nursery rhymes and eight-year-olds discussed quotients and lowest common denominators with enthusiasm. Soon, interest spilled over into mathematics and eventually encompassed other subjects. More and more children left secondary school with excellent exam results and eventually, British universities achieved renown throughout Europe.

It is not too much to say that Jimmy Wheeler's brilliant idea changed the face of Britain and re-established her in the eyes of the world. A knighthood was suggested, but Jimmy was content to bask in glory at the Saracen's Head on a Saturday night, re-living his lecture to the PM.

As he said repeatedly to his weary fellow-tipplers,

"Surr, Jimmy disnae sound like a bloke wi' a stall in the Barras, noo dizzit? An' Ah'm no' wantin' a new career at ma age, am Ah? Naw, Ah wiz jist happy tae gie thim a wee tip. Help thim oot, like. Aye, Ah'm jist gled it worked sae weel an' solved a' thur wee proablims".

The lasers were switched off. Most of the crowd had dispersed. Apart from the looming circular building, the scene now held little interest.

The Edinburgh man stood stamping his feet and looking sharply from side to side with his fierce red cheeks. What a disaster of a night! Not even picked for the slates! He looked in vain for his wife, but she was drinking tea in Twickenham.

The thin bespectacled London girl was furious with herself, "Wotta damned fool I was! Why did I make that bloody mistake? How could I? I practised it over an' over! What a fucking wally! An' I was so nearly right!"

Her companions tried to comfort her and when the usual consolation of a drink was suggested, she finally smiled. The four girls linked arms and rushed smoothly away from the Dome, their pale stockings flickering in the darkness as they shouted,

"Champine! Champine! Let's 'ave some more Champine!"

The family from Norwich showed every sign of despair. The young man, untidy and with head hanging, walked alone, while his sisters whispered behind him. His parents strode ahead with stony faces.

The farming couple from Yorkshire were now several miles away, smiling and sitting close together in the back of an obscenely long limousine.

The cheque for £50,000 was carefully tucked away in Peg's handbag.

# THE CRUISE · 1

" Perhaps you'll meet a millionaire and we'll never see you
again!"

"I don't know that I'd like to be in the middle of all that
ocean. Scary."

"Perhaps you'll put on a stone with the masses of delicious food!"

"I hope you're not sea-sick, I mean to say the Bay of
Biscay in October might be really..."

"Will you have your own cabin?"

"What sort of clothes will you take? You'll need warm
jackets the first week and the next week you'll be basking in
the Med!"

"Lucky old you."

"Will you be dancing every evening?"

"Have you got something sparkly to wear, I bet they'll be
very dressy."

"Will you be sitting at the Captain's table?"

"Won't you feel a bit strange all by yourself?"

"Of course not! She'll meet lots of folk."

"Won't the people that you meet be rather snobby and
play bridge and that sort of thing."

"I'll bet she has an embroidery class started before they
are three days out of port."

Although the talk was girlish and excited, all the ladies
sitting around the kitchen table were, as the French say, of a
'certain age'. Each Monday evening they met in Elsie's house
to pursue their hobby of embroidery and Elsie, who had taken
her diploma at the Art School was, if not exactly the teacher,
certainly the recognised expert. She was the oldest of the
group and also incidentally the only one without a husband
and she was amused that her announcement of taking a
cruise should generate so much excitement. At the same time
the mixed reactions touched on issues which had not
occurred to her. It was strange that no one in that well-
travelled group of middle-class ladies had ever been on a

cruise and this invested Elsie's holiday with adventure and glamour. The soft wools, brilliant silks and coarse linens were laid aside for the rest of that evening and all creativity was diverted to extravagant speculation and fantasies concerning the delights or horrors of the cruise. It was a hilarious and enjoyable night.

Elsie had met a few people who had indulged in marine holidays. One friend who had consoled himself with a trip on the QE2, after his wife of twenty-five years had left him, found, from the moment of embarkation, that he was bombarded by free drinks, billets doux, even cabin keys from unknown ladies.

Another acquaintance had, ad infinitum, recited the story of her torrid love affair afloat. Awash with drama and emotion, the affair had continued from one cruise another. As the protagonists were older than Elsie, as near seventy as dammit, it struck her as unseemly if not obscene. But then that woman had always been a nymphomaniac.

It was twenty five years since Elsie's divorce and she prized her independent life and no matter what the romantic magic exerted by those billowing ocean waves, she had no intention whatever of finding another husband.

Another oft-told tale of cruise ships was the delicious quality and decadent quantity of the food made available at all times of day and night. This she saw as a more real problem, as her tendency to plumpness could be horribly accelerated by two weeks' over-eating combined with the less energetic life aboard ship. She would have to be careful.

Elsie had decided to take this particular cruise for three reasons. It left from a port near her hometown. It docked at Lisbon and Barcelona, two cities which she was anxious to see and it finished in Athens where she could visit an old school-friend. Perhaps most importantly, it was inexpensive. Elsie told herself firmly that this was a bargain cruise, that you only get what you pay for and resolved that there would be disappointments which she must accept philosophically.

# THE CRUISE · 2

She had always known that there might be drawbacks but she was prepared for them. That would be part of the adventure. Since Gregor had died twelve years ago, Clare had tried to make her annual holiday unusual in some way. All those long ago summers at Carnoustie, making the best of it on the windy beach with the children, while Gregor golfed. Then the evenings in the family hotel, with Gregor replaying each stroke. Oh! so dreadful. She could never bear to dwell on those suffocatingly boring vacations. No wonder the kids had started to arrange their own holidays in their early teens. And yes, she had fussed and worried about them camping and bicycling by themselves, but mostly she was envious. And it was no use wondering now why she had continued to accompany Gregor. It was easiest. But with his death she realised that those opportunities for seeing or learning or doing something new and exciting were now available for her to grab. And each year she did something that was novel or just a little bit dangerous. You would not have found her mountaineering in the Hindu Kush or rafting down the Amazon because she was physically quite timid, but it was amazing how interesting quite inexpensive holidays could be. Sometimes just the fact of travelling alone created mysterious possibilities. In the twelve years of her widowhood she had enjoyed a theatre week in London, marvelled at the vulgarity of the Blackpool illuminations and wandered delightedly around the imposing art galleries of Liverpool. She had visited the castles of the Rhine and wine-tasted in Burgundy, enjoying the charming countryside from a luxurious coach. She had sampled yoga in a dilapidated mansion in Ayrshire, but had been discouraged by the elitist attitude which those who achieved a spiritual experience held towards those who merely considered it exercise. She had tried her hand at book-binding in Oxfordshire and at haute cuisine in Skye. She had visited Paris in August when all the museums were closed but had found that walking in the streets of that beautiful city was sufficiently intoxicating. She had travelled to Athens and taken various excursions to archaeological sites whose ancient atmosphere was almost overpowering. It was on one of these excursions, just twelve years after her husband's fatal heart attack and when she was still in her forties, that she had been 'picked up' and asked for a date. She was astounded and completely unprepared because it was a situation she had never considered possible. Partly because of this unprepared-ness, she found herself agreeing to have lunch and then to visit the Acropolis on the following day with this stranger. She had been enjoying the challenge of climbing up the punishing slope which leads to the site of the Delphic Oracle when this elegant man, whom she had noticed as one of the other passengers on the bus because of his unusual height, had started to speak to her. He spoke in French which was a struggle for her school-girl attainments.

That he was black added an exotic touch to the adventure.

# THE CRUISE · 3

Aileen stood in the middle of her cabin and reminded herself of her resolve to be philosophical. She would take the rough with the smooth. He who expecteth nothing is never disappointed, etc. It was a cheap cruise and you get what you pay for. The company had had a lot of adverse media publicity throughout the year, publicity which her friends had been swift to point out. Beleaguered by staff problems, technical problems, a fire in the kitchens, even an outbreak of infection in the water supply, the newly-formed company was forced to cancel some cruises. Typically Aileen had swept these unwelcome facts to a distant corner of her mind for, as well as being inexpensive, the cruise visited several charming places in the Mediterranean and once Aileen had decided on a course of action, she seldom changed her mind.

Now, faint forebodings of claustrophobia made her wonder if she should have paid the extra two hundred pounds for a cabin with a porthole.

Keith had always demanded the best, in spite of growing up in a room-and-kitchen. Perhaps because of that. His extravagance had often horrified Aileen with her background of genteel poverty. Now Keith was once again demanding the best, trading in his second wife for a younger model, just as he had done with Aileen thirteen years previously, after fifteen years of marriage. Not for the first time, Aileen wondered if her desire to take a cruise was generated by this news. That honeymoon of twenty eight years ago was her only other experience of being at sea and though brief it had been wonderful. She would never forget that feeling of being adored and of being alone with Keith for the very first time. After the months of back-breaking work on the house and the preparations for the wedding, the unaccustomed leisure to enjoy pacing the decks of the Scandinavian ship, with its marvellous food, seemed so luxurious. There was also the added feminine delight of every article of clothing being brand new.

She particularly remembered the experience of having a bath onboard. It was the North Sea and although not particularly rough, Aileen was entranced to find that the water in her bath heaved gently from one end to the other with the motion of the ship. At one moment the bathwater would envelope her shoulders and chin while her feet and legs would be completely stranded. Next the water had moved to the other end of the tub, leaving her without water from the waist upwards. She had not realised that a bath at sea would behave like this and she found it mesmeric and sensuous. That bath, unique and evocative, was to remain one of the clearest memories of her honeymoon.

However, there was no bath with this cabin. The shower was incorporated in the small toilet cabinet and Aileen had grave doubts about its practicality. An example of the technology of nearly thirty years ago, the shower head hung high above her and when she had tentatively turned it on, the trickle had soaked her sleeve to the elbow. She giggled at her own foolishness and noted that the store of clean towels and extra toilet rolls would certainly need to be removed before using the shower.

There was a gentle tap at the door and,

"Mrs McGregor? I am your steward, Andreas."

The slender Asian's charming smile showed exquisite teeth. She admired nice teeth and when he emphasised the first and lingered over the last syllable of her name, a name which she had always hated, it acquired a foreign and exotic quality. Aileen immediately felt more cheerful than she had done since the long embarkation process had started that morning.

"I hope to be able to help you in any way. I have brought your copy of the daily news sheet. Is there anything else which you require just now, Mrs McGregor? Extra blankets perhaps?"

His voice was a pleasant baritone and his English almost perfect. Aileen liked a nice voice. They smiled warmly at each other as she shook her head vigorously.

"I only sleep with one blanket." she said and then blushed as it seemed rather an intimate thing to say to this handsome young stranger.

"I shall remember, Mrs McGregor." and with the hint of a bow, he left her, closing the door noiselessly.

Aileen glimpsed herself in the mirror, tilting her chin up slightly to sharpen her jawline. A very nice young man. She examined the lock on her door. Could he enter if she locked it from the inside she wondered? Not that she was worried. He was obviously a most trustworthy lad. More than a lad, perhaps late thirties?

She glanced through the news-sheet. Just as she had thought, nothing much of interest for her. Aerobics? No. Line-dancing? No. Bingo-bango-bongo on the High Seas? certainly not. Paper-flower making? possibly. Special offers on sessions of hairdressing, facials, manicures, massage? She would not normally indulge in these sybaritic delights and they seemed very expensive. Afternoon tea served on the open deck at four o'clock? That sounded appealing,

She looked forward delightedly to fourteen days of sipping tea at four o'clock with the weather steadily improving as they neared the Mediterranean.

The news-sheet also advertised that every evening there would be the cabaret, orchestra and dance floor in the lounge bar, a *very talented* piano player in the cafe bar and the disco starting at midnight. For the adventurous there was the casino with its gaming tables and slots. What on earth was a slot? Aileen wondered. She felt very ignorant and determined to find out as soon as possible. She smiled, she could ask Andreas. How lovely to have him to rely on. There was a cinema too showing a film each evening after dinner. There was plenty on offer. Unfortunately apart from the afternoon tea and perhaps the cinema, nothing particularly appealed to Aileen.

"I suppose I'm difficult to please, too set in my ways. Perhaps it was foolish to take this holiday on my own." but it was not Aileen's way to regret mistakes.

After washing her face, she set off to familiarise herself with the layout of the large old ship, tramping along corridors, interior and exterior, climbing up and down flights of stairs, locating key features, the purser's office, the dining room, the cinema, the small swimming pool in the bowels of the ship. The last was a period piece with its dated mosaic murals. Six inches of cloudy water splashed back and forth in a desultory and unpromising way. The twenty-eight thousand ton ship had been built in the sixties and much of the decor reminded Aileen strongly of her youth. The pool would have seemed very modern and impressive to her when she was in her teens.

With a few mistaken directions she eventually returned to her cabin which was the last one at the end of a long corridor in the stern of the ship. Andreas was hovering near her door and greeted her with apparent delight. She wondered if he had been in her room checking over her belongings but dismissed the thought.

"Do you like the ship, Mrs McGregor?" he pronounced it 'sheep', Have you been exploring? I think you are a lady that likes to find out about things. Am I right?"

 "I suppose I am. It's a very big ship isn't it?"

"Yes, but I have worked in larger ships. Certainly more modern ones."

He smiled his charming smile.

She was really exhausted after the long day and her exploration of the seven decks of the ship and had thought she might lie down and read for an hour before dinner, but Andreas stood between her and her door and was obviously ready for a conversation. It was flattering that he should want to talk to her and she appreciated that. They talked for thirty five minutes in a way that to Aileen was strangely reminiscent of her early teenage encounters with shy boys at the tennis club or the Saturday night hop. She and the Philippine steward found out about each other's families, favourite occupations, foods, music. They discussed different parts of the world that they had visited and found that their opinions and general likes and dislikes often coincided. They had both visited America but preferred Europe, especially Spain and Italy. They talked about ballroom dancing which Andreas was determined to learn and about Aileen's latest hobby, bookbinding. It was such an enjoyable and agreeable chat that Aileen almost forgot how tired her legs were.

"Now, Mrs McGregor..."

"Call me Aileen." Even with an exotic intonation she hated McGregor.

"Aileen? Yes perhaps you would like to change now for dinner. It is served at eight tonight, Aileen, I must not detain you." and, pronouncing her name in a unique caressing tone, and smiling his ravishing smile as though he would have very much liked to detain her, he suddenly and silently disappeared around the corner. Aileen felt that there should be a puff of smoke where he had stood.

Aileen threw herself on the bed and laughed out loud. Her legs positively ached but she felt like a girl and, for the first time, she had a pleasant and happy feeling about her cruise. She was going to enjoy it. She hoped that it wasn't a mistake to get on first name terms.

At dinner the sturdy lady on Aileen's left asked in a broad Lancashire accent,

"Art goin' t' Bingo, tomorra?"

"I've never been to bingo..." this statement astonished the lady into silence.

"I'd like to try it if I could come along with you maybe?"

"Aye, glad to, glad to."

Two elderly gentlemen joined them, one was very deaf and the other fulfilled his part in any conversation in the strongest of Glasgow accents. Two younger couples, with a flavour of the Midlands in their voices, kept themselves very obviously apart from the older contingent at Aileen's end of the table. Lastly two ladies from Belfast joined the group. Unfortunately the older, dominant lady, heavily weighted in gold garniture and unwilling to give anyone credit for knowledge or opinions, dogmatically corrected and disagreed with every remark made. She seemed to have remarkable hearing, because while correcting the neighbour on her left, she could pick up on mistakes made by someone sitting three seats away from her on the right and, breaking off her original conversation, would trounce the distant offender's statement and 'put them right' before returning to settle the hash of the unfortunate who sat beside her.

The poor young waiter, who was Puerto Rican, could make very little of the complexities of accents around the table and invariably brought the wrong dishes to the wrong people, aggravating the atmosphere of aggression and hostility. As the food was mediocre, Aileen decided that at least she must have congenial company and would not submit herself to this particular group of people for two weeks.

On returning to her cabin, she felt a slight shock to find her bed turned down, with just one blanket on it and her nightgown laid out on the bed as if on display in a shop window. Tiny perfect pleats radiated from the gathered waist, flaring the skirt out to its fullest width while the sleeves were arranged upwards, as if in a wild dance. Andreas was a master of his art but she valued her privacy and really, personal servants were so much out of her experience. How on earth had the Victorians managed? By ignoring staff completely, she supposed, but then she had been brought up in a more democratic culture, working alongside her once a week cleaning lady and sharing jokes with her over coffee.

That night Aileen lay in her narrow but comfortable bed and enjoyed the thought that she was travelling feet first through the waves, southwards.

At breakfast it was 'first come first served' and she knew no one at the large round table. The complexities of accent and different orders again confused the waiters and most people looked cross.

It was hardly the way that Aileen liked to start her day but she was amused to see the bowls of cereal brought with the milk already added. No one seemed to object to this quaint custom. After demolishing their cornflakes each person was soon doing battle with a piled plate of two eggs, four rashers of bacon, two fat shiny sausages, a mound of baked beans and a fried tomato.

Aileen felt a little lonely as she enjoyed a virtuous fresh fruit plate.

# THE CRUISE · 4

K enneth would never have approved of her taking this cruise. His clear, exact voice echoed in her mind every day with advice and criticism. She had never considered him particularly critical while he was alive, but perhaps she had been unobservant or blinded by her love for him, for she had always accepted his decision-making without question. Now that he was gone, it was surprising how often and how continuously she heard his familiar, clipped accents expressing disapproval of what she planned to do.

"Not safe. My little Molly would be far too unprotected. And it's a cheapskate sort of business. If you must travel on a ship, take the best. How about one of these Scandinavian superships or even better, the QE2. Spend the money and you won't have any regrets. Always go for the best, my dear. It's safest in the long run, you'll find. Just mark my words, you only get what you pay for."

Throughout their life together, dear Kenneth had taken complete charge of their finances and he had always 'gone for the best', insisting that they bought the best house, car, food and clothes. If Molly were tempted, as she sometimes was, to buy a cheap and cheerful hat or some other bargain garment Kenneth would veto it,

"No, no! Commonplace, terribly commonplace. I don't like bargains. That's not the sort of thing for my lady-wife. No class at all! Give it to a charity shop, for God's sake."

Molly had been fascinated and overwhelmed by this attitude to money, for she had grown up in genteel poverty where every penny counted, stockings were mended and old outfits adapted. As he was fourteen years older, it never occurred to her to question Kenneth and it was a charming experience to be so cushioned in life. However, after his fatal heart attack, it was obvious that Kenneth had not looked ahead to a protected future for his little Molly. There were no savings, no insurance policies, no pensions, only the house and car, neither completely paid up. Kenneth had lived for the luxurious moment. Molly moved to a tiny flat, gratefully found an ill-paid job in a flower shop and at forty-eight, philosophically accepted her return to genteel poverty. Kenneth, apparently quite as money-conscious in his new state of being, was less accepting of her penny-pinching and his disembodied voice constantly registered disapproval of each small frugality.

The year after Molly was widowed, her Aunt Beatrix also died and left her four thousand pounds. It seemed to Molly like untold wealth and she looked forward to using it sparingly for little treats and to ease her everyday life for several years. Unfortunately, Kenneth's voice regularly and urgently made suggestions for the spending of the legacy and only the realities of Molly's penurious life helped her to resist him. In the butcher's shop he would whisper,

*"No, no, not the mince. Get a couple of double loin lamb chops or even better a nice sirloin steak. Go on, Molly. Think of that with new potatoes and lots of crispy onions! Really delicious!"*

That had been a meal that he had always thoroughly enjoyed when alive and she felt that by insisting on purchasing her half a pound of mince, she was denying him pleasure, which was of course nonsense, she would tell herself.

However it was troubling.

When shopping in a department store for some small necessity, a tin-opener perhaps or a yard of elastic, his insinuating voice would point out French perfumes and items of silk underwear as they passed near those counters,

*"Go on, Molly, what is forty quid when you have four thousand in the bank? Go on, treat yourself for God's sake!"*

And Molly would find herself shaking her head, though by ignoring the advice, she felt disloyal

It was confusing and Molly sometimes felt very unhappy and sometimes she questioned her own sanity. Perhaps she had not mourned his death sufficiently? She had been so occupied in surviving the financial mess that he had left, that she had not shed many tears for him. Though she had loved him so very dearly, it seemed that his passing had not broken her heart.

Her friends at her weekly embroidery class advised her to do something exciting with her windfall, something to remember all her life.

"But I really need a new washing machine."

"Well, you've plenty for that *and* a nice holiday! What about the Med?"

"Oh, yes! Go to Spain and visit the Alhambra."

"Oh no! Northern Italy is the place, quaint medieval towns, such delicious food and the *vineyards*..."

"Yes, but Majorca is gorgeous in the north and there are caves on the east coast or go in March and see the almond blossom!"

"I prefer Greece myself, those ancient sites! So poetic! and the *root* of all our culture. Do go to Greece, Molly.

The last speaker was Jean, Molly's closest friend.

Molly had not realised her friends were so familiar with distant places. Travel had never been important to Kenneth.

Molly smiled to herself when she thought of how everyone knew exactly how she should spend her money and the conflicting advice was unhelpful. However, when she saw the advertisement for a bargain-price cruise visiting several Mediterranean countries, she phoned and booked immediately. It was certainly an incredibly inexpensive cruise and she would have more than enough money left to buy the washing machine, winter boots and coat from M&S, and also a little nest egg for future treats.

She considered that she had done rather well and her friends agreed, but Kenneth did not and in the weeks before the cruise, she found his relentless carping hard to bear.

*"I cannot think why you're doing it, Molly my girl! Cheap and nasty. You'll regret it, you'll certainly regret it, my sweet one! Wouldn't be surprised if you pick up a bug. 'Spect the water supply will be dicey and as for the kitchens!"*

On the dark, drizzling November day of embarkation, Jean drove her to Greenock.

The passengers from the previous cruise were disembarking, and Molly was asked to come back in an hour.

Drinking coffee, they laughed as Jean teased her about possible romantic adventures. Molly was uncomfortably aware that Kenneth's voice was silent.

They said their farewells at the entrance to the docks.

As Molly walked through a large lonely warehouse towards the three unsmiling officials who waited at the far side to examine her passport, she noticed an item of her own luggage, a small green bag, sitting all by itself on a table, apparently forgotten. Although she resisted the temptation to pick it up, she suspected that she might never see it again

After passport control, she was directed to another enormous draughty shed, where she joined the other two hundred patient passengers who sat self-consciously on incongruous gilt and crimson velvet chairs. The tawdry luxury of the chairs seemed to accentuate the barrenness of the vast undecorated building.

It was cold and they waited for forty minutes before the slow process of calling out names and embarking started. Molly had plenty of time to contemplate her fellow passengers. Most were middle-aged or elderly and their padded jackets and grey anoraks gave no indication that they contemplated a Mediterranean cruise. Joy and anticipation were conspicuously absent from their expressions. They might well have been refugees or displaced people.

Molly felt terribly sorry for them.

*"You should have listened to me. These common swine will be your companions for the next two weeks, Molly. How will you like that, I wonder."*

He had been disapprovingly silent for so long that Molly jumped at his voice, but quickly recovered and replied firmly inside her head,

"I don't know why you're so cruel to them. They're just people like you and me and they're cold and tired."

*"No, no, they're not your class and you know it, Molly. They'll be loud and vulgar, drinking too much and swearing... . I don't know how you'll stand it. You should have gone for an expensive holiday. No doubt about it. I'll never understand why you didn't choose a luxury experience in the Caribbean instead of shivering here with this crowd of losers. You'll regret skimping, I know you will. Why, I don't expect these folk even know what a daily bath is."*

Molly was roused for the first time to reply, albeit silently,

"I can't afford hot water to take a daily bath myself nowadays, Kenneth."

There was no answer.

"And I survive perfectly well."

Just then her name was called and feeling strangely triumphant, she walked up the gang-plank and was escorted through the unknown labyrinth of the large ship to her own cabin.

There on her bunk lay her luggage, miraculously including the small green bag. It was a good omen.

Felipe, her steward, was a charming young man from the Philippines, with a vast amount of information which he was anxious to share with her. His English was excellent and he pleaded with Molly to rely upon him and ask him anything at any time. He was at least fifteen years younger than she was but he treated her like an equal which surprised her, as Kenneth had always expected and received a fair amount of kow-towing from those who served. Molly much preferred this comradely approach, it made her feel young. As he left, she suggested that he should call her Molly.

*"Bad move, Molly! Familiarity with menials never works."*

As she considered this, another disembodied voice broke into her thoughts. It was the intercom advising all passengers that they must now take part in an emergency lifeboat drill. They were to don their lifejackets and go to their designated mustering points.

The bright orange lifejacket was far from flattering, either in colour or shape. Molly was tempted to giggle as she sat in the piano bar and looked around her. Small heads stuck up ridiculously from the vast inflated orange collars. Those who carried extra weight, and there were many of those, looked enormous and helpless, like Tweedledum and Tweedledee. She expected she looked just as bad, herself. They remained there for thirty minutes, vulnerable and comical.

She wondered idly why Kenneth made no sarcastic comments.

After the drill, Molly reconnoitred the ship. It seemed enormous and she was sure she would never get the layout clear in her mind. She noted the dining room, the piano bar and the dance hall, which had a very small stage. She ascended and descended stairways, walked along interminable corridors and took the lift down to the bowels of the ship where six inches of murky water sloshed around in a sad swimming pool. With its unchanged sixties décor, this area had the aspect of a museum, rather a bad-smelling one. Molly was not interested in swimming nor did she suspect many of her fellow passengers were.

She discovered a small cinema, with traditional velvet curtains to hide and reveal the screen. On the upper deck, the Casino glittered silently with shiny leather seating and bright green baize, though it had too many flashing fruit machines to look as wickedly sophisticated and James Bondish as she had always imagined casinos to be.

It was exciting but what thrilled her most was when she returned to the open deck and felt the movement of the ship. The light was now gone and the beauties of the Clyde were invisible, but with the wind and rain on her face, the sounds of slapping waves and the knowledge that the immense weight of the mountains was there in the darkness, Molly was enthralled in a deep and primitive way.

In her cabin she found an impressive newsletter describing the following days' events. Aerobic exercises, paper-flower making, line-dancing in the morning or Bingo, Bango, Bongo on the High Seas. Molly was puzzled by the last event. What on earth could that be? The rest of the day offered self-indulgent (and expensive) beauty treatments, a visit to the library or the 'well-stocked' shop and afternoon tea would be served on the top deck at four o'clock. The last appealed strongly. A vision of dainty cucumber sandwiches and iced sponge cakes, with a white-gloved waiter offering "China or Indian, Madam?" swam through her mind's eye. Almost at once a terse voice broke through that dream,

"*Bet you ten to one it won't be like that, Molly!*"

She had been so absorbed in her surroundings that she had completely forgotten Kenneth. Her mixed feelings of remorse at forgetting her late husband and irritation at his constant carping were interrupted by a discreet knock at her cabin door.

"I thought you would like to know that your dining table

is number ten, Molly. There are seven other people at the table and I'm sure they are all very nice. Dinner is served at eight-thirty and is informal tonight."

Felipe's smile showed his astoundingly white and perfect teeth. They were gorgeous and Molly gazed at them fascinated and for a moment felt dizzy.

"I expect you are feeling quite hungry now, Molly."

He pronounced it charmingly, *Mollee*.

"Yes I suppose I am, Felipe."

His voice was so kind that she felt tears prickle her eyes as he closed the door silently. She was thinking that she had eaten nothing since breakfast when a voice boomed in her ear,

*"That dago's angling for a big tip!"*

"Oh Kenneth, I really think you're wrong."

*"Mark my words, I know the type and you'd better lock up your jewellery safely. He'll have a key to the cabin, y'know. He could be in here at any hour rifling through your things."*

Molly felt tired and unenthusiastic as she made her way to the restaurant. Why had she come on this venture?

A lady in her sixties was sitting alone at table number ten and greeted Molly in a friendly but unintelligible accent. After several false starts, Molly started to understand the broad Lancashire vowels and learned that Gerty was from Bolton, a retired traffic warden, an expert on cruises, this was her fifth, with a son and three grandchildren. She was very fond of and usually lucky at bingo. Not so keen on the slots though.

"I beg your pardon?" Molly had not caught the last word.

"The slots, you know love, the slots."

"I'm afraid..." Molly looked bewildered.

"The slot machines..."

"Oh! I understand."

*"Be careful, you'll find this woman hard to shake off!"*

Molly ignored the voice and smiled warmly at Gerty.

Others now arrived at the table, two elderly men from Glasgow whose accents were as pronounced as Gerty's but more familiar to Molly. Then an Irish mother and daughter, both heavily decorated with gold garniture, took their places beside Molly. A younger couple from the south of England sat at the end of the table and made it clear that they would not be part of the group. The dogmatic brogue of the older Irish woman was quick to correct any statements or opinions made at the table and Molly took an instant dislike to her.

The several disparate accents around the table confused the Filipino waiter entirely. He misunderstood orders, brought dishes to the wrong people, then argued. Molly pitied him and yet felt tempted to giggle. The Irish lady shouted loudly at him, flustering him further and even Gerty became cross when she was served with the wrong plate for the third time.

The food was not very good. It was cold and the vegetables were an overcooked mush.

*"Don't suppose I need make any comment on this dinner-table! Think you can stand it for a fortnight, Molly?"*

The voice was rather distant but she could imagine the sarcastic little sneer around his lips.

At the end of the meal, as Molly rose to leave, Gerty said something to her which had to be repeated twice before she understood. It was an invitation to join her at bingo next day.

"I've never played bingo I'm afraid. Perhaps I would be useless at it!"

But Gerty assured her that it was 'easy-peesy' and she would love it.

Back in her cabin Molly stood transfixed for a moment and then burst into loud giggles. The bed spread had been removed from her bunk and folded away and her pink night-gown, which she had previously unpacked, was artistically laid out as if displayed in a shop window. The tiny waist was gathered into perfect little pleats from which the skirt swirled wide, while the long sleeves were gracefully arranged as if thrown above her head in terpsichorean abandon.

"It must have taken him ages to do it so neatly. Just to give me a moment's pleasure."

Her laughter had chased away all the disappointments of the meal and she decided to have another walk around the deck before bed. Felipe had shown her a short passageway to the open deck quite near to her cabin.

She stood smiling in the chilly darkness, entranced, leaning over the rail and watching the water as it shifted swiftly past. It was so exciting to be heading south for sunny, exotic places. She could hardly believe it.

*"Molly! I must say I think it distasteful that he should be handling your lingerie."*

"Kenneth! I wish... I wish you would just shut up."

This was the first time that she had spoken out aloud to the disembodied voice and she had spoken very loudly.

She looked around the deck quickly, for if she were going to have an argument with an invisible person, better not have witnesses, but no one else had left the warm interior of the ship.

She added, more quietly,

"If you can't say something nice, dear, don't speak at all."

Molly was close to tears and to calm herself she counted the fairy lights which were modestly looped around the deck above her head. Out of fifty six bulbs only twenty three were alight.

"I suppose it is quite a broken down old tub, Kenneth." She whispered apologetically into the night, but there was no reply.

As she lay in bed, she realised she was travelling feet first towards the magical Mediterranean and raising her arms above her head to bring the sleeves to their previous dancing position, she regained some of her former joy.

Next day at breakfast Molly was taken aback when her cornflakes were served with the milk already added! And even more astonished at the magnificent appetite displayed by her fellow travellers. Each cleared a plate piled high with two eggs, five rashers of bacon, two monstrous shiny sausages, tomatoes and bread and *then* started on toast and marmalade. Molly's boiled egg seemed Spartan in comparison though it was more than she would normally take.

Jimmy, one of the Glasgow men was enthusing about the excellent dance band that had played last night.

"It's a Russian band an honest tae Goad, it's jist as guid uz Joe Loass!"

Gerty reminded her to come to the piano bar at eleven thirty for bingo.

The ship had docked in Liverpool early that morning and Molly missed the movement of the ship underfoot. Listlessly she tidied her things as she listened to the strident voice on the intercom.

"Wake up and stretch with Sarah in the gym at nine, hurry, hurry, she's starting right now!!"

"Get those grey cells working! Pick up your quiz and crossword at the purser's desk."

"Backgammon in the Four Ace salon!"

"Line-dancing in the piano bar! Ten o'clock and BE THERE!"

"Shuffleboard on the games deck! Teams forming NOW."

"Aerobics with Gemma in the disco at ten o'clock, don your shiny lycra and get that heart pumping!"

Molly smiled. It sounded so energetic and few of the ladies she had seen were less than size twenty.

"Bouillon served on top deck at ten o'clock."

How could anyone be ready for soup less than two hours after that monster breakfast?

"BINGO, BANGO, BONGO on the High Seas. In the piano bar at eleven thirty!"

"Oh Kenneth, what will it be like?"

But Kenneth was dumb.

Molly went on deck and gazed at the vast docks of Liverpool. Almost immediately Felipe came on deck and chatted to her until eleven thirty. He was very interesting. He had a wife and two children in Manila but he could make good money as a ship's steward. He enjoyed the adventurous life, though the food on this ship was terrible. He described his father's farm, laid waste last year by a volcano which had lain dormant for eighty years. Molly realised what a narrow self-centred and safe existence she had led.

Bingo proved to be simple and lucrative. Molly won twenty pounds and spent it in the shop on ship-bedecked teatowels for herself and Gerty.

At four, Molly, shielding the teabag in her plastic cup from the drizzling rain, stood in the long queue at the hot water urn and laughed inwardly at her dreams of afternoon tea. She could visualise the dropped eyelids and pursed lips of Kenneth's 'I told you so' expression but strangely, he said nothing.

At least she was luckier than the embarking Liverpool woman, whose luggage, too carelessly thrown on board, had missed the ship and disappeared for ever into the filthy waters of the dock!

After a dinner no better than the previous night, Molly listened to the Russian dance-band but could not agree with Jimmy's whole hearted enthusiasm. The centuries of hardship and misery of that melancholy country were encapsulated in every tune. Dancers stumbled as they slowed their steps to the dirge-like-tempo and the five young musicians seemed very close to tears.

The cabaret startled Molly a little as the three energetic young ladies appeared to be so very nearly unclothed.

*"Obscene! Shouldn't be allowed."*

"Nonsense, Kenneth, they do have lovely figures and the important bits are pretty well covered."

That night Felipe had sculpted an ingenious swan from her nighty with the sleeves twisted to portray its curved neck.

"It's lovely!" she breathed.

It seemed a shame to dismantle it.

When the rough weather started in the Bay of Biscay, Molly was surprised to find that she delighted in it and found the constant struggle to walk straight was great fun.

None of her companions came to dinner that night and she had to admit that it was more enjoyable without them.

She determined that she would take the Mediterranean shore excursions alone.

As Molly made her way back to her cabin that night, trying to keep her balance in spite of the unpredictable lurches of the ship and chuckling as she teetered from one side of the corridor to the other, suddenly Kenneth groaned loudly and muttered,

*"Bloody hell, this isn't fit for man nor beast."*

He had always had a weak stomach and it would be the very last time that Molly would ever hear his voice.

That night she decided that the full-blown rose which Felipe had created from her nighty was *much* too pretty to unfold and she transferred it carefully to her dressing table.

Then, lying naked in the wildly rolling ship, her hands clasped on her breast and her feet pointing towards the warm scented South, she imagined herself to be a carved figurehead of yore, poised on the prow of a sailing ship and gently caressed by the salt spray.

A sailor, bearing a distinct resemblance to Felipe, stood at the taffrail, whatever that was, and regarded her reverently.

# A WONDERFUL WOMAN

I live with a wonderful woman. No, no we are not married, but then that does not matter nowadays, does it. What a beautiful life we have together.

We are so happy with our small pleasures. Just little things fill our days with delight. Black olives for instance. Just so tasty! We both adore them, my Clara and I.

That is an old-fashioned name, Clara, but for me it is the most poetic name in the world because it belongs to my lovely lady.

Clara does all the shopping, well most women like to shop, don't they. She goes to Peckam's delicatessen and buys delectable olives prepared with herbs, not vinegary at all. Just the smooth taste of virgin olive oil. When she comes home with them we open up the plastic tub and eat them all up at once. There are stones in the olives and my lovely lady removes them before she pops them in my mouth, laughing. She laughs a lot and while I do not find it easy to laugh, I enjoy looking at her pretty open mouth which has so many teeth in it. I have few teeth left myself, though quite enough to enjoy my food.

The house that we live in belongs to Clara. I have hardly any possessions and most probably never shall have and before you say a word, I assure you that I have no false pride. I do not care about material things. To balance that, I know that I have blue blood in my veins. That counts for a lot I always think, while Clara's antecedents are almost certainly of peasant stock. I assure you this makes no difference at all to my feelings for her. We truly love and respect each other.

Oh yes Clara loves me and I return her love a thousand-fold. The fact that she has a spacious house with luxurious furniture, paintings on the wall and a fairly adequate supply of delicious food in the larder is quite beside the point. She has freely offered to share her home and her belongings with me and if we make each other happy, what could be more

perfect than that? I have no ridiculous need for independence, no stupid feelings of inadequacy. Clara has plenty of
money as far as I can see, I do not ask how much she has or
where it came from. That would hardly be polite. Perhaps she
was married to a rich man who died or perhaps her father was
wealthy. I do not know and I do not care, although I would
prefer it to be the latter. It would be nice to think that I am
the first man in her life. But that would be unrealistic,
because Clara is no longer young. Lovely as she is, fragrant
and attractive, energetic and playful, she is no longer a girl.
She is a mature stylish woman and older than I am by quite a
few years. I hope you will believe me when I say this does not
worry me in the slightest. Just think of all the life experience
she has. That's what has formed her philosophical attitudes,
which I so admire. The wisdom she has gained from inter-
acting with hundreds of different people of all classes never
fails to impress me. She is quite astonishing in every way and
I will speak later of her knowledge of sensuous pleasures.

There are countless books in the house and she's read
every one of them. Some several times over! I admire this
tremendously because I have never been a reader, though I
flatter myself that I am observant and thoughtful. She has
travelled the world, too, and seen places and people of which
I have only heard. And she has an abundant sense of
humour.

Yes I must be the luckiest fellow in the world.

Lucky! Lucky... and yet nothing in life is ever quite
perfect, is it?

Clara goes out a lot, far more than seems necessary. She
goes out all the time and at night when it is dark! Surely not
shopping, for she brings no parcels home. She does not say
where she is going and she does not invite me to go with her.
She cannot know how rejected I feel and how the loneliness
of the evening stretches ahead for me. As she tidies her abundant hair and dons her coat and chic little beret, I hover
hopefully in the hall, but she laughs, kisses me cheerfully and
walks through the door and out of my life and I am left deso-
late and so much alone that it hurts.

In spite of the complete candour and honesty of our relationship, I have found it impossible to discuss this problem

with her. I have a terrible fear. I suspect that she is ashamed of me and does not want her friends to meet me.

It could be my lack of teeth and perhaps if I were fitted with a set of false teeth, she would suggest that I accompany her. I suppose dentures are expensive and sometimes I imagine *if only* I had an allowance, but no, I have always made it plain that money is no part of our love. All luxuries are provided for me without stint and any organised stipend would seem to me sordid. Then it might not be my teeth that is the problem, it could be my lack of culture. I have had little education and I could never discuss books, plays or music with her companions. I am sure that my Clara would wish to protect me from a situation in which I appeared intellectually inferior.

Our relationship is so wonderful in every way that I am quite unable to risk any confrontation or change, call me a coward if you like.

While she is away from home in the evening, I huddle in an armchair until her return. Some evenings there are tasks which I must perform. These are the only demands which she makes of me and honestly those labours are pleasurable and made doubly so by her gratitude and praise when she returns. When I hear her struggle with the front door, which is rather stiff, I spring to my feet and rush to greet her. Why should I blush to say it? We can hardly keep our hands off each other, hugging, tickling, stroking, we indulge in every innocent caress. Then, after she has been properly appreciative of the work which I have accomplished during her absence we are soon snuggled in bed together. I love to lie with our noses just touching, my hand clasping her wrist, while I mutter compliments to my darling. She laughs and traces my eyebrows and ears with a finger and sometimes she pushes me away playfully, complaining that my moustache is too bristly. Sometimes she will sing to me in her beautiful husky voice and I adore that and try to join in, not successfully, I admit. I love that old favourite,

*"My Willie's eyes*
*Are as blue as the skies."*

My eyes are probably my best feature.

Shortly we will fall blissfully asleep, for our relationship is a pure and perfect one.

"Aw, Missus Jones it's right guid o' ye tae come. Whin Ah seen a' they posters oan the lamp-posts oot therr aboot demolishin' the tenement, Ah wis jist at ma wits' end. As sure's ma name's Clare O'Reilly Ah wis thinkin' o' chuckin' masel in the canal, aye, an draggin' Wullie wi' me. Ah wiz, sure as daith. Ah wiz!

Ye might no' guess it but Ah'm near seeventy.

Aye, Ah'm a' that.

Aye, an' ah remember a' they bad times. Ah've lived thro' it a' in ma lifetime. Whin Ah wiz a wean thur wis nae wark fur ma faither and a poke o' chips wis the best meal o' the week. Then the war cam, wi' a' they boambs drappin' an' that wisnae much fun, wis it, an' Ah wiz evacooated but Ah didnae likit an' ma mither brung me hame an' Ah've nae ideer why she brung me hame fur she did a bunk soon efter. An' Ah've niver saw'r again tae this day. It wiz efter she skedaddled that ma faither pit me an' ma twa brithers in the hame an' Ah've niver saw him since neether, nor ma brithers neether. They wur annoyin' wee buggers right enough, but sometimes Ah wunner aboot thim. Ye canny help it, can ye? Jimmy wis aye a guid laugh, so he wis.

Efter that? Ach weel, 's a' kinda hazy. Ah wis oot o' the hame at sixteen an' workin', charrin' maistly, Ah think. Ah don't reely remember but it wis hard, awfy hard, then ah hud the baby. That wis the yin that deed an' efter that Ah hud the ither yin that wiz adoapted. Aye, Ah think aboot him, the wee lamb. Jist sometimes Ah remember'm. He'll be an auld man in his fifties noo an' he wiz an awfy fat wee baby. Nice, he wis a very nice wee fat baby an' Ah liked him fine... Sorry, is that no' awfy. Ah wis greetin' therr, canny help it... whit 's that yer sayin'? Naw, naw niver a drap. Ah niver tak a drap nooadays. Canny affordit. Isny guid fur me noo. Auld age duzzny come alane, duzzit?... Whit then? Ye mean efter the twa weans an' ma opiration? Weel ye kin guess, can't ye, went oan the gemme didn't Ah. Years an' years Ah wiz attit up the toon. Cauld nichts hingin' roon street coarners for oors an' no

much money. They folk thit say bein' a hoor is fun hiv goat it
a' wrang... Aye, weel... Wiz Ah sleepin' therr? Ach, Ah'm
sorry, hen, Ah jist don't remember much... Ah wid tell ye if
Ah cud but Ah canny. Thur wis wan awfy, awfy bad time fur
me an' Ah've furgoat it an' Ah'm gled, reelly gled Ah've
furgoat it, hen. Ah know Ah wis in the hame again fur a
while an' that's no' yisturday eether, aye an' Ah wis in the jile
an a' but yon wis no' ferr. It wisnae ma fault, it reelly wisnae
ma fault, as God's ma witness, it wisnae me that done it, but
Ah wis loacked up. Years it wus an' Ah'm tellin' ye, it wisnae
ferr... Aye, oh Ah've gave up the prostitution, lang since, weel
tak a gander, Ah'm faur ower auld noo whit wi'ma saggy
boobs an' ma yally teeth... aye that's true Ah aye hud verry
stroang teeth an' Ah've still got thim a', right enuff, ivry wan.
No' like wee Wullie therr. Aw ma wee hen, hiv ye only goat
three teeth therr, ma sowl? Ye've been a guid freend tae me,
Wullie. Many's the laugh we've hud, right enuff an' he's
grand and warm on the cauld nights. He likes a wee cuddle,
the auld divil. Mrs Jones, whit wid happen tae ole Blue Eyes
therr if Ah went... he widnae be ... like Ah mean, would he
be...? or would he be cared fur? Proper like? Aw no, no,
Missus Jones how cud I let that happen tae'm? He's special,
ye know, he's been used tae better days, ye kin see that an'
he's no' that auld but he's no jist right, ye know an' he needs
a loat o' love. Aye, Ah unnerstaun, aye. Aw, Ah'd hate
onythin tae happen tae'm, jist *hate* it. Efter a' these years,
whit a shame, tae... Aw Mrs Jones, wad ye reely? Wad ye dae
that? Intae yer ain hoose? Aw, hen ye've set ma mind at rest,
Ah cannae tell ye... Ye're a saint, so ye are. If you'll luk efter
the wee auld man, Ah'm ready tae go, soon's ye like. Mind ye,
Ah'll be right sorry tae leave this wee den here. Ah niver
thocht onyin wid care if Ah wis livin' here... Thanks, aye, it's
quite homey, intit. Me 'n Wullie like it fine... Ah've been
lucky wi whit Ah fund in the tips. See that big chair, it wiz a
right bugger tae struggle hame wi' but it's bloody comfy an'
Ah fund that rid bedspread tae pit ower it, looks smert an it
goes nice wi they velvet curtins. Goat them frae an auld wife
in Hyndlan' wi' mair stuff thin she knows whit tae dae wi'.
An' Ah think she's lonely. Ah jist mosie up therr ivery week
an' she aye huz somethin' fur me, that vase therr and they

twa wee pented chairs an' yon teapot wi' the floo'ers oan it, aye, an' a' they picturs... reel oil pentins, so they ur! Smell thim! It wis hersel that done thim! She wis gaun tae pentin' classes. Daft auld bugger! At her age! Ivry week she wis pentin' mair'n mair picturs, lanscapes she cried thim. Hur flat wis grand and big but she hudnae the room tae keep a' o' thim! Aye an' she gied me a big loada books wan week, murder mysteries an' they look quite nice oan the shelf therr, don't they but Ah wouldnae read them, no' efter whit happened that time an' me gettin' the blame, wisnae ferr, wisnae ferr at a'... an' the food in the jile wiz boggin'. Aye an' she gie'd me a coat an' twa skirts an' a han'bag, reel leather, jist a pity she wis that wee bit bigger'n me but niver mind, keeps me grand'n warm. She'd that much stuff, she wiz aye at the shoapes spendin' money. S'all right fur some, intit. She'll be wunnerin' whit's up wi' me if Ah niver ring her bell again. Ah jist think the auld sowl wis lonely.

Naw, Ah niver thocht this place wad be pu'ed doon 'cos it's been like this fur years an' years an' naebody's boathered aboot it. They kin say it's no' safe if they like, but Ah think it's fine an' its' a crime tae pu' it doon. Aye, thur's folk livin' upstairs but Ah niver see thim... keep well away from that loat, drugs'n all that. Hear thim right enuff, hear the fights, but this wee basement's jist dandy fur me an' it saves ma auld legs gaun up'n'doon the sterrs, know whit Ah mean?

Aw naw, it's no' coasy, ye couldnae ca' it warm at a' an' that's why Ah invited Wullie tae move in wi' me... It's no' sae bad whin thur's twa keepin' each ither warm. Eh Wullie? Ye're grand an coasy even though yer scabby... Aye ye're right enuff, Mrs Jones, that's a Peckham's bag lyin' therr. See that auld wumman up in Hyndland she aye gies me a quid tae masel an' thur this big swell shoape see, wi' a' yon fancy food in big gless jaurs. Ah get some queer looks therr Ah'll tell ye, but they hiv tae serve me if Ah hiv the dough, an' Ah aye buy olives, the black yins wi' the herbs oan thim. Fancy tastes for an auld pro, ye'll be sayin' but believe me or believe me nut, Wullie there, look he knows Ah'm talkin' aboot'm. Aye Ah'm talkin' aboot ye, Wullie. Weel, wee scabby Wullie jist goes mad fur olives... Aye he duz, honest.

Noo, Ah wid like tae thank ye, Mrs Jones, fur ye've been

awfy kind an' helpful tae me an' Ah'm awfy sweert tae leave ma wee palace here. Palace! That's a guid yin but Ah'm heart sair aboot it... see me, it's no' often Ah'm greetin'... Ah'm no' verra happy aboot livin' in a hame again. But Ah kin see it's fur the best. But when ye said whit wid happen tae Wullie... ye know whit Ah mean... Ah wiz ready tae pack ma bags an' go on the lam wi' the wee darlin'. If it wisny fur whit you've offered tae dae for Wullie, Ah'd be oot o' here in a cloud o' stoor. But Ah'm ready tae gan tae the hame noo an' God bless ye, ye'll aye be in ma thoughts fur yer kindness tae me an' Wullie therr. Come here ma grand wee man, till Ah gie ye a last big kiss.

Mrs Jones, thanks an ye'll niver regret takin' him in an' yer generoasity'll be rewarded fur Ah'm tellin' ye, Wullie's goat a lovely personality an' even wi' jist the three teeth he's a great mouser. Rats as well.

✧◆✧

"Ah, so nice to see you again after all these months, Mrs Jones. Decided to take the plunge, have you and return to the ranks of pet-owners, have we? Still talk about old Deuteronomy here in the clinic. He was a wonderful tabby. Truly a character. You must miss him sorely.

And who have we got here in the basket? Out ye get, old fellow m'lad, come along out... *out!* Oh! That's a surprise! By Jove! and what's your name? William? Right, William! Come here, come here! Gotcha! Don't worry old man, I won't hurt you, that's a good boy, yes... uh huh... neutered male... coat's poor, but medication should help that... few fleas here and there, soon fix those... Oh, oh *and where are all your teeth*, old friend?! Not much to be done there, 'fraid there's no such thing as dentures for pussycats! Ha. Ha. Obviously been cared for at one time. How's the general health? Bowels?... Appetite? Good, good... he likes black *what?*... with *herbs*? And he *gets* them, does he? *Spoiled boy!* But you're quite right, pets are for spoiling. Long as their health isn't affected. Well that's fine. Oh yes he's certainly a pure bred Siamese, aren't you, William? Quite an aristocrat! We should call you Sir William! Haw, haw! Shall we do that, eh? Bet he cost a pretty penny as a kitten... obviously had his hard times since then, of course. *Where* did you find him?

Never! *Never*! I say! And are there many squats like that in the city?

Just a stone's throw from the West end, too. Tut, tut. I suppose it's better than a cardboard box... how sad! Sounds almost Dickensian. Tut, tut, we don't know how the other half live, do we.

Well of course *you* have a better idea than most, Mrs Jones. You do a wonderful job! Take my hat off to you.

No I mean it. Fancy that poor old soul... such wretched conditions.

My goodness, tut, tut.

Did she?

Really? Beggars description! She'll be better off in a home. I would think anyway.

Independence?... true... yes... I suppose so, but I really do take my hat off to you, Mrs Jones, you do wonderful work.

Now, as always, Judy at reception will print out your prescriptions and give you the bill. I'll see you again in a couple of weeks.

And as for you Sir William, you've really fallen on your feet this time, old fellow. But then cats always do, don't they? Haw, haw!

When Clara kissed me for the last time and I was imprisoned and hurtled through the streets I was at a very low ebb, I can tell you. At that moment, I could not have *whispered* a purr for a pound of black olives. First of all Mrs J. actually *bathed* me! The *most* humiliating experience of my *entire* life! Next day I was taken to visit the doctor, who prodded my stomach in an impertinent way and other really horrible indignities that I cannot mention and he shouted at me in a loud and vulgar voice. And all my secret hopes were dashed by a chance thoughtless remark that he made about false teeth. So insensitive! Another dream completely crushed!, And for a week I was *so depressed.*

However his medicine certainly improved my coat.

I found that Mrs Jones was kind, but her house was very bare, Spartan almost, white paint and hardly any pictures on the walls. Unattractive! Truthfully too, it smelled rather *peculiar,* an aroma which I later traced to a green bottle beside the sink, the contents of which are added liberally to water which she often sloshes over all surfaces in a damp and dangerous way. Some sort of ritual, I suppose. I may yet persuade her to break this habit.

Then, last week, I decided that our time here on earth is very short and I had better make the most of things. There is good and bad in every situation and I started to concentrate on the positive side. For instance, the food here is delicious and very regular, while Clara's provisioning, though sometimes lavish, was inconsistent and not always quite fresh. Not her fault, poor darling but there is nothing like a newly opened tin. Then Mrs Jones, Barbara as I now call her, never allows me to share her bed. She provides me with a soft blanket in a box and shuts her door firmly at night. Perhaps she fears I might experience feelings of disloyalty to Clara, for Barbara is an extremely perceptive woman. A trained psychologist, I believe.

Like Clara, she spends rather too much time away from home, but I use her absence to enjoy the armchair, (it's a no-go area when she is present). When she returns each evening, we greet each other in a dignified, but warm way. Later she will take me on her knee and brush me with a soft brush, *very* relaxing and therapeutic.

On Friday nights she visits the delicatessen and we share those delicious black olives.

Of course our relationship could never be compared to my passionate affair with Clara, but they do have a lot in common and, in her own way, Barbara is a *wonderful* woman.

# SOUVENIR

In the cramped sitting-room of a typical Canadian clapboard house, two men sat together on the shabby couch. Joe was twenty, Donald near fifty. They could have been father and son, but were not. At intervals, and in perfect unison, their serious, concentrated faces would break into uproarious laughter. Once or twice, when the flickering antics on TV were particularly outrageous, glancing at each other and rocking backwards and forwards, they would slap their thighs to express a more extreme appreciation.

In one of the quieter moments, a dark-haired young woman entered the room. It was the boy's sister, Elaine, who looked at them with distaste and hurried upstairs without a word.

Ice-cold air suddenly flooded the room, as the front door was opened and closed.

"Hullo-o! I'm ho-ome! Coo-ee! Anybody there?"

Susan, an attractive woman in her early forties, blonde and plump and laden with shopping, burst into the room. She dumped several bags behind the couch then kissed each of the men enthusiastically. She was Joe's mother and Donald's third wife.

"Kettle on, please." and Susan gave a push to the large youth who reluctantly stood and, keeping his eye on the screen for as long as possible, slowly headed for the kitchen.

Susan took his seat and snuggled up to Donald.

"I've been buying such nice things, today. You've *no idea* how nice..."

"Mmm." He smiled, but his eyes were still fixed on the cartoons.

"Things that will make you happy. Things that you've always wanted!" She rubbed her cheek against his.

"Ah-huh?"

"And they sure didn't cost much, they were real bargains. Just you wait till you see them!"

"Mmm." As he seemed so uninterested, she stood up again and ruffled his hair.

"I'll make some coffee and show them to you, shall I?"

In the kitchen Susan experienced the usual pang of misery. Before their marriage, Donald had lived in this house for fourteen years with his previous wife. When he had explained to Susan how financially strapped he was and how sensible it would be to stay on here rather than incur the expenses of starting afresh in another home, she had agreed. What she had not realised was how thoughts of that other wife would affect her. Each room seemed redolent of that female personality that had inhabited the house before her. Of course they had immediately replaced the frigid twin beds with their very own king size double, but otherwise the furniture and the decoration were unchanged. She told herself how foolish she was, but the cooker where that shadowy, high-achieving woman had stirred sophisticated dishes, the sink where she had prepared exotic vegetables, filled Susan with more misery than she would have thought possible. How many times had that other wife gathered cutlery from this very drawer to set on that very table?

Worst of all was the shower where her predecessor must have stood naked so often, soaping her perfectly moisturised and cellulite-free skin.

Susan shook herself and poured the coffee. She did not know if it were jealousy or lack of confidence which so disturbed her. Guilt was another possibility of course. Perhaps it was quite natural that she should be uncomfortable. Certainly she could not yet feel the house was her own home.

Once or twice she had mentioned this ghost, which existed only in her own head, to Donald. He would always just laugh and kiss her and dismiss it as nonsense, leaving Susan too embarrassed to pursue it further.

The cartoon programme was finished and the TV was switched off.

"Let's see your marvellous purchases then." Donald patted the seat beside him.

Susan grabbed two bags and, forgetting her former negative feelings, suddenly felt full of the delight which her second marriage had brought her.

"I went to the charity shop." she announced happily and

unnecessarily, then started to unwrap various parcels.

Harry groaned.

"I suppose you've bought tons of things that other folk wanted rid of."

"No, no, no. Look at this. Isn't it splendid!"

She produced an onyx ashtray, pale green and massive. Donald stared at it, expressionless. Eventually he mumbled,

"But nobody smokes in this house."

"No, I know that, but someone might visit us that smoked and it is such a handsome object. I think it's very classy. We don't have an ashtray and we really need one and this is the very best, the top of the range. Think how elegant it will look standing on the coffee table!" she finished triumphantly.

Next she unwrapped a large untidy parcel and various pieces of cream fabric scattered over the floor and the couch.

"Now these are table mats, hand embroidered, and they were a terrific bargain. Some are not quite finished yet but I'll..."

"You don't intend finishing them yourself do you?"

"Yes I do. I don't think it would be too difficult. See those cute little stitches! I could do that. I could be doing that while you watch your silly old cartoons." she looked at him sideways and pouted. She looked so pretty that he kissed her and kept his arm across her shoulders.

"I've never seen you pick up a needle since I've known you."

"But I could learn, I'm sure. I know I could learn and I do so want to make this our own home, our very own with our own things in it."

"It is our own home, silly girl. Couldn't be more so."

She gazed at him for a moment. How could he love her and yet be so insensitive, so terribly unaware of her reservations about the house? And yet he was not a mind reader. She had screwed up her courage several times, but she could not bring herself to mention how strongly, how bitterly she felt the presence of that other woman who had shared his life in this house. How she would have loved to hear him say,

"Darling if you don't like this house, of course we'll buy another one, lets buy it straightaway."

But that was wishful thinking. He was much more likely to chuckle and protest that she was surely not serious. The house was just dandy, he had put a lot of work into it and to move would just be money wasted. She knew she would have found that answer very difficult to bear.

She turned back to her parcels and produced another few small knick-knacks, which elicited a disappointing level of enthusiasm from Donald. Finally she reached for a large flat parcel and held it high in front of her like a sacred offering.

"This is the *piece de resistance*! This is what you have always wanted, honey, always *needed.*"

"What on earth is it?"

"Can't you guess?"

"No, no idea, tell me."

"Something you always need on a Sunday..."

"A Sunday? Haven't a clue."

"Guess!"

"No idea at all."

"Try!"

"No! Show it to me at once." and he hugged her tightly and made a mock growl at her.

With a flourish Susan removed the paper from a large china dish, flat and oblong. It was decorated with a delicate blue and white Scandinavian pattern. On the edge was a tiny chip.

"It's for you to carve the Sunday roast or maybe the chicken and then the turkey at Thanksgiving! Isn't it great? It was only three dollars. Aren't you pleased! You know you're always complaining there's nothing in the house big enough... and it's so pretty I think. Isn't it? D'you like it? We'll try it out this weekend with something really special, won't we?"

"Sure, that'll be great. You've done really well." but Donald's arm had slipped from her shoulders and soon he reached for the TV control,

"Time for the news."

He leaned his chin on his hand as he gazed at the screen and drank in the political scandals and violence of the world, as though for the first time.

Feeling foolishly like a child dismissed by its teacher,

Susan sat with the heavy plate in her lap. There were tears in her eyes as she gathered up her purchases and their wrappings. None of them was as attractive or desirable as they had seemed to be in the shop, she thought sadly. She still loved the plate and she laid it on the table behind him, but the other things were cleared into a cupboard.

"Elaine, are you going to phone Dad tomorrow?"

"No, Joe! Why should I?"

"It's his birthday."

"Yeah! Does he phone us on our birthday?"

"Sometimes he does."

"If he remembers. Joe, are those two sweety pies cuddling on the couch downstairs again? It's disgusting. I don't think I can't stand much more of it!"

"Well I think it's great. Mum's happier than she's been for years. Donald's not bad at all. He's a good guy. I like him."

"Just because he gawps at cartoons with you and kicks a football around. You like him! You would! Well I don't trust him."

Elaine looked so fierce as she said this that Joe laughed.

"He's a really nice fella, you don't give him a chance."

"He's not so very nice. What about his kids? He has four of them. Does he phone them on their birthday? Does he send them any cash? What does he know about them? Anything? I doubt it. As much as our stupid old father knows or cares about us, I suppose."

"I wonder what they're like anyway."

"Who?"

"Donald's four daughters. Are they our stepsisters, I wonder? I wonder if we'll ever meet them? We're real short on relations. It's kinda fun to think we have some new ones, all girls"

"They're not girls, they're women, far older than us. No romance there for you, Romeo. I expect they're all ugly dogs, anyway."

"P'raps they'll visit him?"

"I don't expect so and I don't care. I certainly hope not."

"Lainey, why do you give Mum and Donald such a hard time?"

"Because Mum is so... I don't know... I worry about her."

"But you're angry with her for marrying him."

"No I'm not. I just think she should have thought harder before she committed herself. What do we know about him? How did he treat those two other wives? We know he walked out on what's-her-name, the last one."

"I suppose that was partly Mum's fault?"

"Oh, Donald's very persuasive, and attractive... in an elderly sort of way. Then the first wife, what happened there? All those kids? They were young when he left. How did they feel about losing their Dad? And his wife, how did she feel? Did he give her enough money to bring them up?"

"I expect she was earning, Lainey, you're so tough on him."

"Well it sure couldn't be easy bringing up four kids and earning money as well. Then what about his old mother. She's *ancient* and he says he'll visit her *next year.*"

"He's been busy."

"Joe! when our Mum's in her eighties I'll want to see her every week. There's no next year when you're in your eighties, not to depend on."

"Well I think he's good news for us, Elaine. We'll soon be leaving home and she'd sure be lonely without someone around. You know Mum needs company."

"I'll certainly be off soon, soon as possible and as far as possible. I hate this set-up. How can Donald live in the same house with two different wives!"

"Not at the same time!"

"Of course not, stupid, but one after the other in the same house."

Joe screwed up his face and scratched his short wiry hair.

"I never thought of that.."

"You wouldn't. Men don't."

"D'ye think it worries Mum?"

"Probably. I'm going out now."

Joe sat for a long time thinking about two wives in the same house. Simultaneous wives and serial wives. It had all seemed so idyllic before Elaine had spoken. His mother's marriage had brought welcome masculine company and a sense of future freedom to Joe.

He wondered what further unknown complications awaited him in adulthood.

The news finished and Donald stood up and walked to the table.

There was no mistake. What a bizarre and unfortunate coincidence! He had recognised the plate immediately and the sight of it had affected him strongly. His thick grey hair still bristled on his head and his knees felt weak. The plate was exactly the same pattern as the dinner service that he and his first wife, Ruth, had bought when they emigrated to Canada. It had been their first joint domestic purchase in the new country and they had agreed it was symbolic.

He had been twenty-two then, newly married and just arrived in Canada and he and Ruth had chosen the inexpensive china from various different designs in a Winnipeg department store. There had been a more brilliant and dramatic set which Ruth had preferred, but he had persuaded her to take this one. Dinner plates, side plates, soup bowl, cups and saucers, six of each and a serving platter for meat, a perfect replica of Susan's purchase. The weight and texture of it were so familiar to him that it was like meeting a long-lost relation. He had carved up pork, lamb and beef on... what was it Ruth had called it? An ashet was it? Yes an ashet, the word was related to the French assiette. There were quite a few old Scots words like that. For some reason, he was particularly glad that he remembered the word. He also remembered, only too clearly, carefully serving the slices of beef on to the dinner plates and how Ruth had craved beef in her first pregnancy. At first only two plates were needed, but eventually, as the children arrived, the whole six were in daily use. Using the six plates had given him a strange sense of satisfaction and they must have been careful for he had no memory of breakages. He shook his head as if to shake these memories away.

My God! this might be the very same dish! Unlikely, as Ruth had returned to Scotland. Besides, she never threw anything out until it was broken. He smiled bitterly as he remembered that there had been a good few dishes broken in that last stormy year of their marriage. But there had been good times before that, wonderful times, even. The day that they bought the dinner service was very clear. He could remember the smart dress that Ruth wore, patterned in stylised peacocks' feathers and her unreserved enthusiasm for each department in Eaton's vast store. Afterwards they had indulged in smooth Java coffee and a delicacy entirely new to them, cheese cake with black cherry topping, and laughed delightedly as they compared the luxuries available in Canada to the dull and simple life they had left behind in the Britain of the fifties.

He remembered that Ruth had been a wonderfully exciting cook. She seemed to produce great food in moments. She had been determined to learn how to make cheesecake and when she did, it was even better than Eaton's. But of course he had not married his wives for their cooking skills, although Ruth's talent was an added bonus. He smiled as he remembered that cooking was an accomplishment that his second wife Wendy had never acquired. She had tried awfully hard, using expensive ingredients and following exactly the recipes of world famous chefs, but somehow she never quite got the knack. Susan had relied all her life on ready cooked supermarket meals, which were probably more edible than Wendy's sophisticated failures.

Donald shook himself and looked guiltily towards the kitchen where Susan was still preparing dinner. He felt ashamed of himself, comparing his wives like that, as though he were a Sultan with a harem at his command.

Again he looked morosely at the plate. What was he going to do about it? It would be a constant aide-memoire. Those deeply buried scenes of his first marriage always seemed too painfully sharp when they rose to the surface, and it was never easy to blot them out again. Those years with Ruth had been his youthful, adventurous years, sharing the unique experience of living in a new country as well as the joy and tribulations of parenthood. They had grown up together and he often struggled to remember where it had all started to go wrong. He had probably been too young to be a parent, though he had enjoyed it to begin with. He supposed that he was a difficult bugger, always wanting to try new things before it was too late, afraid that life would pass him by. Eventually Ruth just seemed to be exhausted by it all. He supposed that he had not listened to what he did not want to hear. He had always seen her as a part of himself and had made decisions accordingly, but she had been a different person, with different priorities and goals and too many domestic responsibilities. He supposed he might have helped around the house more, but in those far-off days, housework was seen as un-masculine.

Finally Ruth had rebelled and returned to Scotland to make her own life.

And now this plate with its wrenching memories had appeared and would continue to appear regularly on the dinner table. He must do something about it.

Involuntarily he turned his head sharply aside.

As for his second marriage to the ambitious Wendy, strange that after only a year, memories of his second marriage had faded so much that it might have been an ancient Hollywood movie that he had once watched in his youth. Peculiar that though they had lived in that house for nearly ten years, nothing in the whole house recalled any incident of his second marriage to mind, compared to the sorcery of this blue and white dish.

Should he just knock it to the floor and say it was an accident? An unlikely one! Besides, it would not break on the carpet. He could hardly dash it into the fire place. Should he say he hated it and it should be returned for some other charity shop trawler? But who could take exception to such an unobtrusive pretty little pattern? Truthfully it was quite a boring design and he wondered if Ruth had always secretly regretted the more exotic dinner service. No use feeling guilty now but it did show that her description of him as domineering and 'always wanting to have things his own way', had some basis. He denied it strongly when she first accused him but, yes, he did like to have his own way. Didn't everyone?

But what to do about this damned plate?

He jumped as Susan came into the room with a bowl of salad and the cutlery.

"You're a nervy old boy. Did I give you a fright? I think you're hungry."

"I suppose I am hungry, hungry for you!"

He grabbed her and kissed the back of her neck.

Notwithstanding, he was unhappy to be addressed as 'old boy'. He preferred not to be reminded that he was fourteen years older than she was.

He had been two years younger than Ruth.

Elaine came downstairs at that minute and averted her eyes as she put on her coat.

"Elaine!" her mother squeaked as she disentangled herself from Harry's grasp.

"Elaine, the pizza is just ready and here's salad on the table. I thought you were eating with us, honey."

"No, not tonight."

"Will you be late, sweetheart?"

"Probably."

The front door banged with another icy blast of air.

"She hates me, you know, Susan."

"Oh, Donald, of course she doesn't hate you. I expect it embarrasses her a little to see her staid old mother in your arms."

"She certainly doesn't care much for me."

"She'll learn what a loveable old devil you are. And Joe *really* likes you. You've been so good for Joe. He needed a mature man around. He admires you. You're his role model!"

"Not sure how fit I am to be a role model for anyone..."

"Well he really likes you, I know that."

But when Joe came downstairs he did not catch Donald's eye once, nor did he respond to a mock pugilistic attack, nor laugh at a terrible pun. Eventually the boy went into the kitchen and came out chewing a large hunk of pizza and shrugging himself into his jacket.

"Said I'd meet the guys at the rink, see you later, folks."

After the door slammed behind him, Susan popped her head around the door and whispered dramatically.

"It's just us two! Isn't that great? *Romantic*! And I have yummy desert for afterward!"

But Donald knew that she would miss her children at the supper table. A happy family seated around a table was her favourite image.

She returned for a moment and picked up the blue and white plate, exclaiming,

"Gorgeous!"

Donald felt relieved when it was out of sight and determined that it could not be too difficult a job, once a reasonable amount of time had elapsed, to destroy a china dish. Then he would buy an extravagantly beautiful one to replace it, richly coloured and without uncomfortable associations. Perhaps a unique piece by a local potter or perhaps an antique. With this decision he felt happier and seating himself at the table, he picked at the salad. He was starving.

In the kitchen Susan hugged the plate to her. She felt this was the real start of their marriage. This was the first thing of beauty that they both owned and so useful too. She giggled to herself with sheer happiness. Who cared for the cooker and the pots and pans and the empty shower upstairs. That faded unhappy lady drifting around the house had had her chance to make Donald happy and *she had failed*. That previous wife would never lay food on this wonderful plate, never watch Donald carve a chicken on it, never use it to display peaches and grapes, never present a surprise birthday cake on it. This plate belonged only to Susan and Donald. It was a symbol of their love!

As she carefully dried and polished it, she whispered fondly,

"You'll never be chipped again, little plate."

Then she shouted,

"Come get the pizza, darling, you must be hungry."

As Donald carefully carried the hot pizza tray from the kitchen, his step was slow and hesitant for a man still in his prime. He had seen the dessert.

Susan was pouring black cherry topping over the two large pieces of Eaton's cheesecake which lay resplendent on the blue and white ashet.

# LEAVING THE ISLAND

The white-haired old lady, who had searched with such slow and painful thoroughness through the myriad small boxes and crumpled paper bags, smiled her sweet smile to Louise and with a shaky upward gesture of her hand, disappeared through the blue door behind the counter. Little gasps accompanied her heavy footsteps as she ascended an unseen and echoing wooden staircase.

"Jessie, Jessie! Are you there, Jessie?" her voice sounded as hollow as the stairs.

Louise blamed herself. She should have realised the impossibility of making a swift transaction in this tiny village store. With less than two hours to catch the ferry back to the mainland, she simply did not have the time and she should have known that. With floors to sweep, food to collect, several doors to lock and the last few minutes fraught with the pre-basket struggles of her tabby cat, leaving the cottage after a long weekend always took more time than she bargained for. She supposed that she was getting a bit slower than she used to be. At least she *chose* to take more time.

And yet she was tempted to buy the buttons at this shop. It was the shop where the wool had been bought to knit her very first cardigan. She could still remember the excitement of choosing the colour and watching the lady skilfully stretch, twist and roll the hanks of blue double-knitting into a large knot, before parcelling them neatly and accepting the money from Aunt Minnie. In those far-off days there was also a white-haired lady, perhaps the grandmother of Jean and Jessie. Then, the shop had sold only wool and linen goods, but gradually it had extended its stock as, one by one, the other shops on the island closed. Now the diminutive premises could hardly accommodate the array of goods and the two modest shelves of wool nestled amongst packets of sugar and flour, while tins of cat food and tomato soup were balanced on top of a display case of embroidery threads. Standing room had dwindled to a space scarcely adequate for the six feet of three customers.

When Louise was six, the bombs were falling on Glasgow and her parents decided that she should be sent to stay with her Aunt Minnie, who lived on the island. Aunt Minnie and Louise were delighted with each other and shared long chilly walks on the shore and hot baking sessions in the kitchen with equal enthusiasm. Aunt Minnie taught Louise to knit and had encouraged her to persevere and produce the first oddly-shaped little blanket for her doll. Then Louise graduated to a striped scarf, to rather square-toed slippers and then to the sublime blue cardigan. She had been quite a child prodigy as far as knitting was concerned. And though knitting might be considered one of the lesser arts, the compliments which Louise had received from everyone for her skill and application had laid a basis of self-confidence which was to help form her character and support her throughout her life. Her daughters now teased her about her early achievements for none of them had ever knitted anything. She would retort that knitting was hardly suitable for a modern young woman and she herself hardly knitted at all now. However a new grandchild had inspired her to pick up her pins and it had seemed only right to buy the buttons for the tiny jacket at the island shop. Continuity was important to Louise, or perhaps it was only sentimentality, she scolded herself. She should have allowed herself more time. It would be very inconvenient to miss the ferry.

A large old clock slowly ticked behind the counter. It was probably the same one that she had heard as a child. It made Louise even more nervous and aware of the passing time.

Not a sound came from the regions beyond the blue door. Obviously Jessie could not be found. The small yellow garment lay on the counter before her with six unsuitable buttons lying beside it. They were too large and they were red.

"Those are the closest I have." Jean had whispered confidentially with her white curls quivering. "I am sure there are some others that would be better. I'll just go and ask my sister, Jessie."

And now Louise felt that it would be rude just to leave the shop before Jean came back. Poor old soul, she was so anxious to please. She was not even sure if Jean was her

name, it was something like that. Louise was struck afresh at
how unfitted she was for small-town living. She never
remembered names.

At that moment the shop bell jingled and a man and
woman entered the shop. According to island etiquette Louise
should have turned and greeted these newcomers, but her
worries made her unwilling to enter into a possibly lengthy
conversation. She threw a vague and undirected half-smile
over her shoulder. She was aware that it was rude. These were
possibly people that she knew well. What a predicament. She
was normally a decisive person and she now felt like a child
that could not make up its mind. What should she do? If she
did not return to the cottage at once she would not catch the
ferry and her presence in Glasgow tomorrow morning was
vital. It would be unkind to walk away now, after such a diligent search, and Louise knew that she would buy some
buttons, however unsuitable. And if she turned to leave, she
must confront and exchange pleasantries with this couple
who stood so close behind her. That could take ten minutes
and that would certainly mean that the ferry was missed.

She could not remember the last time that she had felt
defeated by such trivialities. Life in the city was easier.
Perhaps it *was* time to sell the house and say farewell to the
island.

After carefully placing the ugly red buttons on the small
jacket for a second time, she gathered them up again and
piled them neatly at the far edge of the counter and, biting
her lip, fixed her gaze steadily on the knitting.

The ticking clock was the only link between the three
people who stood motionless and almost touching in the
restricted area.

Walter Hood stood behind Louise and carefully examined
the luxuriant coil of hair at the back of her head. How well he
remembered the shape of her head and the curling tendrils
escaping in all directions. The golden glints of her girlhood
had vanished, but her hair was still thick and glorious and he
could smell its faint delicious fragrance. From the age of six
Walter had been in love with Louise, although he had not
realised the fact until he was thirteen. He, too, had been sent
away from the dangers of the air-raids to stay with a relative,

his grandmother. The boy and girl from the city were very different from the island children. They were more sophisticated, knowledgeable and articulate and, unwilling or unable to hide their superiority, they were not popular with their classmates. Walter had welcomed the bond which inevitably formed between them, a bond which enabled them to withstand the taunts and ridicule which they suffered when beyond the protection of their teachers. Walter did not have the same close friendship with his Grandmother that Louise had with her Aunt and he was a lonely little boy. He wove many fantasies around the games which he might have shared with the girl with the long golden curls. The other girls all had short hair and those curling tresses impressed him. Louise's general knowledge impressed him. Even her knitting impressed him.

He studied the back of her graceful head. Why did she not turn and speak? Surely she could sense his presence.

He had a sudden clear vision of a bright blue jacket which was held up by the teacher for the admiration of the class, while Louise stood with her head drooping forward unhappily. One of His Majesty's Inspectors was visiting the school that day and the atmosphere of the school was electrically charged, as anxiety flickered between teachers and pupils. It might have been God that had descended to hear them recite the Ten Commandments or the books of the Bible and each child in the school could have recited both satisfactorily, if required.

The tall thin inspector with the dark moustache had looked sternly down at the nervous eight-year-old. She had been summoned that he might see and appreciate the wondrous garment which she had knitted.

"And what is this stitch called?" he asked in a deep voice.

"Stocking stitch." whispered Louise.

"Excellent", he boomed enthusiastically, "And the name of this stitch is...?" and he pointed to another part of the garment.

"Garter stitch."

"Very good, very good indeed. And this one here looks very difficult, how would you describe it?"

"Cable." the child's voice was almost inaudible.

"Cable? And it looks rather like a cable too, doesn't it?" And he laughed in a forced way and nodded vigorously. "And what about this bit, does that have a designation?"

Louise looked silently up at the tall man and Walter could see the line between her lips tremble. He willed her not to cry. He sympathised with both the girl and the man. It was horrible for a shy girl like Louise to be so much the centre of attention. She would suffer for it later in the playground too, when the taunts and jeers would follow her home.

"Teacher's pet!"

"She can knit like a wee auld wifie, so she kin."

But Walter could also see that the inspector knew nothing about knitting and found the whole situation as embarrassing and intimidating as the child did. Walter felt proud and grown-up that he could understand just how awkward the man was feeling.

After what seemed a long time, the teacher spoke,

"That stitch is called one-and-one and it's quite elastic, very handy for edgings." Her voice seemed high and loud.

Walter remembered her words exactly. He did not understand them at the time, but they had stayed in his memory.

"How convenient! Very fine, very fine indeed"

The inspector's voice was serious and deep.

"Well, you are certainly a clever little girl and hard-working too. Well done and..."

He paused for a full minute while he chewed and contorted his lips in a way that Walter had never seen before, then said,

"And keep it up."

The vision faded and in the claustrophobic space of the shop, Walter willed Louise to turn towards him as he had willed her not to cry in that distant time, but her shoulders remained squarely towards the counter. He noted that it was an expensive coat which she wore, although not new. He could have afforded to buy her expensive clothes too. His career in banking had been successful. He glanced at his wife beside him, but Isa looked straight ahead with the strange empty expression which she had worn for ten months now. His hopes that a holiday on the island might cheer her had faded. Yes, she dressed well and she was, as always, well-groomed, More so than Louise in fact, though hardly as stylish, but how sad she looked. A man could scarcely count himself a success when his wife looked so habitually sad.

Walter moved backwards slightly and his heels kicked a box of carrots. The noise seemed immense but neither woman reacted.

His thoughts wandered to summers at the swimming pool after the war, when, as teenagers, he and Louise had returned for holidays. The locals were now more friendly and welcoming. They became part of a crowd that swam and danced and played tennis. Louise always seemed pleased to see him and for three or four years, Walter did not doubt that a shared rosy future stretched ahead for himself and Louise. He was seventeen before he faced the truth that Louise smiled on him no differently from the way she smiled on other boys and that she did not share his vision.

Before that realisation came to him he was in the habit of playing a little trick on Louise. He would step up behind her unexpectedly and placing a hand on each side of her sinuous waist, grasp her firmly and hoist her light frame high up into the air, as high as his arms would stretch above his head. No matter how unexpected it was, Louise would never struggle nor scream, as another girl might. She was wonderful, cool and controlled. Stretching her legs and arching her back she would utter a delicious laugh as though the whole thing were expected and rehearsed. Walter had never tried the trick with any other girl. Nor did he repeat it too often with Louise or the element of surprise would have been lost. He smiled as he remembered clasping the fragile waist and the sensation of his own strength and power. He was sure that Louise enjoyed it too, but once the knowledge dawned on him that she did not share his dreams of the future, he stopped lifting her.

As he pondered those passions and disappointments of over forty years ago, his eyes dropped to the neatly-fitted waist of her dark coat. A waist no longer sinuous, but compact and well-defined. An attractive waist above gently swelling hips. Not the slender girl of the swimming pool of course, but an elegant woman. Walter gave a quiet cough and straightened his shoulders. He would have smoothed his hair with the well-remembered gesture of his youth had not the restricted space made any movement of his arms inexpedient. His hands stayed in his pockets. Besides, there was not a great deal of hair left to smooth.

The sound of the large clock above the tins of tomato soup beat through Isa's thoughts. For a few moments she found relief in concentrating on its melancholy irregularity, but soon the sadness poured back into her mind, filling it to the brim like icy water.

No one had ever suffered such a loss as she had and no one could realise her misery.

No one could understand or help her.

It was ten months and three days since her twin sister, Julie, had died. They had not been particularly close. Friends agreed that they had never been what you would call affectionate sisters. In fact they had quarrelled regularly and lost touch for weeks at a time. When together their conversation was nearly always laced with disagreements, corrections and criticisms. Everyone agreed that Isa was the clever twin and she would regularly use a magnificent sarcasm towards Julie, who would then explode in fury and walk out.

And yet Julie's death had disabled Isa. Although she lived her life as before, cooking, cleaning and shopping as before, visiting the theatre and even playing cards as before, a veil hung between her and the familiar tasks. On the veil was projected the transparent and hazy image of two similar little girls, like a series of snapshots. Sometimes the girls were infants, sometimes young schoolgirls, at other times young women, but always they stood close, smiling at each other with hands joined or arms linked and always presenting a picture of loving harmony. Two cherries on one stalk.

These idyllic visions were not based on actual photographs. There had been no camera in the family in those austere years and there was hardly any documentation of the twins' early life. It was her imagination which generated the recurring pictures of close sisterly love. Not one scene displayed the least suggestion of discord. Now these marvellously happy times that they had shared were gone, irretrievably lost. Just as her youth was lost. Walter, affectionate and unselfish, could not help her. Nor could her

handsome sons and their kindly wives help her and she knew
their patience was wearing thin. Even her darling grandchildren could not blot out those interminable pictures of the two
smiling girls and the terrible feeling of loss. Recently, a
daughter-in-law, braver or more impulsive than the rest, or
perhaps driven to distraction after hours of sentimental
reminiscences had blurted out,

"My God, Isa, there was plenty strife between you and
Julie when she was alive. You were always at each other's
throats as far as I could see."

For a brief moment the expressive face of ten months ago
lit with anger, but Isa's misery was too deep to take offence
and folding her hands on her lap she meekly said.

"I expect that we had our disagreements, sisters always
do. But it wasn't often and I don't remember those times.
Would you like a cup of tea now?"

Her sons had suggested that she might talk to the doctor,
but they too were quickly silenced.

"A doctor has no pills to cure misery, I'm afraid." And a
small condescending smile had ended that conversation.

Louise folded the tiny jacket yet again and smiled to
herself. Still no sound from that hollow stairway. Could it
lead to heaven where Jean had joined Jessie for ever? Less
than an hour till the boat left now. Who were these silent
people who stood so close behind her? She could hear them
breathing. Why did they not speak? Strange. But then she
was not speaking either. What an intolerable situation. She
steeled herself to turn quickly and brush past them with a
bright smile and a brief apology. With this small decision she
made a larger one. She must definitely leave the island for
good. She must sell the house and relinquish its problems and
its memories. But it was certainly not the first time she had
made that decision and she smiled at her own lack of determination.

Normally Walter watched his wife's stone-still face carefully, but now he had ignored her for five minutes. His
untiring patience of the last ten months was forgotten. He
had moved his feet further apart and his left boot was braced
against a crate of milk. He was flexing his shoulders and his

hands were no longer in his pockets. He, too, had come to a decision. Walter, the least impulsive of men, was preparing to repeat that wonderful lift, that long-ago expression of love and strength and youth. His hands closed firmly on the well-corseted waist in front of him.

Louise shrieked and grabbed the edge of the counter to steady herself but only her heels had been lifted from the floor. Walter's decreased muscle power, together with her increased weight, had defeated his intention.

Nevertheless it had been a terrible shock to her. She turned and pushed past him with a dramatically outstretched arm and a vivid stare of fury more eloquent than any words. The door banged behind her and the small bell jingled in a desperate way.

The woollen jacket lay forgotten on the counter.

Louise rushed over the cobbled streets towards her house, her nervous tension forgotten in an all-consuming anger. That horrible old man must be the same detestable boy that always used to terrify her by throwing her into the air unexpectedly! And what an idotic girl she had been, too ridiculously polite to tell him how much she loathed it. Why did he not throw other girls into the air? He was such a little know-it-all at school too and a teacher's pet of the first water. She could never stand him. She was spitting mad!

That settled it, she would see an estate agent this week.

It was time to leave the island.

Walter clenched his fists and swayed slightly. There was a roaring in his ears. He could hardly believe what he had done. What a way for a respectable bank manager to behave

But strangely, his impulsive action had most effect on Isa.

When she was fourteen, she and Julie had *longed* for Walter to lift them up into the air like that. They had both been madly in love with him and would talk of his strength and beauty for hours. The summer was the time they dreaded, for of course he was besotted by the conceited city girl.

Five years later, when Louise had stopped coming to the island, Isa became engaged to Walter. Julie, always a jealous girl, had behaved abominably and had at first refused to be bridesmaid, although she was eventually persuaded. And a very doleful bridesmaid she had been. The wedding photographs were a disaster, with Julie standing with her back to Isa, her bouquet dragging on the floor and that glum look on her face. That was a real photograph and it had never been projected on Isa's veil of misery.

Isa shut her eyes and that black and white photograph of long ago grew brightly coloured and enormously large in her mind. It eclipsed all those falsely remembered sentimental snaps of her imagination. She could even see Julie's protruding lower lip and she was reminded of years of manipulation by that pouting reflection of her own mouth. There was something else which she could not quite recall, never mind, it would come to her later, some memory of Julie being difficult long ago.

Isa felt strangely light as though some burden had suddenly fallen from her shoulders.

But what a peculiar thing for Walter to do to that strange and rather fat woman! Shabby too. She must be a visitor. One of the summer visitors or perhaps one of the "white settlers", as the locals called them. It was apparent that the woman had hated it and no wonder! But she would say nothing to him about what he had done, because he was obviously embarrassed.

Isa slipped her hand through Walter's arm and moved closer to the counter just as slow and unsteady steps sounded on the wooden staircase.

The blue door burst open and the sparkling curls reappeared.

"I just could not find any... oh!" Jean touched the buttons and the tiny garment lying on the counter and her puzzled face searched the little store as though Louise might be hiding in some corner.

Smiling brightly, Isa said,

"Jean, that woman had to catch the ferry, I think. She seemed in a hurry."

Then she turned to Walter and looking up into his face with an expression which he had not seen for ten months, she squeezed his arm gently.

"I think we're needing Nescafe, Walter, and let's have some chocolate digestives, too, darling."

# TOIL

It is strange that you, whose culture and background are so incomprehensible to me, should have learned those thoughts and feelings of mine which I have never shared with any member of the elite corps to which I belong. I have never felt the need to speak to others, and I expect that fact has been noted by those above me. When I return to the Centre at nightfall, because I do not join in the evening conversation, I am marked as different, marked as 'wrong' in some way, because conformity is everything to our squadron. Conformity in dress and behaviour, conformity in working hours and leisure, conformity in the death which overtakes us all at a comparatively young age.

I hate it, I hate it.

Our work is sometimes dangerous and always arduous, demanding our utmost exertion at all times on this alien planet. Not one of us returns to our crowded quarters at the Centre but in a state of exhaustion bordering on despair. Our duties are not finished until we have communicated our findings of the day to each other – how to navigate to the rewarding areas, how to avoid dangerous side-winds and unexpected upward draughts, as of course we fly everywhere, and most important, the location of the poisonous plains. Fortunately there seem to be few predators on your world, or certainly not predators who see us as their prey. We are of course issued with S.D.E. – Self Defence Equipment, but that seems rather a black joke on the part of the Authorities as we are as much at risk from the equipment as anyone else, should it be deemed necessary to use it. I find it interesting that in all the conversation that hurtles around me in the short sleepless nights, mainly complaints and disgruntlements about the impossible work load, the inadequate flight gear, the ridiculous uniforms (and certainly they are bulky and highly impractical and personally I find them embarrassingly gaudy) no one to my knowledge, has ever mentioned the fatal design flaw in the S.D.E. Perhaps it is too terrifying a subject to discuss in the loud, free-and-easy, rather bawdy chatter which disturbs and distresses my nights so much and to which I never contribute. In their alternations of useless self-pity and relentless coarse humour, no reference is ever made to the S.D.E., or to the possibility of activating it. I smile inwardly as I listen and congratulate myself that I have at least the courage to contemplate the finality of using this weapon. My own opinion is that the Authorities have deliberately built in the lethal flaw in the mechanism as a psychological lever, forcing us to work harder and refrain from personal aggression or individual expression of any kind. How clever they have been, creating in each breast an attitude of helpless fatalism.

I hope that I do not give the impression of disliking those around me. That would be untrue. To be so surrounded in my brief leisure hours is horrible to me, certainly, but there are one or two of the multitude who stand out as different, and whose friendship I might value if I cared to break my silence – my silence which is my only protection and privacy. I shall describe them to you.

In the next sleep-lair to mine, lies a worker whose faded uniform stripes proclaim her long service. She has nearly reached the end of her work and of her life. One day soon she will leave the flight platform and not return – her strength will be insufficient. There will be no search-party for the body, we cover far too wide an area daily for that to be practicable. There will be no ritual or service to mark her passing – she will simply be scored off the active service list and forgotten, by me probably as quickly as by others – and yet she might have told me many exciting stories if we had ever spoken. As we work individually in the field, her loss will affect none of us.

Not everyone finishes their career in this way, though I hardly like to speak or even think of the horrible alternative. Sometimes, without warning or explanation, several members are withdrawn from field work and transferred to the vast Temperature Control depot at the lower level of the Centre. No one ever returns to flying service from such a transfer, but it is rumoured that the maintenance work is boring and requires great stamina. I can only vaguely remember my youth and the duties which I performed in the domestic and childcare departments. I did not enjoy those repetitive chores. I found them stifling and I consider my real life only started when I was promoted to reconnaissance and foraging. Such adventure and independence! Such demands on my strength and intelligence! Few careers can be so stimulating and rewarding. How I have loved it and I dread a transfer and the subsequent loss of all that is beautiful, exciting and creative in this hard life.

I close my mind to the possibility of a transfer.

My ancient and infirm neighbour obviously need not now fear such a living hell, but for myself, there are benefits just now in sleeping beside her. Her exhaustion causes her to sleep profoundly and protect me on that side from the inane conversation. No doubt when she is replaced – as must be soon now – by someone young and energetic, the stupid complaints, bemoanings and adolescent sexual innuendos will interrupt my thinking and destroy my dozing. I dread this change and gaze at her ragged faded uniform and pathetic stick-like limbs, while listening to the uneven snore which tells me she still lives. I almost hate her for threatening me with the change in my nights which her death will inexorably bring.

Amongst the crowd there is one who is smaller and paler than the rest – she is noticeable because of her physical difference and also because of the attitude of the others to her. While she shouts, boasts and complains as much as anyone, the others act as though deaf to her voice. Heads are turned away from her just before the necessity arises to give that agreeable nod in answer to a rhetorical question, which makes up such a large proportion of our everyday conversation. In the middle of one of her long sentences, the couple whom she is addressing will suddenly start an animated conversation on a totally unrelated subject, ignoring her from that moment on. She is repeatedly disconcerted, humiliated and confused – walking away, pausing, turning, hesitating. Sometimes her reaction is to blurt out an attempt at sexual humour to the company in general. Her jokes often have a suggestion of rape – it is rather easy to parallel our searching and gathering work with the act of rape. She will be met with

stares of silent reproach from the company – which I consider
sheer hypocrisy. Besides I often find her jokes rather amusing.

One other of my colleagues I would describe briefly. Her
back is considerably deformed and her voice is unnaturally
deep – whether or not because of these facts, she is certainly
treated with a degree of respect by her fellows. While not as
aware as I myself am of the philosophical aspect of our situation on this no doubt marvellous world, she does voice
suspicions regarding our employment and the motives of the
Authorities. She questions the necessity and the rationale of
our unremitting labour. Perhaps if she spoke less and thought
more, she might approach the truth, as I have.

It is wrong, dear Listener, if my story so far makes my life
here on your beautiful planet seem altogether gloomy. My
working life – away from the Centre – has many glorious
advantages and moments of almost painful delight in the
wonders that I see around me. If the work itself were not so
physically demanding, and even the physical challenge is
enjoyable for the first part of the day, I should count myself
fortunate. Indeed, I can remember no other life – nor imagine
one. I know my duty and the unremitting toil which that day
demands. But duty and pleasure can be combined and I gain
all the happiness that my life holds from my work of
searching and gathering in this infinitely fascinating world.

As I have said, we fly, sometimes great distances, to
collection points which have been discovered, often by
chance, by other members of the squadron. The Authorities
insist on our use of the ancient ritualistic and painfully slow
methods of communicating those locations to each other –
and the impatience to be airborne is a tangible thing each
morning on the flight deck. For myself, of course, the
exquisite freedom to leave that jostling noisy crowd, the
liberty to soar away and use my intellectual and athletic skills
– that is my life and my sanity – that is when I live! Yes we
must have athletic skills as well, and I see that seems to
surprise you, because of my uniform, I suppose. Yes, the
uniforms are out-moded, too brightly coloured, too warm, too
cumbersome, but that only means that our bodies must be
stronger and our sense of equilibrium more finely developed
as we climb and clamber and straddle and sometimes cling

practically upside down in the Vessels where we work. Every day is a challenge, and each different type of Vessel has its own problem to solve. The largest Vessels are the simplest to enter. However the aroma, which is present to a greater or lesser degree in all Vessels, can be overpowering in the largest ones and the narcotic air, combined with the surrounding brilliant colours and luminous glow, often induces a swooning sensation, not at all unpleasant, but not conductive to performing one's duty. Some Vessels are so small that there is no possibility of entry, but with special instruments, quite rewarding amounts can be gleaned from them. My favourite type of Vessel – what I call the Secret Vessel – is of a moderate size and is so constructed that it appears to have no entrance. Experience has taught me that there is a special spot on which to stand when, magically, the Vessel opens and I can step easily inside the cool interior, whereupon it shuts once more, enclosing me in a small deliciously scented casket, where I can work in peace and delight.

It was in such a secret Vessel that I was working today when tragedy struck – a forceful blow, ejecting me from the Vessel and throwing me to the stones below, where I lay stunned. Then another blow, and another, then I knew no more until I awakened to the reviving perfume of this tiny Vessel, my favourite amongst the smaller types.

How could you know to bring to me such a revitalising Vessel?

That is a mystery – a greater mystery is how you – who are so vast that I cannot comprehend your size – how can you and I communicate, dear kind Listener. Physically all I see beside me is a large smooth pale brown animal with four limbs, one of which is encircled with yellow metal and three white crystals. This animal moves slowly and carefully nudges the fragrant Vessels towards me – now it has flown away! Perhaps my wits are not yet clear from the violence which was done to me... now it returns gently alighting, making no noise of flying. I do not understand... it has little wrinkles and blemishes and yes, another short fat limb that was hidden before – each limb has a shell-like protector at its extremity... it is too difficult to understand and I am still very weak. Your kind and caring thoughts which flood my mind

are easier to understand, dear Listener, such feelings of love
and succour seem an echo of some experience of long ago,
not quite forgotten... so very unlike my life with the
squadron... so very strange... and your self-description, the
concepts are too difficult... you are unable to walk or fly and
unproductive for the community? And yet you live happily,
cared for by loving descendants?... ancestors and descendants
we may have... but we have no contact with them, no knowledge... and you express sorrow for my accident? Some friend
of yours, but of a different race, caused my distress in play,
you say?... we have no... concept... I am very weak... of play...
but luckily, as you say, your descendant has saved me, kind
Listener, and given me such a glimpse of... happiness my
favourite little Vessels never toss in that noisy... sleep-lair
again – such a glimpse of love.

*These thoughts entered my head as I sat in my wheel-
chair in the sunny garden, watching the distressed bee which
my little grand-daughter, Katy, had saved from our over-
playful cat. Although the poor bee seemed to sip from the
thyme which I pushed close to it, sadly it did not live long.*

# THE GIRL IN THE PINK HAT

Tom hated weddings. He felt alone and unhappy, and yes, angry, in this crowd of chattering people. The very word wedding was unpleasant in his mind.

Because he was tall, he looked down on a sea of enormous soup plate hats, with hardly a human face visible.

Why did every woman follow such a bizarre fashion? Some brims were almost as wide as the wearer's shoulders! It needed height to carry off such an extreme style and most of these women were far too small. They made him think of walking mushrooms.

Here and there a taller figure emerged from the seething mass of pale buckram and there were momentary glimpses of part of a laughing female face, but really it was a peculiar scene – with all those over-sized platforms of primrose, sand, lime green, powder blue bobbing and shaking like a quagmire in a science fiction film. What unknown horrors lay hidden beneath that flower- and feather-strewn surface?

Tom shook himself. Bit over-dramatic surely, but that's how he felt.

Lonely and angry and slightly fearful.

He just hoped nobody mentioned anything about his own matrimonial plans.

He had not wanted to come to his cousin's wedding, but his Mother, who was usually the most undemanding of mothers, had insisted.

"I'll wear a dark suit", he had replied to her question, "I'm a lowland Scot and I haven't worn a kilt since I was six and I don't intend to return to that garment for any ridiculous and unnecessary ritual."

She turned away to look out of the window, and shrugged expressively.

Tom was sure her DNA would show a strong French background.

"I'll look highly respectable, you know. You needn't worry that I'll wear anything you'd hate."

He meant jeans. For as long as he could remember, his mother had expressed astonishment that respectable people, with good salaries, should spend their money and *be seen wearing* those ugly garments, originally designed for labouring navvies.

"Your conference suit? Yes, I know you'll look very good in that, it's splendid."

"It certainly cost plenty. Have you got your own outfit organised?"

"Oh, yes. All fixed up."

"D'ye want me to pick you up and take you there?"

"No thanks, darling, Jean and I will take a taxi."

"Will you both be shedding tears at your niece's wedding?"

His own bitterness had prompted the question and he immediately regretted asking it. His Mother smiled slightly,

"I don't cry at weddings."

Tom felt rebuked. It was only a year since his Father's funeral where many tears had been shed.

"I'll see you there, then. In the church."

His Father's death at fifty-eight had been a terrible blow.

His parents had always seemed so much younger and more energetic than other parents. They were so happy together with many shared interests, yet they also pursued independent hobbies. It was a wonderful partnership and he was proud of them. Since his teens, their obviously successful marriage had inspired his own determination to find the right girl and marry while he was still young.

Eight years ago, when he was just twenty, he had expressed these thoughts to his Mother.

At the time she had laughed.

"Oh well, it's not all wine and roses, Tom. You have to work at it and there are good times and bad times in all marriages. Our first year was shockingly bad and difficult. We were always rowing and moaning at each other."

"*What?* I can't believe that. Surely that was the honey-moon period."

"It was a period of adjustment, which is never easy. Your Father had to learn that I was not his adoring subservient mother and I suppose I had to have some of the girlish nonsense knocked out of me!"

Her son looked so horrified that she burst out laughing.

"Oh, we worked hard at it. Lots of quarrels and intense discussions and sulks and walking out, then kissing and making up again. Eventually, over the years, I suppose we pummelled each other into the right shape to suit each other. I expect we listened to each other more carefully than some folk do. It's a terrific marriage now and I hope we can continue to enjoy it until we're old and grey. Ninety four at least, I confidently expect. And I hope you can have the same sort of relationship in your life, dear Tom. Not for a while yet though. You're a bit wet behind the ears still. You don't even know what you want for yourself yet, do you?"

He had remembered that conversation word for word and, since his Father's death, the poignancy of her light-hearted advice and optimism frequently recurred to him.

Tom was honest enough to realise that in a strange way, his Father's death had shaken him out of the apathetic and self-centred mental state in which he had wallowed since his broken engagement.

A death clarified the priorities of life.

For the first time that he could remember, his mother had needed his support. He had come to understand her more clearly in the last year, perhaps understand women in general more clearly. They were certainly very different from men in their outlook. That was something that he had not considered before, believing fully in the equality of the sexes. Equal, but strangely different.

Yes, he had helped his mother through quite a few of her difficulties this last year. Not that she herself could not have dealt with the various necessary tasks, but she had no spirit to do so. The legal paperwork seemed so futile, compared to her loss. She had leaned on her son and was very grateful to him.

It assuaged some of his guilt. Only a month before his Father's unexpected death, it was he who had decided that his marriage to Eve Harper would not take place. He was still not sure how justified he had been in dealing the final blow to what had seemed to be a perfect relationship for more than two years. Though unconnected, the two disturbing events were united in a dark blank space in his mind, a space which he avoided visiting, yet was aware of at all times. It was as if a gloomy cloud overspread all the other aspects of his life.

It sometimes seemed to him that supporting his mother had helped save his own sanity. At least he had been able to hide away all his regrets and the never-ending self-questioning. Surely that was for the best.

Tom looked at the predictable plate in front of him. Chicken breast with a colourful heap of finely shredded salad beside it, three miniature potatoes, sprinkled with pulverised parsley, a small heap of black pudding and some overcooked broccoli. The bare parts of the plate were decorated with small splashings of a greenish sauce as though a child had been asked to add its naive artistry. On either side of Tom the plates were exact replicas of his own. How did they do that? How many guests? Perhaps eighty? Ninety? All those plates exactly like each other and all tasteless. He imagined a moving belt in a factory, with each plate slowly turning to receive the various elements in exactly the perfect spot. Perhaps to add importance, a chef would deposit the chicken, but after that the vegetables would tumble down a chute or a spout as the plate travelled along. Possibly the black pudding would be extruded from a metal tube, followed by the final decorative green squirt. Disgusting.

He was not hungry.

He should never have come.

The young lady on his right had tried to make conversation but he had not helped her and finally she gave up and ignored him. The elderly lady on his left seemed intent on enjoying her meal. Good luck to her. He hoped she had her indigestion tablets in her handbag.

As he pushed the food around the plate, he found himself thinking of Eve's fantastic plans for the wedding that they might have shared.

That was dangerous ground.

The wedding was the rock on which they had wrecked their wonderful relationship.

For the first time in over a year, Tom allowed himself to remember how intense and rewarding their love affair had been, passionate and companionable. It seemed miraculous that they should have found each other.

That was before the wedding plans started, those complicated, impossibly ambitious wedding plans that seemed to
cast a spell over Eve. He had thought that he knew her so
well.

What had happened to that witty, smartly dressed, energetic girl who loved her job of teaching? Who was a demon
on the tennis court? Who took an interest in literature, music,
politics? That girl who would cook splendid meals and make
him laugh and laugh easily herself, yet who could show such
sympathy and compassion to those less fortunate than
herself? Why had the thought of marriage changed her
completely? It certainly had changed her.

She had become obsessed by the idea of a perfect wedding
day.

His suggestion of a small informal celebration, sooner
rather than later, had been the first time that they had found
themselves completely furious and miserably apart in two
years. Tom had been dumfounded at her vehement rejection
of this idea. His joking remark that it was 'only a bit of paper
to make us legal' brought a reaction of hysterical tears.

When he saw how terribly important it was to Eve, he
back-pedalled furiously. Of course he would be happy to fall
in with any plans she might want.

She wanted everything. It would take at least eighteen
months to plan and organise this event.

She had actually called it that.

"Good God, a year and a half! I don't want to wait a year
to call you my wife! And what sort of event! Who d'ye think
we are? Royalty?" Tom had yelped in disbelief, generating
another flood of tears.

His problems increased, for all discussions were related to
the dress, the church, the guests, the flowers, the food. Eve
seemed fixated on the wedding day. She was uninterested in
what happened after that. Even the honeymoon held no charms.

"I don't mind where we go, darling. You decide and
surprise me. I have quite enough to organize with the
wedding."

"But tell me what you'd prefer. Would you like a quiet
little hotel in the Highlands, or would you like a sophisticated

few days in Paris, or perhaps some really exotic spot on the other side of the world with white beaches and lagoons? I've got that money tucked away that Uncle Henry left me. Let's make it something we'll always remember."

"No really, Tom, don't bother me with those problems." She sounded quite irritated, "Surely you can arrange all that yourself."

Tom felt snubbed, but then he had no work to do for the wedding preparations and perhaps he was being helpless and selfish. He just could not find the same enthusiasm for what was really only a big party which would last for just one day. There was all the rest of their life together to plan.

When he found just the right little flat for them, he did expect her to be interested. He organised three flats to view that night, but was positive that Eve would love the one near the park as much as he did. It was small but close to Eve's school and Tom's office.

Eve walked around the three bright rooms with a preoccupied air. At least no mention was made of the wedding for the twenty minutes that they spent there.

"Did you like it, darling?" Tom asked nervously, as they took the shortcut through the park.

"I don't really know, Tom. It's hard for me to think about anything other than the wedding just now."

"Yes, but that's months away and we've got to think about where we're going to stay. You're sharing with all those other girls and my pad is just a dump. I think that one was great, clean and sunny and the price not too exorbitant. Didn't you like it, looking out over the trees?"

"I suppose it was all right. I can't say I was mad about it. I just don't know if I can be bothered thinking about it just now."

"Well, I'll keep looking. We need to find somewhere to start our wonderful life together."

He kissed her, but she broke away quickly and started to discuss the type of flowers that she would like to have in the church.

"Then I suppose it would be best to have different, less perfumed ones for the reception. I wouldn't like them to smell too strongly and spoil the flavour of the food. Do you remember what those large orange daisies are called! They're so spectacular and they have hardly any scent. I'd like those with masses of gypsophila in the hall, then posies of those little tiny purple hyacinths on the tables."

Tom grunted. He knew nothing about flowers, nor did he think them important compared to their future home.

"Tom, have you booked your morning suit hire yet? You won't get a good fit if you leave it to the last minute. Do try and remember tomorrow."

"I have seven months yet to arrange that," he grumbled, but she had stopped and was looking in a stationer's window at designs for invitations. They looked grotesque to Tom, with superabundant ribbons decorating each one.

"You'd need awfully big envelopes for those fancy ones. Might not even go through the letterboxes!"

She looked at him coldly.

The day came when Tom became really angry. It was when he heard that Eve had objected to the outfit which her Mother had bought to wear for the wedding. Eve insisted that it was returned to the shop and she accompanied her Mother to choose a more acceptable one.

He heard about this from his own Mother, who joked that she was now a bit nervous about what she herself should wear.

"Do you think there will be an inspection parade beforehand? I hope my blue suit comes up to scratch."

"There had better not be anything like that!"

Tom could hardly believe it. He was furious.

"She's gone mad. Nothing matters to her except that this bloody wedding should be beyond any wedding that ever was before! Honestly, it's all she thinks about. It's as if our lives don't exist apart from that one day. That one bloody special nonsensical day. As though the rest of our lives together isn't important. She doesn't care about where we stay or what furniture we buy and she can't even let her mother choose her own outfit. It's outrageous! Surely it's not natural. We have seven months to get through and she can't talk about anything else. Not with me, anyway. I wonder if she's able to keep off the subject with her pupils? She's absolutely crazy, she's obsessed. She doesn't want to play tennis or go to the

cinema or anything. If we meet friends, we talk about the
wedding. All she ever talks or thinks about is that one
damnable Special Day. She hasn't cooked me a meal in
weeks."

And there were other neglected aspects of their relationship, which he did not mention to his mother.

"Now Tom, she's probably nervous about the whole thing.
Marriage is a big step for any girl and Eve hasn't had such an
example of parental stability as you have."

Eve's parents had been divorced when she was three.

"Besides you must admit that her Mum is not renowned
for her dress sense."

"Nevertheless... what a fuss... it's humiliating... taking her
mother back to the shop... I had no idea Eve was like that. I'm
very disappointed."

His brow was darker than his mother had ever seen it

She sighed deeply.

Tom's thoughts were brought back to the present, as his
half-full plate was removed by the plump waitress,

"Did ye no' enjoy yer meal, surr?"

"Not really hungry..." Tom mumbled.

The conversation buzzed around him. He must seem a real
skeleton at the feast. He should never have come. Guiltily he
hoped his mother had not been watching him. He looked
around, but could not see her. Leaning forward he peered past
the large pale brims to the far end of the table, where a vivid
pink felt hat caught his eye. It was so extremely different
from every other hat there. The crown was deep and the
waving brim swept back from the face with a swashbuckling
vigour. The fabric was soft and sympathetic compared to the
ubiquitous buckram. The unsmiling face under the pink hat
looked back at Tom with no sign of recognition. The clear cut
chin was determined. The deep set eyes gazed at him for
longer than might have been expected, then her head turned
slowly away.

Perhaps her unfriendly stare was a challenge, for as soon
as the meal and the interminable speeches were over and
dancing had started, Tom made his way through the crowd to
the girl in the pink hat and asked her to dance.

"I think that's a terrific hat you're wearing. The very best of all the hats here. Do you intend to dance the wild Scottish reels in that hat?"

"I expect to leave before they start those stupid energetic dances." She looked up at him, glared almost. She was still unsmiling.

She wore no jewellery and her pale grey dress was simple and elegant. Tom thought her the most stylish woman in the room. He hesitated then stammered,

"Did you enjoy the lunch?"

"It was awful. Wedding meals generally are awful, I think. How do they manage to spoil good food like that?"

Tom smiled slightly. This girl's mood seemed to match his own.

"I take it that you dislike weddings as much as I do?"

"Hate them."

"Why do we come to them, I wonder?"

"Relatives expect it and also partly to wear a nice hat, I suppose and partly..." Her voice trailed into silence.

"And partly... what else would you say?" Tom bent towards her to hear every word.

"Partly to help the bride feel that she's the most important person in the world for that one particular day and also to..."

He waited for the rest of her sentence, raising his eyebrows questioningly.

"And also to help her deal with her fears for the future."

"Wouldn't you agree that those fears should melt away once you meet the right person?"

"I suppose so. In fact you're absolutely right."

"And these big wedding shindigs are just a waste of money and energy that could be used for real living."

"Just a waste, ridiculous, really."

"I believe there's a wonderful marriage suite here in the city. It's a magnificent Italianate house where a small civil wedding can be performed in a circular chamber, with only the couple and their witnesses present."

"That sounds perfect to me."

"Don't you think that as we both hate big showy weddings so much, it would be sensible to leave this one right now?"

"Yes, I do."

She looked up at him from under the brim of her hat.

"Tom, I was such a damned fool. I don't know what came over me. All that idiotic nonsense – what was I thinking about?"

"We were both idiots, Eve. Let's walk round by the park and we might see a FOR SALE sign."

# KUMIHAMA

I was in a train travelling northwards to the holiday area on the coast of the Sea of Japan before I finally found myself alone. I like to be alone. It was the natural state of a shy, only child, and I have not changed with age. After several days in the company of others, however pleasant that company may be, I long to be alone, for then it is possible to absorb so much more, to bathe in the very essence of what is strange in the environment and to recognise and appreciate what is unexpectedly familiar.

Of course it is too difficult to tour a country when one has absolutely no knowledge of the language, spoken or written, a language impossibly and utterly different from the scraps and scrag-ends of the various European tongues which lurk in our consciousness. In Japan you need a lot of help from your friends. I had now been in that mysterious and delightful country for six days and had visited Tokyo and Kyoto. I had been wonderfully well cared for by several different people and led from one interesting place to another in much the same sort of helpless and dependent way that a dog or a small child is taken. It was an unusual experience for someone who has lived a long life of peculiar independence and I realised the horror of being lost or forgotten that must strike the heart of a creature who, unable to communicate, finds itself in an unknown environment.

On my journey from Tokyo on the bullet train which shoots between the new and the old capitals, I was unaccompanied but not exactly alone as I had entered into conversation with an Australian couple, who sadly appeared to be on the brink of ending their coupledom. Perhaps my presence saved them from outright violence.

Rather than be caught in the crossfire of their mutual sniping I should have preferred to inspect the smart interior of the train and enjoy the hypnotic effect of an endless scarlet stream of electronic information in both English and Japanese, which appeared above the doorway. The Japanese language seems particularly suited to be rendered in small red dots, but then, it always does look so much more aesthetic than our mundane ABC.

As the Australians and myself were probably the only English speaking people on the entire train, I wondered if the diligent Japanese travellers used this opportunity to improve their English Throughout the journey there was a constant parade of smartly dressed young people offering sustenance in the form of the obento box, a beautifully wrapped box of sushi. Even the uncountable miles of industrialisation which stretch south from Tokyo have a boring fascination, though I missed my chance to glimpse Fujiyama in the distance.

After a few energetic days in Kyoto, the next stage of my journey was accomplished on a much smaller and slower train. As I trundled across the plain and looked back at the beautiful city and its surrounding mountains, I was alone and deliciously happy. There was no problem of deciphering the names of stations to know when to alight, as my station, Kumihama, was fortunately the last on the line. My mind was full of the previous few days of non-stop sight-seeing. It was interesting and flattering that none of my enthusiastic guides had expected that someone of my advanced years might suffer from jet-lag or sheer fatigue. There were no gaps allowed for rest in my full itinerary, and I will admit that the thought of now sitting for four hours doing nothing but watch the passing scene seemed very like heaven to me. And I was alone.

*Soporific train*
*Travelling smoothly onwards,*
*Past ancient scenes.*

Since I had left home I had developed an irresistible need to put my thoughts into the haiku structure, the traditional dense Japanese verse of seventeen syllables, which must refer, though perhaps obliquely, to the season and should also express some philosophic thought. Needless to say, my verses were in English, pretty low in philosophy and referring to the season only by chance, but what they lacked in quality was balanced by quantity. By the time I was on my way to Kumihama, it had become a compulsion and a close observer would have noted my fingers continuously beating out the five, seven, five syllable lines of the haiku format, before another few scribbles were jotted down in my notebook.

*I see wet rice fields.*
*Reflecting the passing hills.*
*And providing food.*
*So strange to my eyes,*
*A tractor, hub-deep in mud,*
*Prepares the rice-fields.*

I was happy in my harmless pastime and delighting in the strange scenery which passed me. I felt relaxed and yet adventurous.

The barren hillsides of Scotland must look strange to the Japanese eye, for, after the plain, we came to mountains which were thickly wooded to the summit. This is not a modern railway line and the many tunnels which allowed our train the pass this barrier of mountains were impressive. It must have been a daunting task for the engineers to design and build them.

*I pass the mountains,*
*Piercing through them in the dark.*
*My ears feel their weight.*
*Immense mass above me.*
*I scurry like a fast mole*
*Under pine-tree roots.*

Sometimes the vista of a long river valley would materialise at right angles to the tracks and almost immediately be swept away again by encroaching mountains.

After charging miles through thick and varied forest, a charming small town would suddenly appear like a theatre transformation. Every bit of ground around the houses appeared to be used for the rice crop. The reflecting watery fields were amazingly close to the houses, almost on their doorsteps and the use made of hilly or uneven terrain created beautiful shapes. I learned later that the water recedes as the crop grows but in May, at planting time, the atmosphere is appallingly damp and there is a constant struggle to protect clothes and household fabrics from mildew.

Later we passed small stations, obviously holiday resorts where families and their luggage waited on the platform, but no one boarded my train as it was a special sightseeing train. The last part of the journey was run by a private company on a private track and when we reached the changeover, a most exquisite young conductor, dressed from top to toe in pristine white serge, boarded the train and asked me in beautiful English for extra money. Although I had not expected to pay another fare, it was a pleasure to give it to him.

*As young and tender*
*As the foliage of Spring,*
*He takes my ticket.*

At last we arrived at the tiny station of Kumihama. There were only four or five passengers by that time and I was in no doubt that I had reached the end of my journey. The station building formed one side of a small deserted square and was straight from a production of the Mikado. I learned later that it was a historic building which had been in danger of demolition in a different location and had been moved there to act as the railway station office. I certainly saw no other station as charming as Kumihama.

I knew that my hotel was outside the town, though not how far and I was armed with a note in Japanese, to give to the taxi driver, which asked him to take me to the Hotel Resorpia. I felt like the prince in so many fairy tales, who has been given some unlikely charm by an old witch in a wood. A precious talisman which must not be lost, as it will facilitate his journey through untold dangers. I clutched the scrap of paper more tightly at the thought that those hieroglyphics that looked so elegant but so unmeaning to me, were my only lifeline in this small empty town. The other alighting passengers had snatched all the taxis and I stood in the silent village street with a distinct hollowness inside me.

I should interrupt my narrative to explain why it was that I found myself heading for an unknown hotel in a small Japanese coastal resort. Firstly, the fact that two friends were resident in Japan at that time had generated the idea of a holiday. I would stay with Edward in Tokyo and with Chihoko in Matsue, an old-fashioned city of many bridges, some five hundred miles from the capital. While still planning the trip, I was introduced to a Japanese lady who was studying in

Glasgow. She insisted that I must visit Kyoto and volunteered her sister as my guide. As it was a once-in-a-lifetime visit I decided to stay in Japan for three weeks. Then a close friend in Scotland made a kind suggestion. As she has a time-share apartment in Torremolinos which she does not always use, perhaps I might exchange it for something in Japan and such is the organisation of the modern holiday industry, that this was not at all difficult. It was not exactly a pin-sticking choice as I wanted to be at the seaside and Kumihama was on the sea and seemed to be not too far from Matsue. Chihoko would travel from Matsue and spend a few days with me in this hotel before taking me back to Matsue. She would not arrive until the following day.

As I stood outside the exquisite wooden railway station with its vernacular roof, not a soul was in sight. I had no idea how far away the hotel was, how much a meal would cost in the hotel or how much the taxi would cost. Would the hotel be within walking distance of the town? Would there be a beach near the hotel? Would anyone speak English? Most terrifying was what I would do if no taxis returned to the square? What use would my scrap of paper be then? Yes, I felt very like one of those fairytale princes as he prepares to climb the steep slopes of a glass mountain, or encounter the dog with eyes as big as soup plates.

Eventually a dilapidated taxi wheeled into the square and I produced my magic note. The driver read it slowly, as if unwilling to believe what he saw, I had the opportunity to gaze at a most extraordinary face. It was not at all a typical face of Japan, though certainly Japanese. It was a very long, thin face with an aquiline nose, and dramatically framed in a wild mass of pure white curls, the style that was referred to in the seventies as an Afro. His hair was like a wig, appearing to be several inches long and the same length all over his head. His suit was formal but shabby and he was neither young nor old. It seemed as though the only proper place for him would be the stage, for his gestures and his looks were those of an actor and he drove the car with a showy elegance. He obviously spoke no English and after reading the note, invited me to enter his cab with a curt nod and an airy wave of his beautiful hand.

We drove at least three twisting unpavemented miles along
the coast to the hotel. I realised that I would not be walking
into Kumihama every day. Close to the shore and almost
continuously, were regular lines of wooden stakes in the
water, presumably for fish or seaweed farming. I saw no
beaches as we drove. The hotel was built high on a hillside
and the last quarter mile was very steep. I began to feel less
adventurous and more like the fairytale princess who waits
passively to be rescued. I was really glad that Chihoko would
come to my aid the next day. Perhaps I was tired.

It was a most impressive and luxurious hotel. At the foot
of the spacious staircase, two Rennie Mackintosh chairs stood
against the wall as if to welcome me.

I climbed the stairs and crossed an enormous foyer to the
reception desk. Not a soul was in sight. Acres of grass green
carpet disappeared in all directions. Glass walls surrounded me
and all was silent except for a distant sound of falling water. I
could see the fountain shooting high into the air and plum-
meting harshly back into a free form swimming pool on the
patio below. I rang the bell.

The beautifully dressed young woman spoke no English,
but there seemed no need. I was obviously the only Western
guest expected and I was given my key and pointed in the
direction of the lifts. As I entered the lift I was aware of music
playing, but it was no longer audible inside the lift and I had
not quite recognised it. However, when the lift doors opened at
my floor, it flooded once again over me and I greeted it and
with great delight. In the previous year I had choreographed a
dance for a group of children that I have taught for several
years. I have known most of them since they were three and I
am very fond of them. This music now playing in a hotel so
distant from my home was the same piece of early and little-
known Beethoven that I had used for their dance. I found it
almost supernatural that this music with which I was so
familiar should be in my ears as I walked along the corridor to
my room. In my imagination the corridor was peopled with
those dear children, dancing and skipping around me. When I
entered my hotel room it was as though I were returning to a
welcoming home and all my feelings of timidity had disappeared.

What a wonderful room it was. Three or four times larger than a normal hotel bedroom, it had the capacity to sleep four people comfortably. One quarter of the rectangular area was the small entrance hall and luxurious bathroom. One quarter had a large wardrobe and dressing table, desk, minibar and TV, as well as a soft leather three-piece suite. Beside the wardrobe were slippers and a neatly folded yukata, which is a simple and informal cotton kimono, also a dark blue warm woollen tanzen, which is the same shape but short, like a jacket. These were for my journey to the bath house. Another quarter had a balcony opening from it with a stupendous view. In this quarter were the twin beds with their pretty covers of deep rose-pink, the bedside tables and excellent reading lights, always of great importance to me. I might almost say I judge a hotel by its bedside reading facilities. The last quarter was the typically Japanese tatami area. The floor of this unique Japanese feature is always raised above other floors and is carpeted in the straw matting called tatami and one *must* remove shoes before walking on these mats. In the old houses which I visited in Kyoto, the entire house was covered in tatami and shoes were removed at the front door. I suppose this would be less possible in a hotel. Tatami mats are of a uniform size and are used as a unit of measurement. A room might be a four, six or eight mat room. Mine was a six mat and in that area there was a low traditional table and cushions for a meal to be served and that is also where the futons would have been laid if required. Everything looked absolutely flawless, as though it had come straight from the shop. I walked around my demesne with a delightful feeling of ownership. This would be my private space for a week and I would be able to offer hospitality to my friend.

When I stepped out on to the balcony, the sun shone radiantly on a vast breath-taking view. To my left was an inlet of the Sea of Japan with steep mountains and the sea disappearing in the general direction of China or Russia. In the foreground were the wooden structures in the water which I later learned were for seaweed farming. Ahead and to my right were hills and in the distance mountains with every hue of forestry on them. Because I was high on the hill, there was that broad vision of space and distance all around me which suggests that the power of flying without the help of machinery may yet lie within the human grasp. Below me on the terrace was the free form swimming pool with the relentless fountain. That was the fly in my ointment for an impressive amount of water was shooting up into the air and returning noisily to the surface of the pond. Its continuous uproar was intrusive in the peaceful silence of the mountainside. It had no discernible rhythm, but every few minutes, electronically no doubt, it changed its pattern of falling and just as one became used to one type of clattering, another started. One might have learned to disregard the sound after a time if this regular change had not demanded ones attention. Even with the window closed the noise was impossible to ignore. I lay down on the wonderfully comfortable bed but the irritating uproar banished sleep and I decided to unpack and explore the hotel. I wondered momentarily if I had the courage to take a swim in the noisy pool and at least have some good of it, but no other guest was to be seen and I baulked at dipping my elderly person in the pool in full sight of all the balconies, unoccupied as they probably were. Besides, though the weather was pleasant it was not hot and with that ever freshening fountain, the pool was likely to be icy cold.

As I walked around the hotel and found the dining room I was impressed anew at its luxury and perfection. I saw one or two staff but not a guest. I decided that not only did I not have the courage to have dinner by myself that night, I did not need it. I had some sandwiches which had been purchased for me in Kyoto and fruit and chocolate. I would just have a very quiet night, write my diary and read my book.

On returning to the room, darkness was falling and added to the changing sounds of the fountain were changing coloured lights. I cannot say that the lights were any more aesthetic than the noise. However it did give me a feeling of deja-vu, which often happened to me in Japan, a momentary flash of memory of things that had existed in my childhood of fifty-odd years ago and were no longer part of British life. Fountains with changing patterns and coloured lights were very fashionable in the thirties of my childhood.

# EMBARKATION

She stood for a moment, hesitating in amazed incredulity at the vast space which lay before her. The sheer absurdity of the proportions of the place made her smile and also tremble a little.

The architect who designed this building had been given a very free hand and had obviously cared nothing for the economics of saving space.

At her feet, a daunting stairway, broader than a city street, fell in three equal flights directly to the floor of the immense hall. She guessed that each of these flights must have more than twenty steps, perhaps twenty-five, and she determined to count them as she descended.

Although each step was luxuriously shallow, thus adding to the length of the flight, the staircase was dwarfed by the hall which it served. It was certainly the largest indoor space that Amy had ever seen.

As she stood motionless and gazed at the breath-taking spectacle she realised that the ceiling was as high above her head as the floor was far beneath her feet. The far end of the great chamber was so distant that the mist of aerial perspective transformed the rich blue of the floor covering to grey.

It seemed to Amy that the air contained within those immeasurable walls was almost palpable and she smoothed her hair, as she often did when nervous.

Below her, scattered knots of people stood as if waiting. These groups appeared sparse and unimportant in the almost limitless concourse.

An assorted crowd huddled behind her on the narrow landing. It surprised Amy that the landing should be so narrow.

No one was ascending or descending the stairs and she felt herself strangely unwilling to be the first.

However it was useless to stand doing nothing, so with a quick glance over her shoulder at the others and a familiar feeling of being the reluctant leader in an unpleasant but

necessary action, Amy stepped forward and started downwards.

No one followed her.

There was no handrail! When she was younger, Amy had
been proud of her ability to float smoothly down stairs, using
her muscles to disguise all apparent effort but now, at sixty-
eight, she preferred the confidence conferred by a
lightly-touched hand rail.

Oh! They were *wonderfully* easy stairs and it was a pleasure to descend them. She felt she was flowing downwards,
almost as she had done long ago.

Amy's normally unpredictable knees were quite happy on
those shallow stairs! She straightened her shoulders and felt
some of her former grace and elegance return to her. As a girl
she had entered and won several beauty contests and as she
glided downwards she experienced that old, long-gone
feeling of self-confidence and delight in being the cynosure
of all eyes. Some of the people below turned towards her and
gazed at her in an admiring way – or so it seemed to her.

As she descended, she became aware of music which,
though not recognisable, was charming. By the time that she
had reached the bottom of the first flight, she realised that the
enchanting bell-like sounds were a pattern of descending
chords. Though not loud, these reverberations seemed to fill
the endless atmosphere of the place, echoing and re-echoing
until the separate chords blended together in a complex
fugue. As Amy crossed the landings between flights the
sounds died away, only to start immediately again, though in
a different key, as she stepped on the first step of the second
flight, and she realised with embarrassed delight that it was
her weight on each step which produced the melody.

How fantastic it seemed! No wonder the people were
looking at her. It was not her elegance after all, she smiled to
herself.

How strange that no one else was using the staircase!
Could it be shyness?

Amy had a sudden urge to move back up a step or two
and change the direction of the chords. Or perhaps she would
vary her speed or miss out chords altogether by taking two
steps at a time, then she might jump twice on each step

coming down, finishing off with four big 'Beethovenish' jumps on one step! What fun she could have on those stairs but the audience and the sheer size of her surroundings excluded any such flippant behaviour.

Also, she doubted her own agility.

When she reached the very last step of the third flight, she considered turning around and going sedately up again, just to enjoy the ascending chords, but she had not the courage.

The vivid blue floor surprised her. Though looking like vinyl, it felt like carpet and she had the sensation of sinking into its soft depth. She found this worrying and rather unpleasant, like walking through snow.

Though the centre of attention while descending the staircase, Amy found that she was now ignored. No one in any group glanced at her.

"Just as if it were a supermarket or a railway station." She told herself, though it was much too clean for either and everyone seemed very well dressed.

Amy had no idea where she was or where she was going, and, strangely, she was not worried.

Perhaps this was what it was like to lose your memory? Or, horrible thought, could it be the onset of Alzheimer's? But that was nonsense for she felt absolutely fine and surely, if she could analyse the situation so clearly, there was little wrong with her. She certainly felt perfectly clear-headed and logical.

Perhaps she had taken a wrong turning and quite soon she would realise her exact location.

Should she ask for directions? But directions to do what or to go where?

As she walked towards the far end of the hall, she had the unnerving feeling that people turned to watch her after she had passed. She refused to turn around quickly to catch them out. What would she say to them anyway? She slowed her pace to glance back at the soaring staircase which was empty and even more impressive from here. The group at the top of the stairs had grown larger and still showed no ambition to descend. They reminded Amy of those erstwhile bathers of her youth who, lacking the fortitude to leap into the icy North Sea, crouched unmoving on the seaweedy rocks until the east wind so chilled and paralysed them that they were forced to clamber stiff-legged back to their warm clothing on the beach and return home ignominiously. She had despised them.

The far end of the hall was further away than she had realised. What with an imperceptible upward incline and the dragging floor-covering, it was tiring. How easy would that blue stuff be to clean? How many industrious Mrs Mopps set to work when the crowds cleared away. Not a really big crowd, of course. It seemed foolish to have such an enormous area for two or three hundred people but perhaps this was a quiet time. But all that space above one's head! Why? All so beautifully maintained, too, in pristine white. So much scaffolding required for painting! What unnecessary expense! Amy had struggled with maintenance costs on a restricted budget for most of her life.

Suddenly she noticed a series of white doors on her right with a list of names pinned beside each. She brought out her glasses and saw that the names started with the initials A to C and she felt distinctly relieved. Some logic at last. She need only find the list with her name on it.

That took longer than she had hoped, as the list on the next door was from R to T and on the next it was all Macs. Very Scottish! She was torn between anger and despair and walked past many doors, removing and replacing her spectacles and fuming. Like so many other things these days, this place, with all its impressive opulence and apparent professionalism, was so damned un-business-like!

Still with the uncomfortable feeling that many of the bystanders were watching her as she wandered from door to door, she at last found the list for J to L and there was Amy Jack at the very top!

Delightedly she grasped the handle of the door, turned it firmly and pushed. The door did not open. She turned the handle and pulled. Nothing. She could have wept with frustration.

It was a long time since she had eaten or drunk anything. How she would have loved a cup of coffee.

She tried the handle again, with no success.

She felt a light tap on her shoulder. It was a slender woman who had detached herself from the nearest group.

"Perhaps I could help?" she said in a quiet voice that sounded very sweet to Amy.

"Oh, please, that would be so good of you! Thank you!"

The woman smiled and with no apparent effort, slid the door sideways.

"Thank you so much, I'm terribly grateful."

But the woman had hurried back to her friends with hardly a nod and Amy felt over-effusive and stupid.

Amy stepped into a narrow, low-ceilinged corridor with a feeling of excitement. Walls and floor were a murky purple and it was such a contrast to the outer hall that Amy felt like an escaping mouse and giggled at the thought. Her grandchildren would enjoy hearing about this adventure. Ahead of her was a deep pink door and she knocked timidly. A faint voice bade her enter. A middle-aged man sat at a large desk shuffling through a sheaf of flimsy yellow sheets of paper. He glanced at Amy but did not smile or invite her to sit down. He had round pale blue eyes and a large nose and reminded her of her bank clerk who was a constant irritation, for he seldom gave her any sign of recognition, in spite of years of dealing with her account.

She sat down and waited, assuming a quizzical look and ready to be cross.

"Now, Amy Jack, we have a lot of work to get through here." His voice was loud and unfriendly and Amy, who was used to a title, felt herself tensing. This man was abominably rude and she would certainly be complaining about him. He wore no name-tag, but she would ask for his name in due course and meantime try to control her anger. Better to show an example of good manners to a boor like this.

She answered as pleasantly as she could.

"I daresay we do have work to get through, but I am afraid that you must explain to me what it is exactly, because I am completely ignorant of where I am or the reason for my being here. I'd like to say I'm usually addressed as *Mrs Jack*."

The man laughed without opening his mouth and it was unpleasant to see.

"Oh, I think you know where you are, Amy Jack. Or if you don't, you soon will. Now to business. First of all..."

"Excuse me," Amy interrupted him and saw immediately

from his look of surprise that he was unused to interruption, nor did he like it! However, she continued,

"I am really not used to being called Amy Jack like a school girl and I would prefer Mrs Jack, please. Although I suppose it is more fashionable to use first names nowadays, so if you want to call me Amy... I must just accept it."

He shuffled the papers noisily and dropped one or two, grunting as he bent down to pick them up. She could see that she had surprised and upset him but 'in for a penny in for a pound' and she added,

"And perhaps you could inform me of your own name... and position."

She did feel she was being mischievous asking the last because she could see how old-fashioned and authoritative he was. She did not care any more. She crossed one knee over the other and smoothed her skirt down. Perhaps her knees were a bit stiff but her legs were still shapely, strong walking legs with neat ankles.

He neither answered her questions or noticed her ankles but slowly tapped a few words into his computer with two awkward index fingers.

Amy had noticed immediately that it was a strange, antiquated computer, but she almost laughed aloud when he gave several turns to a handle at the side of the machine. The handle was reminiscent of the comptometers that bright young women without much education learned to operate in the days of Amy's youth. She could remember the columns of jobs advertised for comptometer operators. What a tongue twister that was. But she was becoming impatient. This man had assured her that there was a lot of work to get through and here she was waiting, waiting for him! When would he start? Had she so insulted him that he was going to sulk until it was too late.

But too late for what?

Suddenly he leaned across the desk and gazing into her face, spoke deliberately.

"We are here to discuss your sins."

"*I beg your pardon.*"

Amy uncrossed her legs and sat forward in her seat with a jerk, her eyes and mouth wide open.

"Yes, I see here that as a child, you picked your nose and ate it."

Amy closed her mouth with snap and shook her head a little.

"Is that not the case?"

"I was only four or five at the time! All children do that anyway, they go through a stage and then they stop, they grow out of it. All my children certainly did." She felt embarrassed and also indignant.

"Did you *know* it was a wrong thing to do?"

"Surely we are talking about a bad habit and not a sin?"

*"Did you know that it was a wrong thing to do ?"*

"Not at first but eventually I did, of course. Certainly there were enough people telling me to stop."

"And yet you continued to do it ?"

"It is a habit that most children develop and then discard. *It's a normal phase of childhood.*"

"Please do not lecture me on child development. I know only too much about *that*." He looked down and shook his head and suddenly looked much older than he had seemed at first. "Let me ask you a question," he continued, "Is a crime more to be excused because many people are committing it?"

"Certainly not!"

"If ten cars are exceeding the speed limit does that allow you to exceed the limit?

Amy had a momentary vision of herself as a young inexperienced teacher, confusedly facing a group of undisciplined louts who had misbehaved, each proclaiming piteously,

"Ah wisnae the only yin, miss."

She remembered her difficulties and felt the first flutter of sympathy for the man.

"I certainly think we are spending a great deal of time on a paltry childhood habit, that I acquired innocently when very young."

"True, true. That is very true." He crumpled one of the yellow papers and dropped it in the wastebasket. Again he paused and Amy could hear herself breathing.

"Then there was that incident with the mascara brush that you stole. You were eight then, I believe."

Amy sighed.

"*Stole!* You mean the little brush that I found lying below the bed in Aunty Elsie's house?"

"Don't play for time, Amy. That's the only brush that you stole."

"It was just such a perfect little brush and just the right size for my doll Tilly, and it was lying there far below the bed. I was sure that it was lost or... forgotten. Anyway Aunt Elsie was very fond of me and I know that she would have given it to me if I had asked for it."

"But you did not ask and you seem to remember the incident very clearly. Did you feel it was wrong at the time? Did you know that you were stealing. Was it your *intention* to steal?"

"I did not intend to steal, but I wanted the little brush very badly. I had never seen anything like it before. My mother did not wear make-up."

"Amy, there is no time today for conversation."

"Conversation? What do you mean?"

"I mean that I do not need to know whether your mother wore make-up or not. Please stick to the subject under review."

"I was explaining why I was so taken with the little..."

He held up an admonitory hand.

"No conversation. Please continue without conversation."

"I worried for a long time before I put the brush in my suitcase. In fact I put it back below the bed twice, then brought it out again. It was such a nice little brush and I always wanted the best for Tilly. There were so few things during the war."

"Please! No conversation and no justification. At the third time of handling the mascara brush, you finally succumbed and stole it?"

"Yes."

"You knew you were stealing? Or perhaps you did not realise it was wrong? I am trying to help you here."

"Are you? I have always understood that ignorance of the law is no excuse. Anyway, yes, I knew I was stealing. I have never stolen since."

He looked up sharply at her.

"Are you sure?"

Then for several minutes he tapped at his keyboard and Amy examined the room which was pink like the door and otherwise bare apart from a large glass vase of white lilies which stood on the floor in a corner. She disliked the unpleasant colour of the room and the overpowering smell of the lilies.

After turning the computer handle noisily a few times, he made a noise of irritation and pushed the keyboard away from him impatiently. Then gathering up the papers and repeatedly tapping them on all sides to make a neat bundle, he laid them aside. Then, groaning slightly, as though the task were too much for him, he covered his mouth with his hand and gazed aside at the vase of lilies for several minutes.

Amy tapped her foot slightly. What a big production he was making of all this. Just like a man to assure her of how little time there was and then to waste it shamefully in these over-dramatic pauses. She shifted in her seat and re-crossed her legs.

He coughed slightly, shrugged his shoulders and once more looked straight at her.

His eyes, though pale, were clear and piercing and though he seemed to be somewhat at a loss, his gaze was commanding.

"I have some questions I should like to ask you."

"Yes, certainly. I shall do my best to answer them." She smiled, but there was no answering smile.

"What are your thoughts on the seven sins?" He demanded in a deep voice.

The question was so unexpected that she giggled slightly

"This is not a laughing matter!" He almost roared at her. Then in a more gentle tone he added,

"Just tell me what you think of the seven deadly sins. It is important."

Amy longed to ask why it was important but his shouting had frightened her a little and her courage had evaporated.

"I'm not sure that I can remember them all."

"That is a very strange admission, but I shall refresh your memory if required."

"Well," Her mind had gone blank "Gluttony!".

She had seldom thought of the seven deadly sins although

she remembered a very funny French film of that name that she had seen in her twenties. It had not been nearly as naughty as many French films were. In the story which illustrated Gluttony, a couple had eaten their way through an enormous soft cheese. That was the only part of the film she remembered.

"Yes, and have you been guilty of Gluttony?"

She blushed when he spoke, for Amy was sitting in a small plastic armchair and since the start of the interview, she had been aware that it was a snug fit for her hips. That familiar resolution to cut back on the fattening delights of life had passed through her mind, as it had done several times each day for so many years.

"I expect so."

"Yes or no."

"Yes."

"Next sin?"

"I cannot remember them."

He tut-tutted just as her irascible Grandmother used to do, almost sucking his teeth in a most violent and objectionable way.

"Anger. What about anger?" he barked.

"Surely anger is an important tool to deal with the evil of the world." She answered just as peremptorily.

"I must advise you that you are not here to indulge in philosophical arguments. Anger is one of the sins and I can see immediately that your weakness lies in this direction. Is this not the case?"

"Yes and it takes one to know one! Certainly I am angry and you are making me just about as angry as I can be with your impossible manner, your rudeness and *your* anger. It's very obvious that anger is one of your own greatest sins."

His mouth fell slightly open and he gazed at her in absolute astonishment for nearly a minute before he spoke

"I *beg* your pardon!" His voice was dangerously quiet.

Amy's experience of emotional teenagers stood her in good stead and saying nothing, she tilted her head, raised her eyebrows and looked at him questioningly.

His face changed immediately, his whole body relaxed and she wished, not for the first time, that she had used that gambit with her dominating Grandmother.

He seemed at a loss and dropped his eyes to his desk as he crumpled several sheets of paper, then discarded them. It crossed Amy's mind to ask if his waste paper was recycled, but decided it was the wrong moment.

Then, with something like a smile hovering on his lips, he asked,

"What about Avarice, my dear?" His voice was much more polite than previously, though she did not care for the endearment.

"I'm not exactly sure what that means." Her words were honey-sweet, for she had always found it a good idea to hand the power back again after winning a stand-off.

"Eager desire for wealth." Obviously a definition he had repeated many times.

"Chance would be a fine thing!" but noting his pursing lips she continued quickly, "There was a time, after I received that legacy from my uncle, that I was very interested in money and making it work for me. I thought a lot about stocks and shares and looked up the papers and well, everyone was doing that in the eighties and nineties, weren't they?"

"I suspect we are back to that previous syndrome of "Ah wisnae the only yin, Miss"."

"I suppose so. Well I had better say 'yes' to Avarice. I did feel ashamed of being so money-grubbing, but I had never had much money before and also I was doing it for my children too..." she felt she was babbling and stopped.

"No self-justification and no conversation." It was more of a request than an order and though there was no please, the words were kindly said.

There was another long pause while he wrote something down and Amy was struck by his reference to her memory of the loutish schoolboys and their excuses. She had not mentioned that phrase to him but only thought about it. He had called it a syndrome, was it a well-known syndrome?

"What about Envy?"

"Oh, I could never accuse myself of that sin. I don't think that is something I have ever been guilty of. I have always been very pleased with my life and my family and my friends. I have had good health and generally there was enough money, I think that I have had an enviable life. Look at me too, hardly a grey hair while most of my contemporaries have been white for years. Oh I'm really a very lucky person, it would be silly for me to be envious."

"H'mm, lucky, are you? Certainly unusual to admit to luck." He looked at her carefully then continued. "I have often wondered if there should not be a sister sin of smugness, but in truth I think we are dealing with Pride here and I wish to return to Envy for a moment."

He looked over his glasses at her with almost a playful expression, then leafed through the papers once more.

"Yes, yes, I was sure it was here. A little girl named Dorothy, with long ringlets. Now did you not feel envious of those ringlets?"

Amy suddenly felt very tired. It was all so long ago.

"Yes, I did. I used to lie and think about them before I went to sleep and imagine that my short straight hair fell to my waist in those long delicious rolls, but I was a very little girl then, seven or eight."

"Ah yes, the excuse of youth again."

"And is youth not an excuse for ignorance and less than perfect behaviour?" Amy was very indignant, "Surely childhood is innocent and unknowing and that is what education is for. We must learn and improve throughout our lives. I am still learning."

"I am pleased to hear it, my dear."

"I think it is very hard lines to drag up facts from over sixty years ago."

"We will say no more about ringlets or nasty nose habits."

"I think not!"

He looked at her over his glasses.

"Thank you," she added.

He crumpled several more yellow sheets and popped them into the waste basket with a dramatic flourish. His mood had improved.

"Yes, yes, yes, now what was next on the agenda..."

"Pride? You mentioned Pride."

"Oh, Pride, I don't think we need bother too much about Pride. I believe a good seasoning of Pride is important to see us through life." He smiled for the first time and he had beautiful teeth.

Amy suspected that pride was his own strongest sin, as he was so ready to dismiss it. He had also demonstrated that he was quick to anger so she asked, with a touch of mischief if he would agree that Pride and Anger were both rather useful sins.

"Yes, I expect they are both very useful." He answered surprisingly.

"And another useful sin is Lust." Amy stated boldly.

His eyes opened enormously and he seemed struck dumb.

"Yes," Amy continued, "Marriage needs a little lust now and again to keep it stimulated."

"You mean within the relationship?" His voice was faint.

"Yes. Although I should not use the word marriage, I suppose as it is so out of fashion. In any serious relationship there should always be a spark of lust."

"Indeed?"

"Yes. Of course, I don't approve of lust leading to promiscuity or one night stands or anything like that. That's rather nasty and I don't expect any of my generation would approve. That sort of lust is definitely a sin."

"Yes, well, I think that perhaps... I myself... I am not experienced enough..." he seemed very flustered and his neck was red. "One-night-stands? Incredible! You seem better informed than I am... and I think we will now move to the last sin. Can you tell me the seventh?"

She felt herself returned to the state of an ignorant pupil as she shook her head.

"But I do remember the eighth!"

"*I beg your pardon...*"

"I used to tell my children that the eighth sin was Procrastination."

"Indeed!"

"It can lead to missed opportunities, inadequacies, carelessness and... chaos."

"It's an interesting concept. I have never come across it. However, the seventh is...?"

"I have absolutely no idea."

"Sloth!" he announced triumphantly and with one more glance at his papers, he positively beamed at her.

"No problems there for you, I think. I exonerate you completely from Sloth. Always happier to run rather than walk, to lift rather than lay and to go up rather than down. I congratulate you. I find you have been a most active woman throughout your life."

"But not everybody liked it."

"No they wouldn't! Because your industry made them feel guilty and perhaps rather useless and inferior."

"Is avoiding sin such a very good idea if it makes you unpopular and unloved and makes other people feel guilty?" she asked glumly.

"Never mind, never mind, my dear." She no longer resented the familiarity.

He laughed, showing his excellent teeth and stood up, smiling paternalistically. Amy realised the interview was at an end.

"Now have you got change in your pocket? No? Right, my dear, here you are." And he handed her a fifty penny piece. "Well, off you go and have a good trip."

She was reminded of receiving her Saturday shilling from her Father and being sent off to the children's matinee at the local cinema. She rather enjoyed it.

On returning to the great hall, its immensity struck her afresh. The people still stood around in quiet groups. A crimson rope now barred the crowd hovering at the top of the stairway from descending. Pity. She would have liked to hear those beautiful chords again. Could she perhaps step up one or two stairs herself, but she decided not. She was exhausted.

She wondered what he had meant about change in her pocket and a trip. What sort of trip was it? Perhaps this was an airport after all. For a woman, well organised all her life, it was horrible to be so unsure. The coin which he had given her was all the money that she had. How careless! For the first time in her life, she must have left her handbag somewhere with her wallet and her credit cards in it!

Just then the level of noise and movement around her changed dramatically. All eyes turned in the same direction.

To Amy's amazement and delight the entire wall at the opposite end from the staircase appeared to dissolve. It must be an enormous pane of glass! Revealed now was a bright view of the sea, or it might as easily have been a very broad river. It was just the sort of day that Amy loved, windy, with scudding clouds and rough little white-tipped waves. On the distant horizon was a ship.

With the sudden view of sky and water, the large hall became less important, less real.

As though hypnotised, everyone, apart from those restrained by the barrier at the top of the stairs, had started to walk slowly towards the great window until they were crowded close to the glass. Amy followed slowly. By hanging back, she had a better view.

The ship was approaching steadily though not swiftly. She saw that there was a large beach outside the window and the shallow water lapped on it in little wavelets. This was a very large ship that would be unable to come anywhere near such a beach. That would make embarking difficult. There must be some smaller boats out of sight. She thought they were called tenders.

Amy shivered a little.

There was a breathless silence and a terrific sense of anticipation in the hall as the ship drew nearer and nearer. It was now apparent that it was travelling towards them comparatively quickly. It was a smart vessel, newly painted in black, white and red.

But why did the ship come on so relentlessly, Amy wondered? There was no apparent slackening of its progress. Amy knew how cautious captains usually were when nearing land with a large unwieldy vessel. The ship now loomed very close to the shore with no diminution of speed. Amy started to feel uneasy and in fact moved sideways towards the wall as the ship was directed at the centre of the window. Then, without too much haste, she walked back towards the foot of the staircase. When she turned again towards the window, she saw that the ship was very large and close and had almost reached the sandy beach *which it mounted* and continued onwards, travelling over the sand as easily as it had over the water, heading inexorably for the centre of the great window and the crowds gathered there. Amy supposed that in spite of looking like a traditional ship, it must be some kind of amphibious sea-going transport that she had never come across. Surely it could not reduce its speed in time to avoid crashing into the glass!

Amy gasped at the tragedy which was about to be enacted before her eyes.

The waiting people now at last seemed to realise their danger and with cries and exclamations surged backwards, pushing and tripping over each other. Some fell to the floor, but were helped to their feet again. It was fortunate that the numbers were not greater. Amy felt like closing her eyes but it was too horribly fascinating. The huge ship drew closer and closer until its silhouette filled the entire window and its bulk completely blocked out the sky.

At last it stopped abruptly, just a few feet from the window.

Amy took a deep breath and realised she was filled with an ambiguous mixture of relief and disappointment.. She pitied the folk who now dusted themselves down and tried to assume their previous dignity. How foolish they must feel. Amy, however, felt happy and in control, exhausted but relieved.

She now knew her destination.

In her pocket her hand cradled the coin for the ferryman, as she joined the queue to embark on her last journey.

# DIMINISHING RETURNS

They had been married three weeks when she whispered her secret to him and he did not care for it at all. "That's a very strange thing to do! I think it is anyway."

"Oh Raymond, it's just because I love you so much."

"I mean to say... you don't still... even now that you have the real me right here beside you in bed? The real *big* me."

He laughed in spite of his annoyance, for he was self-conscious about his modest height and slender build.

"Yes always. Do you mind? It's because you're so dear to me, darling."

Gail had admitted that ever since she realised how much she loved him, she had gone to sleep each night imagining that he was a little creature about the size of a 'large kitten' or a 'teddybear' and that she held him close to her breast to protect him.

"I just cuddle you up, kiss the top of your little head and fall asleep."

"I don't know what to say exactly. You mean you have two husbands in this bed. One adult who is taking up half the bed..."

"Rather more than half, my pet." She giggled.

"And one teddybear sized husband that you clasp to your bosom?"

"Am I an awfully foolish, greedy little wife? Please forgive me."

Her contrite words were uttered in a light-hearted tone, for Gail did not appreciate quite how upset her husband was. Up until that moment he would have marked their marriage ten out of ten, for Raymond was a teacher and fond of grading situations. But his diminutive stature had always been a problem to him and now suddenly he was beset by memories of teenage inadequacies and he lay there feeling empty and alone. He also remembered that one of Gail's many boyfriends had been a rugby player of tremendous girth.

His wife's even breathing told him that she was asleep.

"Clutching a damned teddybear that looks like me!" he thought to himself.

Raymond tried to shake himself out of his depression. After all it was reassuring that the teddybear was his own doppelganger. Nevertheless, over the next few weeks he often thought of the small being that was pressed to his wife's bosom and his bridegroom's ardour was cooled. Instead of clasping her passionately every night, he sometimes turned away and fantasised about being taller and broader, just as he had as a teenager. He imagined his deltoids and pectorals expanding satisfactorily and he dreamed of shirts that would not fasten and muscular thighs stretching the fabric of his trousers.

Meanwhile Gail slept quietly with imaginary little Raymond under her chin.

For the first few months, the marriage followed the usual pattern of misunderstandings and quarrels, followed by loving reconciliations. By the following spring Gail had forgotten her quaint conceit, but the miniature Raymond still lingered uncomfortably in her husband's memory.

They took a holiday in Spain and travelled to Ronda, that tiny fabulous city perched high above a plain which is surrounded by mountains.

After a breath-taking journey, they reached their hotel in the late afternoon.

"No more than five out of ten for this room, Gail eh?"

"I just love it, it's so... *atmospheric*."

"Well I suppose that's one way of describing the shabbiness, but first of all we must get a map!"

"Do we really need a map, Raymond? It's not a big place and I'm happy just to wander..."

"We *must* have a map, Gail."

But the information bureau was closed and no maps were available at their hotel.

Nearby, an ancient bridge spanned the ravine which split the town so distinctively and they stood on the small spectator's balcony and gazed downwards at the perpendicular cliffs, tumbled rocks and rushing water far beneath them.

"This is the New Bridge, Raymond,"

"Wouldn't like to see the old one, then."

"Isn't it wonderful, all that water constantly pouring down. Where does it come from? We are so high up! I could watch it all day."

Gail was entranced and did not notice that Raymond had stepped back slightly from the flimsy railing, for he was not fond of heights.

"It's a devil of a nuisance that we don't have a map."

Gail looked round with a laugh as she was sure he must be joking. The quaint streets and buildings and the fantastic surrounding landscape filled her with such delight. It seemed to her that walking in any direction at all in this aerial city would be exciting.

To her astonishment, her husband looked in a thoroughly bad mood.

"Look, Raymond, let's go down that hill over there. We can go right down to the plain and if we keep beside the gorge, we only need to come up again to get back to the hotel. We can't possibly get lost. Ronda seems just like a big mushroom to me, with a split in the middle..."

Raymond's lips tightened and he shook his head.

"We'll get a map tomorrow and explore properly."

But after some cajoling, he agreed to her suggestion.

Down and down they went, passing charming houses and gardens. Eventually they came to a flight of many rough steps and continued the descent.

"I'm going to count how many steps on the way back up, Raymond I bet there must be a hundred and fifty at least."

"I wish I had a map and we would know where we were going."

"We're going down and down and down, Raymond and isn't the changing view *fascinating*! I love it so much. The mountains around the plain seem to be growing upwards... and all the animals and trees have changed from toy-size to reality"

"I expect the bureau will open early tomorrow, although I'm not sure about any of the hours of business in Spain. They have pretty strange ways..."

"Oh, look at that notice, it is a direction to the Arab bath-house. Must be near here, but it isn't open just now, it says it's under construction. What a pity."

"I never knew you could read Spanish!"

"Raymond! Of course I can't, but... a smattering of French and some guesswork..."

They reached the lowest level and paused. Raymond suddenly shouted,

"Come on, I'll race you up the stairs."

But Gail had seen three beautiful horses and wanted to photograph them.

"Just look at the railings round their paddock. They've used bits of cars and old brass bedsteads and all sorts of other furniture. Poor things, I wonder if they mind. They look like such aristocratic animals."

"For God's sake, are you going to hang round here all day? Race you to the top!"

Raymond won easily but Gail counted the steps as she toiled upwards. There were one hundred and fifty and she found a satisfaction in knowing her estimate had been correct.

The following morning they had coffee in a pleasant square, while Raymond studied the map.

Gail gazed around her in delight and remarked that it was a gorgeous morning and what a lovely noise all the birds in the trees were making.

Raymond was too engrossed to reply and frowned and bit his lip as he folded the map to a manageable size.

Gail threw crumbs to the birds, stroked the café cat and watched the passers-by. She felt very happy. There were five different streets leading from the square and she would have loved to explore any one of them, but she waited patiently.

At last, Raymond heaved a deep sigh.

"Right, I've worked out an interesting route for us to take."

When they had walked purposefully for six or seven minutes and turned two or three corners, Raymond stopped and opening out the map fully, retraced the last fifty yards, looking down side streets, gazing at street names and referring back to his map. The walls of the houses were washed in delicate colours, with beautiful old stone-carving around the porches and Gail brought out her camera. She realised that

Raymond saw her photography as a time-waster and a nuisance, for he was always impatient to move on and see more, but holiday memories and interesting scenes were important to Gail.

Now, however Raymond stood stock-still, peering at the map. He even turned it upside down, something he had warned her that no educated person ever did. The morning was still pleasantly cool but he was unusually red in the face.

He marched towards her flapping the map.

"Something pretty peculiar about this map!"

"Surely not. Are you looking at the right place on it?"

He did not reply and his face got redder. Shaking the map vigorously and gazing vaguely to right and to left, he suddenly started off so quickly that she had to run to catch up.

After ten minutes walking, he again stopped and frowning at the map, shook his head then grunted with frustration.

"Shall I look and see if I can make any sense of it, Raymond?"

As soon as she had spoken, she realised it was the wrong thing to say. He was furious and bundling the map roughly under his arm he again moved off at speed.

After a breathless walk uphill, they started downwards again and the road became steeper and steeper.

Once more Raymond stopped and looked at the map.

"It's absolute bloody rubbish, this map! Either that or they've changed all the street names."

"Perhaps they've printed it the wrong way round?"

"I *don't* think that's likely! It could almost be a different town, only it's not. Whatever it is, it's scrambling my brain."

"Darling, put it away and forget about it and let's just wander and enjoy ourselves. Look there are some ruins over there, Moorish ones, I think. Though it seems so inaccessible, this place has been invaded by everyone from the Greeks, Romans, Vandals, Visigoths, right up to Napoleon and they all left some architectural mark on it. Fascinating, isn't it. And there used to be lots of bandits who plundered passing travellers."

Raymond made no comment.

"And the bullring is the foremost in Spain."

"Is this some guide book you've been reading up?"

"Yes, there was one in the hotel foyer this morning and I skimmed through it while you bought the map."

"I expect every Spanish town has a guide book that makes the same claim for its bullring."

It had been a mistake to mention the map because he brought it out once more, determined to de-cipher it. But after some mumbled swearing, he folded it tightly again and set off downhill. They had now reached the outskirts of the town but were still high up and the way now led through a ruined archway, then steeply downwards beside high ramparts which cut off any view of the plain below.

"Perhaps if we go down to the lower level, Raymond, we'll come to those steps and the Arab Baths we found yesterday."

"Nonsense! We're going in the wrong direction."

There was no path and Gail, walking cautiously on the uneven ground was soon left behind. Her concentration was suddenly interrupted when she glanced up for a moment and exclaimed with delight.

A small rectangular aperture high up in the ancient city wall, gave a totally unexpected and perfect view of a tiny white horse standing on the bright green grass of the plain far beneath her. It appeared incredibly small and yet very detailed in the clear air, even the flowers at its feet were visible. It seemed like a painting or perhaps a magical vision in the middle of the grey stone wall.

"Raymond! Raymond come back up here and see this!"

Raymond had got rid of some of his bad mood by jumping and leaping down the steep incline but he had no idea of how they would get back to the town centre and he was hungry. He returned to his wife ungraciously, huffing and exclaiming over the more difficult obstacles.

"This better be good, whatever it is you've found."

Predictably the miniature horse did not impress him and almost as soon as he reached Gail, the animal moved out of sight.

"You've brought me all the way up here to look at a square of grass!"

"You did see the horse before it moved though, didn't you.

It looked so wonderful... like a mediaeval painting only real...
I just loved it and I wanted you... to see it too..."

But Raymond was again leaping down over the broken
ground.

In his mind there was a great resentment against his wife.
What *was* her preoccupation with miniatures? It was
unhealthy.

At the bottom of the hill, with his right ankle twisted and
hurting abominably, he was infuriated to find the Arab
Bathhouse and the familiar flight of one hundred and fifty
stairs.

Gail's delighted cry of pleasure and recognition did not
help his mood.

That summer they visited Gail's parents. Their seaside
cottage was built on the top of a cliff with houses stepping
down from it to sea level, as in a Cornish village. The garden
overlooked the lower roofs to an uninterrupted view of the
sea. When sitting, a waist high stone wall at the foot of the
garden obscured the lower houses completely, apart from a
few chimney-pots.

One day, after lunch in the garden, Raymond noticed that
Gail was sitting in a strange way. She seemed abstracted and
she was slumped peculiarly in her chair.

Gail's mother was prattling her usual stream of consciousness.

When the older couple went off to the garden centre for
yet another clematis, Raymond and Gail were left alone.

"Are you quite comfortable, Gail?"

"Oh darling, I've just discovered the cutest thing."

Raymond winced. He disliked the word cute. Too
American.

"Look, here, see if you can do it. You've got to sit well
down in your chair, put your chin on your chest, Raymond.
We might have to wait for a moment or so... oh, no, here's
one now, look!"

"I have no earthly idea what you're going on about, Gail."

"Look there, Raymond, there's a good one. See! If a
seagull is walking along the ridge of the Bowman's house
down there and you can line its feet up with our garden wall,
it looks like the *tiniest seagull* you could imagine is walking

along *our* wall. There's one now, darling! Look! Push yourself down in your chair and make your neck shorter. The illusion is perfect. It's *just so sweet!*"

"Have you been doing that for the last half hour?"

"Yes and look now, it's flown away and it still looks small somehow."

"That's because it's far away. Things that are far away look small. Were you miniaturising seagulls all the time your mother was burbling on?"

"Yes, but my mother doesn't *burble* on! She can be very amusing."

"That's a matter of opinion and I think you're making yourself ridiculous, hunching yourself up and miniaturising seagulls."

"Raymond! It's hardly a crime."

"It's undignified."

"I can't understand why you're so angry!"

"I don't want you to do it anymore!"

"*I beg your pardon*! How dare you tell me what I can or can't do."

When her parents returned they realised that all was not well with the young folk.

"Perhaps Raymond is hungry. We'll have an early dinner."

But in the garden that evening after dinner, they were horribly disturbed when all at once Raymond jumped to his feet and shouted at Gail,

"Stop it! Stop it at once! I hate that sort of thing, I tell you. I won't have it!" and stormed into the house. Gail burst into tears and ran after him.

What could have caused his outburst? To the puzzled parents it seemed that while their daughter had been smiling and deeply relaxed in her chair, their son-in-law had suddenly gone mad.

"What a very strange way to behave!" said Gail's mother.

"I never considered the fellow quite stable!" added her husband.

Back home Gail and Raymond made up and agreed that staying with the parents was always stressful and for another three months they were comparatively happy. Until the day that Raymond wakened and became aware that Gail, lying beside him, had her arm stuck up in the air in a very unnatural way. Her elbow was bent and her hand was six inches above her face with her fingers placed as though she held some small thing between index finger and thumb, perhaps a button or a coin, though there was nothing to be seen. She also had one eye closed.

"What the *hell* are you doing?"

"Oh, you're awake are you darling? I was just making the handle on the wardrobe into an earring. Look, the brass handle is much the same shape as an earring and if I can keep my hand very steady, though it's difficult 'cos my hand shakes a bit, and place my fingers... just so, it looks as though I were holding a pretty brass earring, doesn't it? Don't you think? Perhaps you can't quite see it from where you are. But it's awfully difficult to keep steady. And I can make the big blue jug on the mantelpiece into a teeny-weeny blue jug. That seems easier somehow. Perhaps because it's bigger. It would make such a sweet jug for a doll's house."

Raymond jumped from the bed, took a noisy shower and left for work without breakfast.

That night Gail sat silently as Raymond poured his white hot fury over her.

He reproached her bitterly, saying that, right from the start of their marriage, Gail had tried to minimalise him in every way. From the moment she spoke of the ludicrous *'teddybear Raymond'* and he spat that epithet out with venom, she had put him and his achievements in a poor light, trivialising every statement, never giving him credit, never appreciating him for what he was, reducing everything he did to minor importance.

"Look at what happened in Ronda! That damned map! You had no faith! *You* wanted to take the map. Oh yes, *you* knew all the history of the place. Visigoths and bullrings! Then dragging me back up that hill to see a bloody hole in the wall. And as for the seagulls and the earring and the teeny weeny blue jug... I've had enough, I've had it up to here. I'm leaving. Now!"

And he proceeded to pack his bags. Gail said not a word. She was stunned. Had she really denigrated him constantly like that? She had never intended to insult him. She had no idea that he had harboured all this resentment.

Was it justified, she wondered, as she listened to him banging drawers and stamping back and forth?

He *was* impulsive, careless and lacking in judgement and on many occasions she had smoothed over his mistakes, while assuring him that they did not matter. He was pompous and self-righteous and furious when proved wrong. He categorised everything and was often judgemental, even prejudiced.

What a lot of time and energy she had spent in making excuses for him or ignoring his failings! He was young, but then so was she! What a waste of effort! Perhaps life would be easier without Raymond? Yes, she decided it would be much easier. She felt astonished but not really sad.

It was snowing as Gail stood at the window and watched Raymond march down the street.

Her left eye was shut and her right hand was raised to eye-level and her husband's receding figure was contained between her steadily poised finger and thumb. As he disappeared into the distance, her finger and thumb slowly approached each other until they touched. After a moment, she rubbed her fingers and thumb together as though ridding them of dust.

# A Talent to Amuse

My grandmother Agnes was a supreme raconteur. With her large dark brown eyes and graceful gesturing hands, her observational skills, her timing and command of language, she could rivet an audience with the simplest of anecdotes. Throughout her long life, she seemed to find dramatic content in everyday life and by adding just a soupçon of malicious seasoning to her fascinating tales, she bewitched her friends and often reduced them to helpless laughter. She would have made a wonderful actress or comedienne and she might have been a happier person in that rôle, but she lived at a time when the stage was thought not respectable. At fifteen, she saw an advertisement for chorus girls. As she had long legs and was proud of her high-kicking capabilities, she informed her father that she was going to the audition.

"Aye, you'll go, and you'll go with two broken legs!"

Fathers were stern and strong in those days.

She married at nineteen and as the wife of a society portrait painter, her bright amusing chatter was useful to welcome and relax the prospective sitter, who was often nervous and ill-at-ease. My grandfather specialised in painting important fellows in impressive robes and a Lord Provost or a Brigadier-General and more especially, the Moderator of the Church of Scotland, must look serious in perpetuity. Thus, when the real work of painting a 'speaking likeness' began, my grandmother was banished from the studio, for a smile would linger on the sitter's face as long as she was present and practising her undoubted skills.

Agnes was only twenty when my mother, Ann, was born. Ann was very different from her flamboyant young mother and I suspect it was never an easy relationship, though Ann, too would have a great power with words. In her twenties, when such young women had many hours to spend together at the swimming club, the tennis courts or the sewing bee, Ann was known for having a bottomless fund of funny stories, many no doubt rather risqué. I remember her humour as more intellectual and sardonic than it must have been in those early days. As I grew up, I was also introduced to several 'naughty' stories, which would no doubt seem incredibly tame to a teenager nowadays.

I have never met anyone else who learned improper stories at their mother's knee.

I knew her best as a mistress of the quiet ironic remark, whose meaning grew deeper as one thought about it. Her arrow-sharp comments were very funny though often too subtle to pierce their target, which was usually my father, hardly ever myself.

And has the talent to amuse been passed to a third generation? Has the gene or DNA conferred its mixed blessing on the writer? The reader must judge. I suppose the fact that I am a writer, confirms the fact that I *desire* to amuse, but ability and desire are two different things, though they must both be part of the make-up of those who entertain.

My education as a jester was certainly started early by my grandmother.

At three I was encouraged to do impersonations. With one hand on hip, a sultry glance over the opposite shoulder and doubtless a cringeingly bad attempt at an American accent, I would invite someone to "Come up and see me sometime!". Or perhaps with half-closed eyes and expressionless face I would aver that, "I vaunt to be alo-o-one."

My grandmother and her friends thought I was brilliant, at least they certainly laughed a lot and for the jester, appreciation is the ultimate payment. To render a group of people helpless with laughter confers a thrill of power which is unmatched and that power is like a drug which demands repeat doses. However by the time I was four I refused to perform Mae West or Garbo. Not even 'one more time'. I must have been stubborn and determined, for my grandmother was a difficult person to thwart. Perhaps I realised that impersonations were not my forte or perhaps I had an inkling that I was being ' laughed at'.

For the next ten years I was a shy rather timid child, reserving my entertainment skills for my mother's benefit alone, delighted when she smiled and euphoric when she laughed out loud.

In my teens and probably to offset my academic deficiencies, I started to work hard at amusing my fellow schoolgirls. Perhaps not a very difficult task you will say. However at fourteen, I became the jester for a small elite group and no doubt the thorn in the side of many a teacher.

I aimed for complete and overpowering giggles and a day was wasted in which I did not achieve this disruptive state amongst my friends. It is difficult for a teacher to pinpoint the instigating culprit in such a group and I have no recollection of being punished or reproached. This phase passed with my schooldays and as a student, I returned to comparative obscurity, with only an odd unexpected play on words or surreal insight creating amusement for my friends.

Probably the unexpectedness of my wit was its strongest feature. I found it very pleasant to be appreciated on these rare occasions.

In my teens I studied ballet and achieved high marks. Those high-kicking genes from Agnes had not been wasted! While appreciating my classical grace, my mother swore that the way that I would become rich and famous was with my 'eccentric' dancing. I could always make her laugh with my uninhibited and crazy movements. Charlotte Greenwood popularised this hilarious style on the screen in the thirties and forties and was the craziest and highest high-kicker of all time and a wonderful comedienne. She was in her middle years by the time that she played Aunt Eller in the film of Oklahoma, and though still a spectacular dancer, had somewhat modified her extraordinary movements. Sadly, dancing would never take me to any pinnacle of success, for my sights were set, unattainably as it turned out, on Swan Lake and Giselle and I could perform in this mad, loose-jointed way, only in private for the reward of my mother's laughter.

And now my own children have grown up and can I see the influence of those genes of entertainment in them? Yes, just as the songbirds at Delfi and the sparrows in the elder tree in my garden echo the voices, abilities and preferences of previous generations, so do my children, each with his or her own modification.

Like many other only children, I became the mother of quite a large family, three boys and two girls. Regrettably, in the limited experience of a mother, the boys have never shown any *ability* with the spoken word, although their school reports always talked glowingly of their written work. Each one has chosen a career which is dependent on their use of concise, yet descriptive language. Indeed the second boy is speaking of pursuing a political career and I presume that he must have a public charisma which has never manifested itself at home. For all I know, my boys may mesmerise the young women in their life with fascinating and witty persiflage, but I have certainly seen no sign of this. Gruff and brief would best describe their conversation, unless of course, it has to do with swimming, cricket or football and then, for rather longer than I care to listen, they become vivacious and articulate. However, those other genes, bequeathed by their great grandmother, those long, muscular, active legs have certainly manifested themselves on many a playing field.

My daughters, though uninterested in competitive sport, are also long-limbed and active. The older girl, a fine gymnast when younger, is sharply observant, with a decisive wit. She uses her gift of spotting the smallest fault as well as the more important ones, with humour and her irony recalls my mother's style. While still in her early teens, she perceptively pointed out that the way to earn the reputation of 'witty conversationalist', and thus get asked to lots of parties, was to watch the eyes of your listener very closely. When those eyes showed the first sign of glazing or inattention, then you must wind up your story immediately. I have always remembered that sensible advice, for the heady drug of appreciation is sometimes hard to resist.

I have noticed that men and women who have been particularly attractive in their youth, can often be very boringly long-winded. Sadly they do not realise that the fascination which their youthful beauty added to their performance, has been deducted by the years and they must now work harder at the necessary ingredient of brevity.

Elsie, my second daughter and last-born child early showed an absolute genius for impersonation. She was not cajoled and bribed as I had been. No one suggested that she should attempt this difficult feat. In fact no one could stop her. At two years old, she blossomed with unmistakable representations of those around her.

It was said that Shirley Temple, the child film star, was constantly urged by her mother to,

"Sparkle, Shirley! Sparkle!"

Elsie needed no such encouragement. Her siblings thought it hilarious as she danced madly, gracefully, sexily, recited strange poems and impressively dramatised the simplest of everyday actions. She even sang, which suggests a genetic permutation, for the phrase 'tone-deaf' might have been invented for this family. By the time that she was four she could sing "Don't Cry for me Argentina" in a deep, torchy voice which rivalled, in both passion and volume, that of Elaine Page, the original Evita. Elsie was a pretty little girl, perhaps slightly less so than her sister, but when Elsie was at her chosen work of entertainment, she convinced the audience of her utter beauty and I think this is a power shared by all great actors, of either sex.

Although the stage seemed the only future possible for this child, suddenly, at the age of twelve, she changed. Without explanation, greasepaint and applause lost their allure. By applying her energies to school work, she turned into a calm, scholarly and very hard-working top pupil and student. Today she is an academic although Elsie will never be staid or dry. She is a most engaging and witty conversationalist and an hour in her company is as refreshing as a peach in the desert. I expect her thespian talents are channelled into her lectures and though it must be difficult to find humour in medical statistics, I have every confidence that she does so.

Elsie and a colleague have evolved certain statistical methods which they are invited to impart to students in universities throughout the world. It was on returning from one of these distant seminars, that Elsie made such wonderful use of her inborn genius.

Unable to book seats together, Philip, her colleague and good friend, was sitting further forward in the plane. The flight was scheduled to land at Hamburg airport and they intended to stay in that beautiful city for two nights and attend a conference at the university. They were due to land

at midday and were surprised to hear the captain announce at
eleven fifteen that descent was about to commence. If they
had been more familiar with his voice, they would have
realised that those were not his normal tones. It is hard to
speak with relaxed and jocular confidence, when three armed
and sweating young men are crowded in the cockpit,
mumbling to each other in an unknown language and
pressing the cold muzzle of a firearm into the back of your
neck.

The passengers were all seasoned travellers and had
fastened themselves responsibly after the captain's announcement, although it was strange that no stewardess came
around to check. However when the plane had landed and
taxied for what seemed a mile, with no further word from the
captain and no sign of stewards, a great uneasiness spread
through the cabin. The engines were turned off and almost
immediately the temperature started to rise.

There was an eerie silence.

Whispers and the small controlled movements of the
passengers enhanced the unreality of the strained atmosphere.

Should they unfasten their seatbelts?

What was happening?

There was no further word from the captain and no sign
of a steward or stewardess.

Something was certainly amiss!

I will let Elsie tell her own story.

"Philip and I sat in aisle seats on opposite sides of the
plane, left and right respectively, and could just glimpse each
other if I leaned into the aisle and Philip twisted round in his
seat. We both knew it wasn't Hamburg where we'd landed.
There were no airport buildings in sight at all. Philip raised
his eyebrows and shrugged and I shook my head and smiled,
without much joy, I suppose. But it was nice to see each other
and I really wished we were closer together, although I
changed my mind about that afterwards. It was all for the
best that we were apart.

Do you know what was the very worst time? It was just
sitting, waiting, with no idea of what was happening, but
suspecting that something was horribly wrong.

At first people were restless, then there were murmurs, even a nervous laugh. The man beside me spoke to the woman at the window, probably his wife. I didn't look round.

After perhaps twenty-five minutes, two young men with guns appeared and started to shout at us in a very unfriendly way and though the words meant nothing to us, we sat very still. I'm sure nobody looked at either face. I know I didn't!

*Hi-jacked!*

That word was hammering in my brain and must have been hammering in every other brain too.

Then one of the men came and stood right beside me, gazing towards the back of the plane in a hostile, yet nervous way. He was so close to me that his jacket brushed against my bare arm. It was a rough sort of fabric and I can still feel it...

He was very young, only nineteen or twenty, and quite well dressed. Just what any young man might wear on an airplane trip. He had nice brown hair, thick and shiny, and his nails were really clean and well manicured. In fact he was far better groomed than lots of guys I've been out on dates with! He'd really taken trouble with his appearance before he went out to hi-jack a plane! Funny when you think of it, isn't it. And he had just a few fine dark hairs on the back of his hand. Yes! I certainly gave him the 'once-over'. He was so close to me but he never actually looked in my direction, too busy glancing up and down the cabin to see that no one made a move. He was terribly nervous, trembling and somehow that made me calmer. Can't think why!"

Elsie laughed at this point, a slightly hysterical laugh, then she cried a little.

"There's no need to go over it all just now, darling." I told her, "Take a break, try and put it out of your mind for a while..."

"No, I want to talk about it. I think it does me good to talk. I would only be rehearsing it all in my thoughts, over and over again, if I weren't telling you.

One thing I was really glad about was that the plane had landed!

I'm always glad when the plane has landed even without hi-jackers. It would have been so much worse to be hurtling through the atmosphere, while those nervous fellows pointed guns at us. Then I wondered if it *could* be any worse than it was already and smiled inside my head. What crazy things your mind considers even in the middle of danger. I thought of how I had never been in danger before and I could hear myself breathing quite quietly in the silence, though my mouth felt parched. I longed for a sip of the mineral water that was in the bag at my feet, but of course I made no move to get it. I suppose we were all paralysed and well-groomed hands that clutch guns can pull triggers. Those were the silly things I was thinking, when suddenly the other gun went off! *Oh what a terrible noise!* Not the gun beside me, fortunately or I'm sure I would have screamed blue murder. And no one was hurt, but we didn't know that till afterwards. The report made an incredible, ear-splitting sound in the cabin and two women started to have hysterics and three kids were howling, poor wee things. No one got a bigger fright than the hijacker standing beside me. He turned and looked down at me for the first time and his eyes were full of tears! Absolutely true! His eyes were swimming with tears. Somehow the gunshot and the tears changed my attitude, made me feel that I had some responsibility to act and not just sit there like a passive victim. Perhaps his obvious vulnerability affected me, anyway, whatever it was, it brought me back to reality, though I suppose that what I did next was hardly normal, for I started to speak to the hi-jacker. I just spoke to him in an ordinary voice, just as I would do to any young man that happened to be standing beside me in a queue or a bar. I spoke in English of course and I'm sure he understood very little, however he gazed at me and appeared to listen to every word. As soon as I started to speak, the man sitting beside me put a hand on my arm, perhaps it was a warning touch, but I ignored it and continued talking. Though I found the human touch very comforting and supportive.

What did I talk about? There I cannot help you. I have no recollection. I just started to go through every amusing anecdote that I could think of. Stories of the family disasters, you know, and the adventures that our pets had. Just in time, I stopped myself telling about the time that the big angel fish was poorly and I had to hit it with a stone to put it out of its misery. That might have put ideas into his head. The fellow looked down at me as though he were mesmerised. His mouth was half open and the sawn-off shotgun, I think that was what it was anyway, was now dangling towards the floor in a very non-aggressive way. I just kept talking and smiling as naturally as I could and I put in all the little amusing bits, even though they meant nothing to him. When I came to a blank in my memory, I started to make up stories about being Scottish and wearing a kilt and making haggis from sheep's innards and harvesting heather and nonsense like that. I have noticed that people all over the world are interested in quaint Scottish customs and will believe practically anything you tell them. Besides, I couldn't decide how much he understood of what I was talking about. I quite often mentioned Coca Cola and Corn Flakes and football and he understood those words and nodded and his mouth even twitched at the corners. Yes, the hijacker almost started to smile as I talked. Sometimes he nodded as if in agreement, not at the right places. of course. Now I can hardly believe it when I think of it! Of course I had been turning on the charm myself, nods and becks and wreathed smiles to the nth degree. Do you know what I was thinking as I spoke? That I was Scheherazade and telling stories to save my life. Well, that crossed my mind, fleetingly anyway, I was too busy chatting to dwell on it. And my neck started to get so stiff because I was looking up at him!

I had no idea what the other hi-jacker was doing. I didn't even know how many there were. My mind wasn't clear enough to think that someone must be keeping the captain and his staff captive. I suppose I kept hoping someone would soon come to rescue us!

The heat was building up unbearably by this time. You know how I hate to be too warm and my neck ached and my lips were dry and cracked, but I kept going. The man beside me was holding my hand by this time and I'll always be grateful to him.

Suddenly a name was shouted, something that sounded like Alf though I'm sure it wasn't and all at once my hi-jacker turned and ran back to the front of the plane. I stopped speaking in the middle of a sentence and just sat there, then the tears started and the nice man beside me passed a handkerchief. I'm not sure how it all ended but the three men were overpowered without any more shots being fired. Philip is a keen rugby player, you know and he was able to give a hand to the captain and his crew to subdue the three terrorists. I was proud of him.

All of us passengers left the plane more thankfully than I can begin to tell you.

How delicious to sip my water and breathe the fresh air outside, although we were half frozen before a bus came to collect us and take us to civilisation. But I don't think anyone minded being cold, I know I didn't. It was just great to be *alive*.

Evidently the silly young terrorrists had no idea of the practicalities of refuelling and not a clue about the strength and bravery of the crew. They were younger even than I had thought and altogether pretty ineffectual hi-jackers. The captain was kind enough to say that I had played an important part in their capture and everyone congratulated me but honestly, I could have stopped breathing as easily as stopped talking after that gun was fired. Some women have hysterics while others talk, I suppose."

I had been hugging my daughter close, speechless as she spoke, but now I broke into her narrative,

"That is the most terrifying and amazing story and I am trembling just to listen to it, my darling, but I want to know why you were glad that Philip wasn't sitting beside you. Surely you would rather have held his hand."

"Oh mother! Philip has heard all these stories lots of times and I would have been editing them in my head and cutting them short in order not to bore him. And when I started all the nonsense about kilts and haggis, he would have interrupted me and corrected me and that would really have put me right off!"

# ASPIRATIONS

They met at Bible class. Carrie was seventeen, with enormous, blue, spiritual eyes. Her demure mouth, which seldom disclosed the tiny teeth within, had nagged her father for weeks to bring her into town in order to attend church. Her religious zeal was a recent development and her parents could not quite understand it.

In spite of a decorously bowed head, Carrie's sharp glance soon picked out slight, sandy-haired Wayne from the crowd of young people in the congregation. He looked presentable, clean, polite and manageable. Might he be the one? Carrie was determined to find a regular boyfriend and few young men visited her parents' farm.

Nor did religion mean much to Wayne Barrett, though the church affected him in a way that he had not expected it would. His aim in coming to church was similar to Carrie's. No woman under fifty lived near his family's farm and he had travelled thirty-five miles of dusty Manitoba back roads in search of romance. A passive boy of eighteen, actively discouraged from taking any initiative in the running of the farm, for a wrong decision might lose precious dollars, his life was dominated by the harsh demands of Prairie farming.

Wayne's desperation to meet some young person of the opposite sex had finally spurred him to action and the church seemed a sensible place to look for a decent, good-living girl. He had no illusions about his own looks and no fantasies about meeting a glamorous or beautiful girlfriend.

There was a break for coffee and cookies after the class. When Carrie dropped her little plastic handbag, Wayne, who stood closest to her, hurriedly picked it up and handed it to her with a shy smile. With a returned smile and a pretty thanks, their fate was sealed. They had each achieved their objective and their religious studies lasted only until their wedding the following year.

Wayne could not know it, but his choice of Carrie as the goddess of his future spelled the death knell of any further decision-making for him. Carrie was very clear about her wishes and ambitions. And more determined and more ruth- less than his parents.

They married in May, unregretfully leaving their remote Prairie homes and renting a small airless room in a clapboard house in Winnipeg.

Carrie soon found a job in a laundry and Wayne worked for the large co-operative dairy.

Marriage and living in a city seemed terrific at first. They felt like entirely different people. Carrie bought eyeshadow, lipstick and high heels. Wayne started to smoke.

After a lifetime of shopping from catalogues, it was heaven to wander the aisles of the Hudson Bay department store and touch the goods. They were still very young and toys still fascinated them. They adoringly handled fluffy bears and rabbits, brightly coloured trucks and gorgeous dolls that they had known since childhood only as glossy pictures. After an hour of regressing, Carrie rode the elevator to 'Household Goods' to caress soft striped sheets and gaze with longing at fifty rainbow colours of hand-towels, while Wayne galloped to the basement to wander blissfully amongst power tools, unfin- ished furniture and infinite pots of paints and varnish.

There was no money to buy, but the reality of the goods was satisfying.

Each evening they walked around the city, exploring the French and Ukrainian quarters and feeling sophisticated as they sipped coffee at street stalls.

Carrie noticed that stars looked less brilliant than those that had hovered in the vast darkness above the prairie and Wayne missed the sound of the wind in the grass and the continuous, comforting chirp of grasshoppers. But they did not share these regrets and spoke only of the luxurious delights around them and how they would very soon be able to afford to buy all those wonderful goods.

The first part of Carrie's dream of leaving the country was now realised. Somewhere far in the future she determined to have a lovely modern kitchen, a Ladies Home Journal kitchen, with several beautifully behaved, perfectly dressed children sitting around the table, munching her home-made cookies.

Wayne changed his job several times in that first year. He was never actually unemployed, but often on the move. Each new job held promise, but after a few weeks he realised he had made a mistake. It was quite easy to pick up work, but because of the constant changes, there was never any advancement.

Carrie stayed in the laundry. It was hard boring work, especially in the summer, when the downtown temperature was in the nineties. By the end of September the weather had cooled slightly, but by then she was pregnant and most mornings between ten and twelve she was sick. She stuck to the laundry job, and by November, when the first blizzard struck the city, she felt pretty good again, just tired. Struggling home through the deep snow, she felt all the steamy warmth of the laundry leave her body and the cold air seemed to strike at the small life within her. The intense cold of the prairie had never seemed so hostile and terrifying.

Their son, Royston, was born in May just as the weather became hot. He was a thin, sickly baby but Carrie thought him perfect and never complained about the extra work and the broken nights. The following year Angela, plump and energetic, was born as winter started. Her parents would never understand where her brown eyes and fine head of dark curls came from.

"She's sure like a little gypsy!" Wayne would say many times and chortle and the baby would smile back at him. But Carrie hardly smiled for she did not like those gypsy looks.

They had made no friends in the city and there were no relatives nearby to help out. The two babies, so close in age, made life hard for the young mother. Carrie continued to work an early morning shift at the laundry, for though Wayne took a second job pumping petrol late at night, not one of his many jobs brought in enough money.

Although Angela was an easy, happy baby, Carrie, full of self pity, blamed her daughter for causing most of her troubles.

Carrie preferred her large-eyed, timid son.

The stuffy little room was still all that they could afford.

They seldom returned to visit their families in the country.

On the few occasions that they did, Carrie was silent and permanently bad-tempered throughout the visit, perhaps

envious of her mother's more comfortable home or unhappy
that her return was not more glorious.

On their visits, Wayne worked obsessively hard on the two
farms. All his old skills came back to him and it seemed as
though he could not rise early enough.

"Bit of a difference from usual." Carrie would sniff sarcas-
tically at five-thirty each morning. However Wayne found a
freedom in this life which he had not apppreciated before. He
was able to choose his occupation and when to start and stop.
His pleasantly aching muscles made him feel young and alive
again.

Strangely, his parents and in-laws were grateful for his
help, where formerly his work had been taken for granted. He
realised they were growing older and more dependent, but he
was too sure of Carrie's answer to suggest a return to life on a
farm.

Back in Winnipeg after the visit, Carrie either ignored his
depressed silence or perhaps commented,

"You've wore yourself out on them farms."

The children had a wonderful time in the country,
enjoying the animals and the freedom. They often discussed
their adventures, but always in secret, for neither parent
seemed pleased by any reference to the holiday.

After a few years in Winnipeg, the small sophistications
and pleasures of those first months were forgotten. Money
was always short. Eventually they moved to a shabby duplex
on the outskirts of town with a small, brown, old-fashioned
kitchen, nothing like Carrie's dream.

Both now worked for Eaton's catalogue store, in the large
windowless building where orders from all over Manitoba
were parcelled for delivery. Though at first the work seemed
almost enjoyable to Carrie, certainly preferable to the
laundry, it soon palled. There was always a push from
management to work more quickly. A fining system, when
mistakes were made, depleted the inadequate wage. However,
they lived nearby and the shift system suited them.

Sixteen years of determined hard work had made Carrie's
eyes larger and her mouth smaller. She was thin and worn
and looked closer to middle age than her thirty four yeas
warranted.

When her parents were killed in a level crossing accident, she heard the news with little emotion.

She knew exactly what she would do with the money from the sale of the farm.

"We'll move east, Wayne and buy ourselves a nice little business."

"You really sure you wanna sell your Dad's farm?"

She looked at him pityingly, without replying and Wayne's secret fantasy of using the money to improve his own father's farm faded and died.

They found a large, but run-down, general store and house for sale in the small Ontario town of Redfalls. Standing in its own grounds with space for customer parking in front, it had belonged to a local family for three generations. For many years, the spacious shop had thrived and had been a meeting place where folk lounged and gossiped. Now everyone had transport to take them to Kingston or Belleville, where supermarkets and cut-price stores displayed their alluring bargains.

Carrie was unaware of this decline. For the first time in her life she had money to spend and with her usual determination, she proceeded to realise some of her dreams. Naively and without any business knowledge, she transformed the shop.

"I guess we want to make it real modern, Wayne. Something like the big self service stores."

Wayne said nothing. It was not his money and he had learned that arguing with his wife was useless.

After a local joiner had worked for three weeks on the shop, Carrie dismissed him.

"He's jist a hick, that fella. He ain't got *no* idea what I wanted. Just lookit them shelves, I mean just *look*... "

Wayne bit his lip and looked at the floor.

A tradesman was brought in from Belleville to finish the work. There were many months of acrimonious argument between Carrie and the local man before he was paid.

It was a bad start to their stay in Redfalls.

Carrie also had the kitchen remodelled by the city joiner, though she was dissatisfied by the finished job and stupefied by his final account, totalling it ten times before she admitted it was correct.

However when they visited the wholesale depot in
Kingston to buy stock for the shop, Carrie regained her joy in
the store and all her previous ambition. She was entranced by
the sheer amount of goods available and acted like a little girl
on her birthday. She almost took leave of her senses.

"Just lookit those Wayne, so cute and this here! Come
over here Wayne, I never thought of... and look here... and
here."

The years of having nothing but absolute necessities were
behind her. She marked down orders for babywear, slippers
and bathrobes, cosmetics, kitchen gadgets, fancy stationary,
salad bowls and lemonade sets, even three fondue sets. She
was deliriously happy as she imagined handling and
arranging these delightful luxuries and then selling them for
a profit!

When Wayne suggested some caution in their first order,
he was snubbed. Later she took his arm and explained,

"You know, honey, we're really aimin' to open their eyes
in Redfalls. They probably never seen such fancy stuff before
*in their lives*! Our store'll beat anythin'! Just you wait'n see!"

It was a long time since she had called him honey and
when she started ordering tins of olives, asparagus, cocktail
sticks and fancy Japanese crackers, Wayne withdrew into his
normal quiet dreamworld.

Everyone in Redfalls came on opening day, exclaiming at
the changes in the old store and even buying a few things.
But they were not as astonished as Carrie had hoped, for they
had seen it all before, and cheaper, in Safeways and Eatons in
the city.

The display stands, the tightly packed shelving, the bins
of toys on special offer, left little space for lounging and
gossiping. But there was plenty of that once the customers
left the store and none of it was optimistic.

"Hey, she don't give out much warmth!"

"Sour as a pickle, any day."

"Guess they've stuck out their necks way too far."

"They'll be movin' on six months from now, Ah'd say."

"Some big prices they're hopin' for!"

"They'll be lucky!"

"Loada fancy trash if y'ask me!"

"Guess they'll cut prices real soon."

"More likely move on."

The customers came each day but they spent little, saving their cash for the weekly jaunt to one of the larger towns.

Carrie was disappointed and her small mouth conveyed disapproval and superiority. She lacked the skill of welcoming customers and her unwise disagreement with the local joiner had given her an unsympathetic reputation.

Strangers who move to a small, close community must tread warily.

After five weeks of poor trading, only a few hundred dollars remained of their legacy. It was obvious that the store would not support their family. Wayne tentatively suggested that he might find some farm work, but Carrie disagreed strongly.

"How'd I manage all the store work myself, Wayne? Besides, everyone 'ud think the shop was *failin'.*"

"I guess it is failin', Carrie."

For once she had no reply and Wayne happily started work on a farm that week.

At fifteen Royston was, tall, thin, strange-looking, with his mother's small mouth and pale protruding eyes. From the start, the youths of Redfalls were hard on him, making him the butt of their ill-humour and small town boredom. He had no real interests and he had drifted apart from his bright energetic sister. Lonely and desperate, Royston was filled with a terrible mixture of sadness and anger, which did not exclude his parents and sister.

His father had a gun for shooting rabbits and Royston often thought of this gun and whether it would be possible to kill himself with it.

Then they would all be sorry.

Angela was the only one of the family to be delighted with Redfalls.

That first week, she made friends with two older girls who, miraculously, had a spare bike and the three girls flew around town every evening. Angela had always *longed* for a bike.

"Angela, I don't want you runnin' round with them older girls, hussies more like, showin' off their bare legs all over town."

As a child, Angela had dismayed her mother with her flir-tatious female ways and now that her figure had matured, Carrie felt even more uneasy. With her colouring and her curves, Angela had more overt sexual appeal than her mother had ever possessed.

"They're only sixteen, Ma!"

"An' you're only fourteen. They're too old, they're near women. Give'em back that rusty ole bike."

"But, Ma..."

"*Give 'em back the bike.*"

That night Angela embarked on an exciting life. She waited until her parents were asleep, then climbed from her bedroom window to join her friends under the clear Ontario stars. For the next four months, by sleeping late in the morning and retiring early at night for a cat nap, Angela managed to find enough rest to escape every night. Her real life was lived in the hours of darkness, cycling madly through empty streets, laughing and shouting on street corners until angry faces appeared at open windows, treating her friends to Coca cola and chocolate bars, stolen from the store.

Within a fortnight, her friends had persuaded her to go out of town to the Spender Hill where young people gathered, arriving throughout the night in cars and motor bikes. Each evening was a party with drink and drugs and inevitably sex.

Quite soon, Angela had tried them all.

Carrie was neither work-shy nor a coward, but she was a stranger in town and unpopular and she disliked the towns-people in return. She could not greet them affably. She knew they would spend only a dollar or two and some wanted to run up a bill. When she refused to give credit, several customers became nasty and pointed out that the previous owners had always been helpful that way.

"It's right necessary for farmers to git credit, young woman, an' you won't keep this shed long till ye learn that fac'." said a tall intimidating farmer to Carrie one day.

Then, with a meaning sneer on his face, he looked around at the unsold household luxuries, the grubby teddybears and other mishandled goods and the empty shelves where everyday commodities had once been displayed.

As he stamped out of the shop, the tears rolled from

Carrie's large eyes.

About eleven o'clock one cold October night just five months after they had moved to Redfalls, Wayne was reading his newspaper. Carrie sat hunched over the accounts, repeatedly adding up the same disappointing sums. Angela had as usual, gone to bed early to prepare herself for the party in the hills. She knew that winter would soon finish these wonderful nights and had been afraid to ask where they would go when the bitter cold of winter set in. Already the meetings were shortened, though a blazing bonfire and whisky helped to keep them laughing for hours.

Royston was alone in his room with his fierce, melancholic rage.

Suddenly there were shouts from the street. Wayne jumped up and ran through the store to the front porch. From the darkness of the shop, he watched nine or ten men gathered in the carpark. Three of them carried flaring torches and their voices were raised in angry discussion. They paid no attention to the store although they stood so close to it. Carrie joined her husband.

"What do those fellows mean, havin' their meetin' in our yard, wavin' them dangerous torches close to our building! I'm goin' out to chase 'em off!"

"No, Carrie, leave 'em be. They look kinda nasty."

Carrie would have walked out the shop door, but Wayne held her arm.

Suddenly about fifteen much younger men, also carrying flaring brands, ran around a corner and joined the first group. The shouting grew so loud that it was hard to know whether these newcomers were friends or enemies. It was too much for Carrie and she burst out of the shop and shouted from the veranda.

"Get yourselves home, you noisy louts, and leave honest God-fearin' folk in peace, can't ye."

Her words were mostly lost in the uproar but her obvious fury made her the focus for their anger.

"Ye'd better keep a closer eye on yer daughter, afore ye claim to be God-fearin'!"

Called one young man and some shouted agreement, while others laughed.

Carrie picked up a broom as though she would attack the speaker, but Wayne grabbed her firmly.

"Let's get back in the house, Carrie. It ain't us is their problem."

Just then a youth full of bravado and whisky, threw his small burning torch on to the side veranda. Wayne immediately swept it off with the broom.

Next, two larger brands landed on the roof, but Wayne was able to climb up and remove them too.

The crowd now lost interest in the store and its owners and moved from the yard to the street. There was a deep discontented murmur amongst them which was terrifying and hostile. Carrie and Wayne stood immobile on the veranda.

All at once the men turned again towards the store with raised faces. They were all looking at the roof and a few took a step backwards.

Although Carrie and Wayne could not see him, Royston stood unsteadily on the ridge of the roof, brandishing the shotgun.

His high-pitched shout was unintelligible, but as another three burning sticks flew through the air towards the store, Royston fired into the crowd and blinded a schoolfellow in the right eye.

Two years later Wayne had aged since that terrible night and lost all ambition and Carrie no longer aspired to status, only respectability.

In a rundown area of Kingston, they had rented a small unattractive corner store with a tiny flat above it. Penny candies displayed on dusty shelves unpleasantly near to the floor attracted children and a minimum profit came from magazines, cigarettes, fresh bread and tinned goods.

Royston's trial had been a terrible experience. It was never made clear why the crowd had gathered. Carrie always felt that if she could have seen him and spoken to him, he would never have fired the shotgun. When Wayne tried to remember that night, his head ached and it was all confusion.

The judge advised psychiatric treatment for Royston and gave him a short reformatory sentenced. Those months away from his family were very happy for Royston and he made a fine model of a covered wagon out of balsa wood.

When Carrie discovered that Angela was pregnant, some of her old energy flared and she arranged that when they moved to Kingston, the baby would be considered as her own, while Angela, still only fifteen, continued school.

She had reckoned without Angela, who wanted to be a proper mother and bring up little Ritchie herself. Angela's ideas about life were every bit as clear and determined as her mother's. She and Ritchie would be vegetarians. They would wear the bright ethnic clothing that was termed 'hippy' and was so popular with young people and such anathema to their elders. Angela would work with drug addicts and help them kick the habit, as she had been helped in the maternity hospital. Perhaps she would eventually find employment in one of the three penitentiaries situated in Kingston. For a hobby she would study Indian dance and philosophy. She was an ambitious girl but as Carrie saw it, it was certainly not a respectable life.

Angela's wild, waist length hair, her second-hand embroidered skirts and fringed shawls, the tinkling bells and the waft of patchouli which followed her everywhere, were a constant affront to her mother.

Mealtimes were a battle of wills, with Carrie plying Ritchie with hamburger and beans and Angela snatching them away from the child, substituting yogurt, fruit and seeds.

"That child'll grow up stunted if he don't eat proper!"

"Ritchie ain't eatin' dead animals. I give him what's healthy and nat'ral."

The wonderful thing was that the little boy ate whatever was in front of him with a good appetite, blinking slightly when a plate suddenly disappeared, but relishing the next offering with a smile.

The hostility was too much and Angela broke first, setting off across Canada on a sad lonely journey for three months.

When she returned, Carrie refused her access to Ritchie.

"How could a proper mother leave her child like that? Leavin' me responsible for all them months? You expect to waltz back in here and take up where you left off? Bringin'im up in heathen ways? No sirree!"

Angela took it to court, but the wild hairiness and extravagant dress of Angela and her friends did not impress the judge, who hardly noticed the sharp eyes and the small embittered mouth above Carrie's respectable polyester suit.

Angela was banned from seeing Ritchie until he was sixteen and Carrie and Wayne Barrett were given permission to adopt the child formally.

Let us hope that the determination in Ritchie's shapely mouth and the glint of mischief in his large dark, gypsy eyes will not create too much grief for Carrie in the next eleven years.

# MISS TOD & MISS BINNS

The two old ladies sat together in the warm secluded garden. Not very close together, perhaps, as although they had shared the same house for many years, their relationship could be better described as acquaintance rather than friendship. They were the same age and had many tastes in common – one was an obsessive interest in cleanliness. They also shared a great delight in mealtimes, although not necessarily in the same foods, and their quick little footsteps always hurried to the dinner table.

Miss Tod was little and plump and had grey hair, almost wiry to look at but quite soft to touch – if anyone had ever dared to be so bold. Perhaps they might not have been repulsed. As she sat almost dozing in the August sunlight, just the tip of her tongue showed between her teeth. That was often a sign that she was about to speak, but as her eyes were now shut quite tightly, it was more likely due to forgetfulness. Those eyes could open very quickly, of course, if there were the slightest movement in the garden. Even an extra large bee exploring the mint flowers might disturb her apparently deep sleep.

Miss Binns, the other old lady, was very different in appearance. She was tall and angular with long legs and tiny feet on which she always wore high heels. Her hair was still very black but bands of grey, carefully brushed and smoothed, gave her an aristocratic and imperious mien which was not at all unsuited to her character. She seldom allowed her eyes to close completely. She never ran to look over the garden wall, as Miss Tod might do if she awakened suddenly. Miss Binns contemplated the garden from where she sat, marking the plants which needed trimming – and there were quite a few of those – her eyes following the flight of butterflies with such disapproval that it was surprising that so many caterpillars inhabited the lettuce. The sudden cry of a seagull – because the sea was close by – might make her leap up with a little start and if you were close to her you would hear the click of

her tongue in irritation at the disturbance. Only one incongruous habit disturbed the magnificent dignity of Miss Binns.
On really hot sunny days, which often come in June in this
country, that elegant lady would, incredibly, throw herself
full-length on her back in the grass and abandon herself to the
sun, her arms above her head, her legs stretched far, her feet
not together. Who knows what deep primitive urges caused
her to throw away her hard-earned character? But during all
those hours of sunshine, she was happy to ignore the dictates
of convention and return to the simple blissful innocence of
Rousseau. Those occasions happened seldom, and when they
did it was Miss Tod's turn to look censorious – which she did
unexpectedly well – from a much shadier corner of the garden
than she usually chose. Yes, little Miss Tod loved the sun, but
not, like her friend, to excess. Glimpses of usually unseen
white undergarments really shocked Miss Tod and the benefits
of living in the same house with Miss Binns, seemed at those
moments of sun-worshipping, perhaps not quite sufficient to
balance the embarrassment suffered. But all relationships
depend on compromise and there were certainly great benefits
to be gained from sharing the pretty house and sheltered
garden.

Not the least of these benefits was the large kindly servant,
Jane, who created the clean peaceful background that the old
ladies enjoyed – indeed took for granted. Jane was always
there, cleaning, tidying, weeding in the garden and, most
important, producing little meals at the right time – the ladies'
delight was not in a large amount of food, but in delicious
flavours, presented several times a day. Jane made her continuous, somewhat cumbersome way on the periphery of their
lives and to tell the truth, though they were fond of her, they
knew little about her. What she did was important to them and
often merited praise, which they expressed in their own individual ways. What Jane thought or what Jane felt did not
exist as far as Miss Tod and Miss Binns were concerned. What
selfish old ladies you will say. Yes, perhaps they were, but
soon we will all be old and only the very young and the very
old can indulge in perfect selfishness. The very young have
beauty and charm to offset their sin and hopefully the very
old have wisdom and charm – and know how to stop talking

sometimes. At any rate, Jane was very fond of her two selfish old ladies, and if they seemed to take her for granted at times, she had other founts of happiness. The very laziness of the old ladies meant that Jane had complete control of the garden. What a heady delight to have power, complete power, over a sunny garden, with excellent soil, after so many years of parsley and geraniums in a window box. Roses, honeysuckle, clematis, black currants grew against the old sandstone walls. Lupins, delphiniums, sweet rocket, stock, marigolds bloomed effulgently and were then replaced by sidalcea, sweet william, loosestrife, nasturtiums. Throughout the garden there was a haze of brown feathery fennel and green and yellow lady's mantle. In every corner white alyssum, dianthus and dark blue bugle sprouted against the unexpected cold grey velvet of artemisia.

All this was Jane's and it meant that she could spend almost as much time in the garden as her mistresses did, albeit Jane was working. The ladies dozed or pretended to sleep in order to disguise their unease that Jane was weeding and the air held no promising aroma of an approaching meal. Feeding the two old ladies was no problem for Jane. She loved cooking – and eating, herself. Being so close to the sea, the fish was deliciously fresh and they all enjoyed it. There was an excellent butcher in the village and Miss Tod especially enjoyed a small portion of grilled liver, while Miss Binns preferred steak or mince. There were many locally grown vegetables available, though Jane found that the ladies cared less for vegetables than she did herself. Occasionally they had fish suppers and they all giggled as they ate them straight from the paper bags cradled in newspaper.

Another aspect of Jane's life which certainly pleased her were the regular visits from Arthur the joiner. It is surprising that in such a small house as this was, there were so many requirements for new shelves, adjustments to window fastenings, replacement of floorboards, mending of chairs, fixing of fences. There it is, however, believe me if you will, there was almost a weekly need for joinery work to be done and fortunately Arthur, a handsome and well-trained joiner, much the same age as Jane, was always able to come along and see to the work. The ladies made no demur about any work which

Jane suggested as necessary, as they realised that the smooth running of the house was of paramount importance. Arthur seemed a gentlemanly fellow and no doubt an excellent tradesman, though his voice rang very loudly in the quiet establishment. Quite often the laughter of Jane and Arthur made the ladies look at each other in askance, moving their hands and feet abruptly and licking their lips with slight displeasure. Arthur was also a keen gardener, although vegetables were more his interest and he often brought presents of beans, turnips or tomatoes to the household. He liked to look around the flower beds in Jane's garden and he drank his cup of tea beside the ladies, speaking to them most respectfully. I think he was genuinely fond of the two of them with their delicate old-fashioned ways. I think he was even more fond of Jane.

We all have problems in this life to bear. The particular fly in the ointment of life for these two old souls might not seem to be a seriously large insect to us, but it made them miserable. The garden, although walled and sheltered from the breeze, was scarcely as private as they might have wished. A little pathway skirted the west side of their garden, where the wall was only waist high – and in a friendly little village, where people have not quite enough business to occupy their day, it is natural for passers-by to stop and exchange pleasantries. Both ladies hated and resented these neighbourly exchanges. 'Intrusive'. This was the word which Miss Tod used repeatedly about the friendly passers-by.

"What can one do? They are so terribly intrusive", she would lament several times a day. Miss Binns, closing her eyes, kept a grim silence.

If only her friend would have some sense, but Miss Tod, when greeted by a passer-by would leap to her feet with a false show of pleasure. It was far better to be honest as Miss Binns herself was. If Miss Binns were not as upset by the intrusion as her friend, it was because she was able to be honest and ignore them. At the first sound of approaching footsteps, Miss Binns would turn her head and gaze fixedly at the beautiful Zephrin Drouin rose which grew against the cottage wall. After a few moments Miss Binns would turn her severe, unwelcoming face sharply back to the hopeful visitor who would mumble a phrase about the weather before walking away. It was rude but it was effective, and the small glitter in Miss Binns blueish-green eyes showed her pleasure in her little victory. If Miss Tod could have developed a similar formula, she might have saved herself a great deal of unhappy resentment, but she was quite unable to summon up such strength of character, and I, for one, cannot blame her.

Miss Tod was particularly distressed by Mrs. Ailes, who had lived in the district even longer than herself and who took it for granted that her presence conferred a grace of its own and would always be welcome.

"She really is frightful with that red hair and staring eyes – when will she stop dyeing her hair? An old woman like that, it's pathetic and frightful and she is so... so... intrusive".

"I don't think she dyes her hair" said Miss Binns dryly.

"Oh she must – it's awful – no one has hair that colour. When I see that pink nose and red hair and staring eyes appearing over the wall – *intruding* on our garden... why don't you think she dyes it? She must surely."

"It has faded over the years."

"Perhaps, I suppose it may – but sometimes, it's awful – so untidy and matted. I hate her."

"She has had quite a difficult life, you know."

Although compassion and understanding were hardly characteristic of Miss Binns, she was not above appealing to those qualities in Miss Tod, especially if it might put an end to what appeared a somewhat hysterical outburst.

"So she has, yes, she has had a hard time, hasn't she, all those houses that she has lived in, and so many children too, and no one to rely on".

Miss Tod proceeded to list the many difficulties of Mrs. Ailes' life, repeating some of them three times, thereby making the list much more impressive, returning more than once to the handicap of having been born with red hair and finishing with the earnest desire that Mrs. Ailes might not intrude so much in the future, poor soul.

There were a few visitors who were welcome. They were always pleased to see young Mr. Black from across the road, for instance. In fact Jane often opened the front door and invited Mr. Black in, as she felt his visit cheered the old ladies up. He never stayed long and seldom spoke much. He stalked around the garden, making a few complimentary remarks as the old ladies sat very still, watching him with little smiles on their faces, nodding agreement. He would not accept a proffered cup of tea, or even sit down. To the ladies' secret delight he often left by lightly vaulting over the low wall at the foot of the garden into Mr. Jobber's garden, looking over his shoulder and giving a brisk unsmiling wave as he disappeared from sight. There was a dashing quality about Mr. Black' s visits to the ladies which seemed to show that romance and gallantry might still be important in their lives. Perhaps they did not discuss this excitement which his visits generated, but no doubt they were each aware of the other's feelings and tended to smile more and sleep less that day. There was more patting and preening, more discussion of the flowers, less wondering if it were not time for supper soon, on a day that Mr. Black came to call. Perhaps that is why Jane invited him in.

Mr. Jobber, whose garden adjoined their own, was very different from Mr. Black – a younger man and much less polished. He popped his head over the wall when least expected. He had moved to the district quite recently and obviously wanted to be friendly. His staccato sentences, delivered in a harsh southern accent had not the calming smoothness of Mr. Black's kindly compliments. In fact, Mr. Jobber's conversation consisted of questions, quite awkward ones. What was the name of this plant? When did that shrub flower? Should the herbs be cut back in September? In their horticultural ignorance the ladies could only shake their heads. Most embarrassing of all his questions – was the compost sufficient feed for the garden or should he get horse-manure? This seemed a shockingly vulgar question and he always asked it. Even Miss Binns' famous neighbour-quelling formula seemed ineffectual with Mr. Jobber and he continued to stand, looking into and around the garden with his rather close-set eyes. With not a word spoken by any one of the three, the situation would become unbearably awkward and after twenty minutes of silence, Miss Binns would stand and walk rather slowly into the house on her little high heels and Miss Tod, after a little flustered twitch of her face – it might have been an apologetic smile – would follow her friend rather quickly, almost trotting. Mr. Jobber would return to his barren garden with no apparent feelings of sadness or discomfort. Once he had caught a brief unforgettable glimpse of Miss Binns sunning herself in her abandoned way. He had at once left the garden, so he must have some gentlemanly feelings. Miss Binns had immediately leapt to her feet and darted into the house putting the unfortunate incident out of her mind for ever. Not so Miss Tod. For weeks her mind dwelt on the embarrassment of her friend's sparkling white underwear on view to Mr. Jobber's masculine gaze. She felt she might be happy if the sun never shone again, tempting her friend to such uninhibited exposure. She thought she could never again meet Mr. Jobber's eye when he spoke. But as we know, time heals all and his visits were quickly resumed and his loud unanswered questions once more echoed around the garden.

Two other ladies, only marginally more welcome than Mrs. Ailes, popped their heads over the garden wall. Miss Tod did not know their names and did not feel she could ask Jane, who probably did know. Jane generally seemed to know most things, although she seldom spoke much – except of course to Arthur. The two visiting ladies were middle-aged and very elegant. Their attire was always immaculate and always 'set off' by sparkling white collars and cuffs. Miss Tod never wore white herself as it was "too much laundering for poor Jane" and Miss Binns only wore white underwear and she herself was responsible for keeping that spotless and snowy. There was little conversation with the two stylish ladies and one might almost wonder why they bothered to call.

Apart from Mr. Black, all these visitors left an atmosphere of nervous discord in the garden. The two ladies would fidget for perhaps ten minutes or more. Jane often stood at the window which overlooked the garden, watching as they tidied their hair with quick little movements, their little hands and feet almost jerking with nervousness. Each avoided catching the other's eye and not a word was spoken for at least quarter of an hour. Only when they had regained their composure would Jane go out to the garden again, and after a little unnecessary dead-heading of the roses, would she suggest some refreshment, which was always gratefully received. It was usually served in the garden, unless Mrs. Ailes had been the visitor and then they both agreed it was better to go inside "... in case that red-haired intruder returns".

Both old dames liked to rise very early in the morning. Perhaps the birds awoke them. Perhaps the remembrance of the perfume of the flowers in the garden called them. More probably they felt hungry. Perhaps when one does no work one needs little sleep. At any rate Jane, although an early riser by most standards, always slept rather longer than seemed convenient to her mistresses. They each dealt with this in their own way. Miss Tod in her little pink fluffy slippers would slip quietly and silently into Jane's bedroom – the conscientious servant always left her door ajar – and just tap the foot of the bed gently and then quickly dart out into the hallway again. No doubt this movement started Jane's long ascent from those depths of somnolence which only a hard day's work brings. Miss Tod would repeat her little manoeuvre several times, forcing Jane's thought processes to the surface in a most kindly way.

Next Miss Binn's high heels could be heard clipping up and down, up and down, outside the bedroom door. That undoubted irascibility which always attaches to the sound of hurrying high heels would make its way rather sharply into Jane's consciousness. Next, Miss Tod would – oh so lightly, like a piece of pink thistledown lay her little hand on Jane's shoulder and tap, tap. That would waken her thoroughly and that was fortunate because Miss Binn's patience would have reached its end. Miss Binns who spoke very little and often very quietly would put her head inside Jane's bedroom door and – I am afraid I can use no other word – *roar* her name. That is a terrible way to describe how Miss Binns greeted her devoted servant each morning, but I must be honest. At no other time did Miss Binns seem so demanding or imperious with her beloved maid. Perhaps it *was* hunger which wakened Miss Binns so early.

There are many aspects of the Scottish summer. In June the days are deliciously long and bright and the three ladies usually shared a democratic breakfast in the small fresh garden each morning at seven o'clock, listening to the small sounds of insects and watching the dew dry from the grass and leaves, as the sun slowly filled the garden. They were often to be found still lingering in the garden at ten or eleven o'clock at night in that month, reluctant to leave the magical translucent blue of the sky which hovered above them and the perfumes which some flowers give more potently, as night approaches.

July, sadly, often brings showers and high winds and those without faith or observation think that summer has gone for another year. Happily in August the heat returns, stronger than before, to compensate for the shorter days. In a good summer, enthusiastic plants recruit their strength, delphiniums and lupins particularly reassemble their indigo spears and delight us for a second time. Exotic lilies unfold, Shasta daisies sparkle from shadowy corners, nasturtiums treble their previous quota of brilliant blooms and late clematis and roses add their rich colours to the celebration. Windy gusts often blow in August and the surface of the deep navy blue sea is decorated with white whipped waves. Those breezy days had a particular effect on the two old ladies. Jane noticed, but of course said nothing to them about it. She did discuss it with Arthur though and they smiled together at the quaint ways of her two mistresses.

When the wind was brisk, Miss Tod stood at the wall at the bottom of the garden, gazing at the wild waves. Sometimes she sat on the wall for half an hour looking always seawards almost as though she awaited the arrival of a ship. Then suddenly she would jump down from the wall in quite a girlish way, run quickly across the grass, dash thro' the long hallway, turning so sharply into the kitchen that her little pink slippers almost skidded as she turned. It was strange skittish behaviour for a mature lady and it was never explained, but Jane enjoyed this manifestation of a younger, wilder Miss Tod.

Eventually the windy weather made Miss Binns stay inside. At first poor Miss Binns would look for shelter in various parts of the garden – under the graceful fennel shrub which was now a mass of feathery yellow flowers, but those flowers made her sneeze. Next she would try the large honey-suckle bush but that blew and swayed and the recurring little knocks on the head were more than she could stand. Lastly she tried the black currant bushes which stood against the high East wall. That wall caught the last of the evening sun and its cream and ochre stones seemed always warm and inviting. Alas, those strong towering bushes which produce the most ambrosial jam fruit of all, were the home of the tiniest unfriendliest inhabitant of the garden – the berry bug. Miss Binns was forced into the unladylike occupation of scratching. She itched behind the ears, on the arms and legs, round her tummy, even between her toes and all those places were scratched – at first unobtrusively, then she forgot her dignity and threw all her energies into trying to find relief. Jane, who did the berry picking and was herself not unaware of the agony caused by the minute creature brought powders and creams and tried to soothe her dear mistress, without much success. Miss Binns stayed indoors for a week, looking miserable and scratching.

As the evenings grew shorter and more unpredictable, Jane could not garden, so she produced her wonderful baskets of wool and knitted vast shawls and made crochet blankets. Sometimes she blended her colours with the bright splash of summer flowers, sometimes the sombre hues of the garden in winter. The old ladies loved watching her and each snuggled into a favourite shawl or blanket. The warmth of the wool helped them to doze happily until Jane chose her next colour, an operation they both watched with some excitement. These evenings passed very happily.

Sometimes Miss Tod would exclaim over the colours, in fact she exclaimed very regularly. "Oh what beautiful soft glowing colours, I could enjoy looking at them all evening."

"Yes" said Miss Binns.

"And what wonderful wool it is, so soft and warm."

"Yes" said Miss Binns.

"And it is very strong too, look now long the shawls last and never wear out."

"True" said Miss Binns.

"Jane's colours are so perfectly blended and the shawls are so fine... they are really just like gossamer."

"Yes, that is the case."

"The wool must be very, very special wool, I think."

"It is Shetland wool", said Miss Binns.

But if Miss Binns seemed less enthusiastic than Miss Tod, she was certainly wrapped up just as thoroughly in the discussed shawls.

The weather had been particularly lovely that summer until the second week in August, which was very strange and disturbed. On Tuesday afternoon, after a splendid morning, the ladies were driven into the house by the wind rising and gusting alarmingly. The sea changed swiftly too. Little white crests appeared – Miss Tod always called them 'the white horses' but soon the waves grew to six feet, then ten feet high and their crashing on the rocks on the shore could be heard distinctly within the house.

The ladies looked unhappily from the window as the tall plants in the garden were blown, bent and broken. Then they turned their backs and refused to watch the destruction. Jane, however, gazed from an upstairs window and thoroughly enjoyed the power and beauty of the natural forces. Suddenly, as though switched off, the wind stopped. The sun shone on the monstrous seas and a perfect rainbow arched across the sky. Within an hour the sea had turned to steel-grey, and the sky was almost black, split at regular intervals by lightning. The thunder was deafeningly loud. By seven, when the fishing boats set off for their night's work, the sun shone once more on a brilliant green and blue sea. The water looked deceptively calm but the spray breaking over the lurching boats bore witness to the earlier instability of the elements. Jane had stood watching the phenomena most of the afternoon, the sheer excitement and beauty of it all had elated her spirit and for once she had neglected her two ladies. I am afraid supper was very late that evening. There was no word of reproach, but the long look of sadness from Miss Tod's large, almost golden eyes did smite Jane's conscience. Miss Binns chose to close her eyes each time Jane tried to make amends by offering some little service.

That night Jane awakened suddenly. Had she heard a little cry of fear? Were those small pink slippers rushing along the corridor? After standing for a few moments in silence in the dark house, Jane crossed to the window and opened the shutters – the moon, which should have been full, was a wire-thin silver crescent, with clouds of luminous burnt orange flaring from each side of it. With a deep feeling of mystery and magic, Jane realised that the day had been the prelude to a complete eclipse of the moon. She clenched her hands and curled her toes tightly as she watched the moon triumphantly reappear.

All good things must come to an end – the triteness of the saying does not make it any less true. Jane cut back more and more of the plants. The evenings started earlier and earlier. Some days the rain and wind beat at the windows for hours, while the ladies, wrapped cosily in shawls, looked wearily out. It seemed as though they had never known any other life than that fragrant flowered garden, that small comfortable house with the appetising smells of cooking and baking, that kind and efficient presence of Jane, realising their wishes almost sooner than they could express them, but summer was ending. Jane packed all the little necessities that her ladies required. She packed her own voluminous flowery smocks and skirts, she tidied her knitting, crochet and coloured wools, almost more methodically than was necessary, but it was a great delight to her. She collected her crayons and sketch books – perhaps I did not mention that she liked to draw in the evenings as well as knit. The honesty and eryngium and agapanthus and poppy heads were hung up to dry. A little feed of bone-meal was given to each shrub. The garden tools were stored in the shed. She cleaned each room in the house and locked each window. Jane's regrets at leaving the summer home faded as she worked and her mind turned with its usual optimism towards the other tasks which awaited her in the coming months in the city.

The first day of September arrived. Jane was dressed very differently from her faded summer smocks and wore a smart tweed suit and rather expensive shoes. She looked unusual but bustled around in her normal motherly fashion, putting boxes and suitcases into the boot of the car which had stood unused at the front door for nearly three months.

"And now my dear ladies, we must leave our summer garden and return to civilisation – the new terms starts next week." There was a faint expression of surprise on Miss Tod's face as Jane brought out the big square basket and gently but firmly popped Miss Tod inside. Miss Binns was much more vociferous and complained bitterly during the entire journey back to the city.

Miss Tod only miaowed once.

# PARIS MEMORIES

It is difficult nowadays to convey the extreme insularity of Britain in the thirties. It was a strange attitude for a country whose culture has been so influenced by centuries of skilled and fascinating immigrants.

Generally only the wealthy had ever left the shores of this 'right little, tight little island' and for the greater part of the population, foreign goods and foods were suspect, even despised by quite educated people. The word 'foreign' was almost always used pejoratively. Wine was drunk on special occasions only, perhaps once or twice a year. As for garlic in cookery! Its addition was terribly frowned upon by some and approached with absurd caution by others. At least one cookery book suggested that a clove of garlic, suspended from a thread might be swung around a bowl for one minute, before placing salad in the bowl. Presumably the clove was then discarded. Any hint of accent in one's speech or too much gesticulation of the hands made most listeners uncomfortable, if not downright amused.

My mother and father were a stereotypical middle-class couple and shared these prejudices. They worked very hard at behaving exactly as they thought they should and as everyone else did in that street of modestly comfortable, but cramped, suburban villas. My Father took the train to the office each day and my Mother, with the help of a charwoman twice a week, kept the house immaculately clean. On entering the house one encountered a strong aroma of lavender furniture polish with faint, unpleasant undertones of Brasso and boiled cabbage. I cannot remember finding it displeasing, for the other houses that I visited smelled exactly the same. I do not think my mother took a great deal of creative pleasure in her home. It was her duty to keep it hygienic, an important word in those pre-war years and she was prepared to fulfil her duty to exhaustion point.

At six thirty each evening, a three course dinner was served with well-boiled soup, meat, also often boiled, with potatoes and vegetable, usually the aforesaid cabbage. These unexciting dishes were followed generally by a hot milk pudding with a spoonful of jam or a cold milk pudding in a 'shape'. I really loathed the latter. Very occasionally an adventurous suet roly-poly made a red letter day for me. I was a picky eater, devoted to sweet stodge on its rare appearance. As I was an only child, my parents followed the strict regime advised by the experts, plain food, regular hours and fresh air. My Mother always seemed to be opening windows. I suffered this discipline throughout my childhood, for those idealistic goals are most easily applied to the only child. Perhaps a child in a larger family might have demanded more independence, but I suppose I was a biddable child and my parents were particularly careful that I should not be spoiled. This may have led to the apparent coldness and lack of physical contact which I remember and regret. I realise now that they were too busy struggling to achieve some ideal, rather than just be a loving couple, naturally taking pleasure in their child. Although I am sure that they loved me dearly, they never gave me that impression. I find it sad and I try to forgive them. Perhaps money was always a worry too, I do not know, because money was never discussed. I suspect that the semi-detached villa and the charwoman stretched my father's modest salary to its limits.

If you ask whether I regret not having had siblings, the answer would be 'no'. I have no desire to be a different person. Those who have brothers and sisters are certainly changed by those relationships, whether for better or worse. That close interaction with other human beings can only be experienced by the only child once it has become an adult, and I believe that by then one's character is moulded, again for better or worse.

Although my paternal grandparents were not French, they lived in Paris and visited us only once each year. I expect my grandfather was an agent for some British manufacturing company, though I cannot say for certain.

Now that I must finally accept that I am an old man, much older than my grandparents were in those carefree, pre-war summers, I realise the immense influence that flamboyant, Francophile couple had on me. It is also apparent now that those annual visits must have been very hard on my parents because Grandmère and Papa, as they insisted that I call them, carried always with them a frighteningly exotic and unmistakeable hint of the Continent.

It is difficult for me to remember exactly why they seemed so different from the other people that we knew. Certainly their conversation was sprinkled with French phrases and references and there seemed to be a stilted quality about their speech, giving the impression that English was not their first language. Also their movements had an unusual dramatic energy and they laughed and spoke loudly, changing direction quickly in the street, pointing and fluttering their hands about. Their clothes were more adorned and more frivolous than those worn by ordinary people. Their hats were obviously not British, Papa's being wide-brimmed and much too large for a man, while his wife balanced a tiny piece of feathered nonsense on her immaculate curls. Altogether, they were much more enthusiastic about life than was acceptable in that pessimistic, self-deprecating society.

My Grandmother was fond of the word *chic* and used it a lot. Very occasionally she applied it to some article that my Mother was wearing. I was always excited and delighteded by the compliment, yet I was uncomfortably aware that it did not please my Mother.

I loved this aura of glamour and fantasy and secretly longed for my Mother to exchange her sensible, masculine, pull-on felt hat for something as crazy as grandmere wore.

My Grandparents' most important 'difference' was in the way that they treated me.

This urbane, effervescent, couple had no foolish scientific notions about not spoiling me. I was granted anything I might wish for, though no doubt my desires were modest. Also I was treated as an equal and included in conversation and decision-making in a way which was delightful though awkward as I had no practice in either. Cakes, fruit, nuts and sweets were bought every day and my Grandparents and I nibbled them greedily and continuously. I was guiltily aware that my Mother feared for the resulting collapse of my health. Yet I delighted in the treats even more becuse of her warning glances.

I delighted in receiving comic papers, pencil cases and cheap tin toys which gave me extreme, if transient satisfaction. They were bought for me on the understanding of absolute secrecy, but of course my parents knew of them and said nothing, though their lips tightened in disapproval. Then how I enjoyed the linked arms, the smiles and winks, the hugging, the shoulder clapping, the cheek kissing, the head patting and the hand squeezing to which I was subjected when my grandparents were there. Even an admonishing finger wagged furiously in mock anger when I was naughty, seemed charming and intimate. Each night in bed, I would re-live those gestures and caresses in my imagination, often until after midnight.

But my feelings were ambivalent, for I was torn between adoration for this couple who seemed so much younger in many ways than my own parents, and dread that I might encounter any schoolfellows in the street when I was with them. There was no doubt my Grandparents *were* different. Too, too different! My Mother must have cringed at their eccentricity, and worried about what the neighbours thought, at the same time as she struggled to play the role of dutiful daughter-in-law.

Perhaps my Father found their presence even harder to bear, for this outrageous couple were his own flesh and blood. I think his office demanded many more late nights during the weeks of his parents' visit.

I believe that I was quite a stolid little boy who seldom cried, but from the time that I was two years old, the end of my grandparents' stay was always a terrible tragedy for me. The sight of their packed suitcases waiting in the hall for the taxi to arrive, was the signal for me to give way to hysterical screams, kickings, tears and tantrums. I was inconsolable for hours after they left and often for long periods throughout the following days This abandoned misery at their departure was repeated, unabated, each year, thus realising my Mother's worst fears about the effects of spoiling. As I grew older I knew that I was 'too big a boy for crying'. I was certainly told often enough. Yet, at each parting, I determined that for this traumatic severance, I certainly *would* cry and give way to the immense sorrow that I felt. The kicking and tears did not diminish with the years and I rather looked forward to that dramatically physical part of the sad farewell. It is not that I was insincere, for their going left a terrible emptiness in my life, but it was an occasion when I viewed it as my right to express the *weltschmersch* and frustration that all children feel... perhaps the only occasion for another year.

I expect my grandparents saw nothing amiss in this outrageous display of grief, but my parents must have been terribly dismayed at my lack of British stoicism. It may have been in order to avert yet another 'scene' and perhaps break the habit (and I am willing to accept that there was a degree of habit in my behaviour) that they suggested, when I was nine, that I return to France with my grandparents that summer, to visit their adopted city.

As you can imagine I was wild with delight when the arrangement was explained to me and my first thought was that I might probably stay in Paris forever and never return to that boring suburban street.

What a magical summer that was!

My grandparents were even more magnificent and outrageous in their beloved adopted city. They wanted to show everything about Paris to their adored grandson and I drank it all in, found it heavenly, and adored them even more in return.

Paris!

Who can pin down the beauty and mystery of that exquisite city?

Surely its aura is there to be enjoyed rather than described or analysed.

For years I had listened to my grandparents' stories of the delights to be found in their adopted city.

I had been assured that every street was cleaner, broader, every building more beautiful, all food more delicious. Even the sun was warmer and the rain delightfully scented.

I was not at all disappointed.

Paris was gorgeous in a way that I had never even imagined.

I was very young and no doubt the vision was coloured by the plethora of croissants and delicate pastries with which I was plied, but my memory of exploring the elegant shops

and streets, parks and museums of Paris with my beloved
grandparents has left an impression only of bright happiness
unmarred by any unpleasant detail.

A few fleeting disjointed memories remain of those four
sunny weeks in Paris and those scenes are crystal clear. They
have occurred to me again and again throughout my life,
flashing in my mind's eye, sometimes unexpectedly, always
vividly and evoking the strongest of feelings. Even the
memory of perfumes is distinct.

As soon as I arrived in that summer of 1938, Grandmere
took me to a large department store and bought me a pair of
black shorts, six inches shorter than the grey ones that I was
wearing, also a close-fitting brown velvet jacket with a
matching cap. It was incredibly and stupendously different
from the typical schoolboy's uniform in which I had spent
most of my life. It seemed to me like fancy dress and my face
must have expressed my horror.

"Worry not, my little one," my Grandmother whispered to
me. "You must have a special holiday outfit for the promenade with Grandmere. You will be *tres chic* and there will be
many other boys dressed *just* like this, you may be *very* sure!"

I did see one or two boys in similar outfits but not many. I
could only be glad that no one paid the slightest attention to
my extreme attire and I was not followed in the streets by
whistles, shouts and catcalls, as I most certainly would have
been, had I been forced to wear those garments at home.
However the clothes were very comfortable and I soon
learned to ignore their existence.

My grandparents lived in a small cramped apartment, in a
narrow side street, rather than the spacious house surrounded
by trees, which I had imagined. However I was prepared to
find their home magical, whatever it was like. Compared to
my parents' rather empty house, the flat was filled with a
great deal of furniture. I was a tall lanky boy and I bumped
into tables and chairs and upset things regularly, breaking
various articles. Two delicate cups, a cream jug, a crystal
bowl and a china cat were shattered in the first week. I also
upset a large scarlet geranium, scattering the earth over the
entire carpet, but my Grandmere was only ever cross about
bad manners or bad taste, never about accidents or mistakes.

She insisted only that I help to clean up the mess. She was very philosophic about the breakages and almost seemed pleased, for she laughed each time and announced,

"Now I am justified in buying myself some more pretty things. We shall go shopping this afternoon."

I felt that she had quite enough pretty things already, with more decorative, useless objects on her mantelpiece than we had in our entire house. However I was glad that my carelessness did not seem to upset her. I could never be critical of her and dutifully helped her to choose some other little objets d'arts, as she called them.

How strange that I have no recollection of visiting Versailles, apart from the train which seemed very unlike any train which I had ever seen. It left from the enormous station at Montparnasse and Papa told me that Mount Parnassus was the home of the Gods. That fact so stimulated my imagination that I scarcely noticed the Chateau or the fountains that we must have wandered around and gazed at from different angles.

We also ascended the Eiffel Tower but I have no memory of the lift or of the misty view of Paris which must have spread below me. What I do recall is afterwards standing on the ground underneath that great feat of engineering and looking upwards into its immensity. Its size and strength seemed beyond anything I had ever seen before. The terrifying thought struck me that it might break and that tremendous weight of metal would plummet down and bury me.

I also remember sailing on the Seine in a little boat and diving under bridges, where the reflections made shifting lights on the green, slimy stones. I felt that I would like to drift forever under a thousand bridges.

One long boring day was spent in a large building with many paintings and a large white statue of a lady with no arms.

None of these recollections has the immediacy of the time that Papa took me to the public swimming pool. I was a good swimmer and so was he. We had a wonderful afternoon and were astonished when Grandmere reproached us for returning so late.

"I was truly sure you were both drowned!"

There were tears in her eyes as she spoke and she rolled her Rs in a very Parisian way, as though she had forgotten which language she was speaking.

I suppose the weeks in Paris held some minor disappointments for me.

I did not speak to one other child during my holiday. Of course I could not speak French, but I longed to make contact with the boys in the park, perhaps help to sail one of the beautiful model yachts on the boating pond or join a crowd in throwing or kicking a ball. My Grandmere did not forbid me to do any of these things, but I knew that she would have disapproved. It was not part of the arrangement, for I was there to be her very own grandchild and to discover the delights of her beloved city. Timidity and laziness made it easy for me to accept her possessiveness.

In Paris I learned to rise early, for Grandmere needed an hour to complete her elaborate toilette and Papa made breakfast a long and enjoyably talkative time. Even on weekdays we had a protracted breakfast and when he left the house, it was still early. Papa must go to work on weekdays, but he joined us at weekends. He was a man who was never in a hurry.

Now we come to the most potent recollection of all, a memory which stands alone in those delightful weeks that have influenced my entire life. You will probably think it a paltry little happening and you will wonder how it could possibly have assumed such importance. Perhaps the previous lack of contact with other children gave it heightened significance. I cannot tell. It is only through living for nearly eighty years that I have unravelled the threads which lead back to that July day in the Luxembourg Gardens, those threads which have, again for better or worse, woven the fabric of my life.

It was ten in the morning, the sun was not yet too hot and my grandparents and I were strolling through the Luxembourg Gardens with no particular aim in view, except to enjoy the day.

We stood for ten minutes, watching five patient little donkeys dozing under the trees, as they waited for the next child to come along and take a ride. I was asked if I would

like to ride but I shook my head. I felt that a boy of nine
should have left such pursuits behind him, though secretly I
should have liked it very much. However just gazing at their
pretty faces and gently twitching tails and knowing that my
grandparents were in no hurry to move on, made me feel
calm and happy.

I appreciated this lack of pressure tremendously for at
home my parents led a terribly structured life. A life which
demanded that they constantly watched the clock and met
deadlines. Father always seemed to rush for his train in the
morning, with Mother hovering holding his hat and umbrella
but looking anxiously towards the grandfather clock in the
hall. Even at weekends time was apportioned. A walk in the
park was always short and brisk, with constant reminders of
the chores that awaited us. No loitering was ever allowed.

Life with my grandparents was very different. There was
always a feeling that time did not matter for them.

I loved to gaze and observe as I walked slowly along. If I
wanted to speak to a dog or watch model yachts sailing on
the pond, my grandparents would happily seat themselves
until I was ready to go. Sometimes I must wait for them as
they pondered and argued over the name of some plant or
tree. Sometimes in an excess of energy, I would take a fast
gallop for a few hundred yards, returning to find them
waiting, smiling patiently, pleased with my animal spirits.

On entering the park this particular day we had been met
by a magnificent display of pink and red geraniums. The first
sight was almost like a blow to our eyes and we stood
delighted with our mouths open. The two colours were
equally divided and the glowing vivid flowers stretched into
the distance. Since my clumsy accident in the house with the
geraniums, I had disliked the flower, but that wonderful
opulence in the Luxembourg changed my attitude and
vanquished any guilt forever. Since that day the bitter smell
of a geranium leaf has been my favourite perfume.

Even as I heard my Grandmere exclaim ecstatically over
their beauty, I knew exactly what my Mother's reaction would
be. Her taste in civic planting was strictly traditional,
geometric and meagre and she would no doubt have muttered
disapprovingly,

"Fancy putting those two colours together! It's ridiculous. And so many of the same flower in one place!"

It upset me that I should think of my Mother and know so well how she might spoil my pleasure. I am sure it was at that moment that I finally cut myself free from my parents and their narrow prejudiced life. Of course as a child I was not logical or rational enough to know what had happened. It has taken me a lifetime to pinpoint and realise the significance of that moment, Though I am happy that it occurred, I am sad that so many years of misunderstanding existed between myself and my parents and that the forgiveness that I feel towards them now, was not expressed while they still lived.

Ah! I am much too serious. Now to the second important thing that happened that day. I was standing apart from my grandparents while they examined an effulgently blossoming tree, when an elegant young woman hurried past me holding a little girl by the hand. The child was much younger than I, perhaps only six years old and like her mother, beautifully dressed. It is strange that, although I had as little interest in female attire as other nine-year-old boys, I was fascinated by this child. I can picture her as clearly now as I saw her that long ago day in the park. Her dress was the simple classical shape that all little girls wore at the time, with a full skirt, plain bodice and puff sleeves. It was made of blue silk, a wonderful deep sky blue and it was patterned with a light scatter of tiny red flowers. She wore a straw hat, similar in shape to a schoolgirl's but decorated with a garland of small red roses. She was a pretty little thing and I suppose that I stared rudely at her, for she returned the stare with unpleasant interest. After she had passed, she looked backwards over her shoulder, still glaring at me. Although the curls which fell on her shoulders were very blonde, her eyes were dark and deep-set and her eyebrows were particularly well-marked for one so young. I was partly surprised and partly amused that this small mademoiselle could give me such an indignant look. In different circumstances I might have stuck my tongue out at her, but she had an adult dignity and such boyish effrontery did not even occur to me.

When they had walked a further twenty yards or so, her mother met a friend and stopped to chat. The small girl again glanced back at me, and finding my eyes still on her gave me another Gorgon glare, then, lifting a determined chin, turned her back on me decisively, firmly relegating me to the unimportant and ignored past.

I waited and continued to watch her, hoping that she might once more look in my direction. If she did, I was determined to smile to her. It was quite out of character for me to pay any attention to a child younger than myself, especially a girl, but there was an attraction about this child that I could not resist. Perhaps after three weeks of the unrelieved company of my grandparents, I longed for some childish companionship. I continued to watch her. I have often asked myself since then what it was about her that so enthralled me.

I have also wondered if my grandparents were observing me in my first romantic essay. I can imagine them watching me carefully, perhaps nudging each other gently and smiling.

Just then the girl noticed that her shoe-laces were un-tied and keeping her knees straight, she bent over from the waist to adjust them. As she bent down, a small gust of wind caught her skirt and blew it over her head, revealing perfect little knickers of the same silk as the dress! Although she hurriedly stood erect and smoothed her skirt down behind her, I was enthralled!

I cannot tell you how delighted I was to find out that she wore matching underpants! What a charming thing! Such an idea had never occurred to me before. As with most nine-year-olds, underwear and the bottoms which they covered, were a source of mystery and interest to me. I felt that I had stumbled on a vital piece of information. Did all little girls wear pants to match their dresses? Surely not. This little girl was particularly special and complete. I felt clever and proud that I had been lucky enough to discover her secret.

On another level I was aghast that such an indignity should happen to this proud girl. I felt tremendous sympathy for her and frustration that I could never voice my sympathy. She must be horribly embarrassed. She must be hoping that nobody had witnessed the incident.

As I pondered these ideas, the girl turned and looked straight at me with a more gentle expression than previously.

What did I do? Probably I tried to look sympathetic, perhaps by tilting my head a little or raising my eyebrows. I cannot remember and sympathy is a difficult emotion for a nine-year-old to convey at twenty yards, but I think she understood, because with the slightest hint of a smile she shrugged, shrugged as only a Parisienne can. I learned at that moment that even a six-year-old Parisienne can shrug with a wonderful wealth of philosophic meaning.

Then she turned and walked away with her mother into the distance.

I stood there, bereft, feeling more alone than I had ever felt in my life, for I felt that a bond had been created between us. Such a bond as a man feels for his sister, his mother, his daughter or his wife.

Were my feelings towards her romantic and innocent? Tender? Paternal? Erotic?

Perhaps a mixture of all these.

Certainly the bond that was created that day has never been severed.

It has shaped my life.

As the years pass, I think about that whole enchanting incident more, rather than less.

Quite soon after that magical day in the park, Papa brought me home to my parents. There were no more than a few tears from Grandmere at our parting. For the first time at our parting, I was dry-eyed, for I was secure in myself and also quietly positive that I would return to France within a few months.

My parents found me a changed boy. The quiet, biddable, obsessively tidy son that they remembered had disappeared. I had become an argumentative, disobedient child, determined to have my own way. I had developed a loud assertive voice when speaking to them. My bad behaviour seemed inexplicable to them.

My father blamed his mother for spoiling me. He refused to discuss the problems which I was obviously experiencing and avoided the issue by spending even more time at the office. I found my Mother boring and irritating, as she blamed herself continually for allowing me to go to Paris.

It seemed to me at the time that both parents disliked me

and as I was acting so obnoxiously, they would have been perfectly justified in doing so. In reality I think that they were hurt and puzzled, with no idea what to do with this changeling.

What a pity that a little boy did not have the logic or the language to explain to them the feelings and desires that he had learned in Paris and the inexpressible need to live his own life.

War was declared the following year and in a strange way it eased the tension in our family.

My father joined the army almost immediately and his letters home were surprisingly entertaining and affectionate and showed a side of him that I had never known. Perhaps my Mother discovered a different person in his letters too, for she received them eagerly and her cheeks were pink as she read them.

My mother, deprived of her charwoman and kept busy with problems of queuing and rationing, dropped some of her ridiculous middle-class standards and was more relaxed. She joined a group of women who organised entertainments and bazaars for the war effort and seemed suddenly to have a busy social life, with laughing friends dropping in, something which was quite unheard of before the war.

I became less selfish and more involved with school work and friends.

We were all happier and foolishly I did not worry about my grandparents. For me Paris remained a magical city of pleasure, where Grandmere would enjoy her breakfast of crisp sweet croissants each morning and masses of pink and red geraniums would always bloom in the sunny Luxembourg gardens. So strange is the mind of a child that even when I heard that the city was occupied by the Germans, this vision remained unchanged and my only regret was that my next visit must be postponed.

We heard nothing from Paris, but I remained optimistic and like so many other people, looked forward to the time when the war would be won and everything would be all right again.

I was thirteen when we were officially informed that my grandparents had been dead for at least a year.

It was a blow from which I have never really recovered and when I learned of the hardships that they suffered in their last months, well, I still cannot speak of that.

When I was twenty, I aspired to be an artist. I visited Paris for a month and tried to paint my memories of those childish years. It was useless. I had so much emotion, but no talent.

I returned to London and studied science and the French language and by the time I was thirty, I had a reasonable profession and had settled in Paris. I have lived here ever since. It has been a good life, although the magical quality with which I endowed the city as a child has faded somewhat, just as a husband, no matter how happy, will find it difficult to rediscover the delicate enchantment of his bride, in the wife of many years.

Sometimes I walk down the street where my grandparents lived and look up towards the balconied window of what was their sitting room. How small that room was, how cluttered, and how the air smelled delicious in the morning, with a mixture of the aroma of strong coffee and the perfume of face powder. I seem to think that the powder smelled of irises but whether my Grandmere told me that or whether the box had a picture of those exotic flowers, I cannot remember. I know it was a small square box.

Every Sunday, for over fifty years, I have walked in the Luxembourg Garden and like every other fellow there, no matter what age, I enjoy looking at the attractive and stylish women. I find myself searching always for a woman who might be three years younger than myself, a woman with well marked eyebrows and deep set eyes. Just occasionally I see one that I think might be that little girl of long ago and I will stare at her until she returns the look indignantly. How happy that glare will make me for a moment. My day is complete if I am fortunate enough to see her shrug her shoulders, as only a Parisienne can.

# TOO FAST!

Because I write poetry and paint pictures, some people expect me to be spiritual, other-worldly, fey. They could not be more wrong. I take pleasure only in the real and solid beauties and delights of this world. I believe they are more miraculous and rewarding than anything that might exist in Heaven or Fairyland.

And now it will be very difficult to make you understand or believe what I am about to tell you, for I have no faith in it myself. I had certainly not been drinking or otherwise manipulating my faculties. Nevertheless this was my experience and I felt no fear at the time.

I was driving from the East coast to the West, as I have done for more years than I care to admit.

Because a lorry had spilled its bales of hay, I was forced to leave my usual route and turn up a small side road, which would take me to an alternative way home. I drove up a long steep, winding hill, lined with trees in their first flush of Spring leaf. At times they arched over the road to form a tunnel. How delicious it was to fly upwards between these graceful shapes. My window was open wide and birdsong and the fresh perfume of May filled the car. To complete my delight, the radio was playing some wonderful music, an exquisite quartet or quintet by Beethoven or perhaps Schubert. I am no expert, but it was glorious. How lucky that I had been forced into this detour, and at this particular moment. I was tremendously happy, almost rapturous with the scene and the sounds. The experience of complete joy comes but seldom and it can conjure up an idealised memory of youth and strength. Such a precious vision should be hoarded for future, more difficult times.

Suddenly, this exalted state of mind was banished by a rather harsh voice shouting,

*"Nein, nein! Zu schnell, zu schnell! Nicht so schnell".*

As I have a smattering of German, I immediately applied the brake, although I had only been tootling along at forty.

*"Immer zu schnell."*

I slowed to under thirty and became aware that the passenger seat was no longer vacant. A bespectacled and somewhat portly young man sat there. I was surprisingly cool-headed about this sudden apparition. I swivelled my head briefly. The glimpse showed me a stranger with a large head, sporting a great springing bush of hair and very thick glasses sitting beside me. In that first glance I thought he seemed a little misty, but I could not swear to that.

"Zey are playing zis music too fast. I want it to go *a leettle slower.* From vere is zis music coming? How can I tell zem it muss be slower."

I swallowed hard and took a better look at my passenger. He was now completely solid, I was happy to note. Dressed in a dark suit of a strange cut with a large white cravat at his throat, he was obviously one of these romantic young people. So many fashions nowadays, I just cannot keep up. I was glad that he was not a punk.

His face looked vaguely familiar.

As it was not my speed he was complaining about, I accelerated once more.

But how could I answer him? My German conversational skills are sufficient for little more than shopping or buying a bus ticket. Fortunately he seemed to speak English pretty well.

Before I could say anything, he again asked,

"Vat music is zis? *Vere are ze Musicians?* Are zey invisible? The trees are passing zo very fast too. How are ve travelling zo fast? I see no pferd or other animal. Vat is zis Hutte in vich ve are sitting? *Who are you and vere are ve?"*

Such a rush of questions! I answered the last one, as it was the simplest.

"We are in Scotland and my name is Gertrude."

"Ach! *Schottland*! How sharming, I haf *alvays* vanted to visit Schottland und hear ze sad songs und ze instrument vit the bag! Und Gertrud, such a nice name! Fraulein Gertrud! My name is Franz. Guten Tag. I am zo delighted to meet vit you. Pleez to explain how do ve travel zo fast and from vere does ze music come?"

"We are in a motor car and it can go a lot faster than this, if you like. And the music comes from the radio. If you push that little button there, it will go off and come on again... if you push it again, that is. The music sort of comes through the air... I suppose."

I was just drivelling on and I felt a complete idiot. How does one begin to explain the internal combustion engine or radio airwaves to someone from 1828? For I knew now who this was. I had recognised the thick lips, the pebble glasses, the enormous muscular hands. Even before the announcer told us that we had been listening to the third movement of 'The Trout', I had guessed that Franz Schubert, or his shade, sat beside me in my Toyota, enjoying his own music on Classic FM.

As the announcer spoke, Franz had taken off his glasses and flipped out his cravat to polish them. The linen had obviously been used for this purpose many times, for it was none too clean.

He smiled happily when his name was mentioned and gazed at the passing trees.

"*Ohne Brille.* I feel... I am... *schwimmen gehen*, ha ha. *Schon, schon, zehr schon.*" He looked very relaxed and happy as we sped along under the trees.

The next item on the programme was modern, a simplistic piano piece, background music in a successful film. I find it incredible that it has become so tremendously popular and is continually requested. Franz listened to the first twenty bars, nodding his head, then mumbled,

"*Praktik vielleicht?*"

Then replacing his glasses, he leaned forward and pressed the button that I had indicated. After a few moments, he pressed it again and the repetitive music once more flooded the car. Almost immediately he shut it off once more and grunted,

"*Schwafeln.*"

By this time we had reached the top of the hill and I had stopped before turning into a busier road. As the traffic whizzed past us. Franz whistled his astonishment under his breath.

"Zo many leetle carts like you have! All going zo fast. You make yours stop now until a leetle space shows, then you jump in fast?"

I nodded.

"That's right."

"But it is *schwierig*? Difficult? To drive one of zese carts? Is it not unusual for a fraulein to hold zis wheel and drive? Und to go zo quick."

"No, no. I've been driving all my life."

"I very much like to make a horse go quick, but it could never go zo quick as your cart. Usually damen, ladies vould not take charge of the driving. Some do, veilleicht, but most like to make sure their frills and parasols are safe. Zey go driving to be admired I zink and not to struggle with a horse."

"I think it's much easier to drive a car than a horse, Herr Schubert."

There, I had said his name! What if he disappeared in a puff of smoke at the sound of his name? What an adventure. I could not tell whether I was enjoying it or not. And how was it going to end...?

"I think you are eine very fine driver, Fraulein Gertrud and extremely brave and skilled to travel at the astonishing speed which you have shown me."

I had not exceeded forty-five in our short journey, but I expect it did impress someone who had only experienced horse travel. It was ten miles till we reached the motor way. What would he say to seventy miles an hour?

He reached forward and pressed the button. Ionardi was still dribbling along and he immediately shut it off again.

"There might be something better on three." I suggested and touched the buttons to change programmes. Beethoven's first piano concerto sang out. That's a piece I can always recognise.

Franz gasped.

*"Ach! Wunderbar! Du bist Zauberin."*

I closed the window and kept my speed low and we sat and listened in mesmerised silence.. I noticed tears on his cheeks when the music finished. There was enthusiastic applause and he murmured,

"Gute, gute. Zey appreciate him. He vas more zan a genioos, he vas ein Gott."

I wanted to say something about how much I loved his

own music, but was unsure how to go about it and he continued,

"I met him just vun time, you know. How glad I vas to meet him after many years of utter adoration. But he vas dying. He died soon after zat meeting. I valked behind his cortege. Such an honour! And he liked my songs! He, the greatest of zem all, liked my poor songs."

"I love all your music and I think your songs and their accompaniments are the greatest of all songs with piano."

"You are too kind."

"No, I mean it truly and I'm not alone. Your songs are considered magnificent and all your work is greatly appreciated. The tragedy is that you..."

I hesitated for I could not say it! I was faced with saying something terrible. I could not put into words that he had died too young, that he was now dead and yet sitting beside me in my car. I felt slightly faint with the ambiguity of my situation. We were crossing Kincardine Bridge at that moment. To our left, the River Forth stretched to the North Sea with three small fishing boats in silhouette against its sparkling expanse. Drifting smoke from the industries outside Edinburgh added a poetic, Turneresque beauty to the scene. To our right, the river dwindled away to distant purple mountains in the accepted picturesque Scottish manner. Above us, the sky was filled with a variety of beautiful cloud formations and seemed impossibly enormous.

"I am zo happy to haf seen Schottland, dear Fraulein Gertrud. It is as beautiful as zey say. *Schon, schon, sehr schon.*"

We arrived at the motorway and I accelerated to fifty, sixty, seventy. I make it a rule never to exceed seventy.

I heard him very quietly say "*Ach*" on a sharply indrawn breath and I glanced round at him.

His lineaments were once more fading. In fact I could see right through him!

Just at that point of the road, the speed limit drops to forty because of a long sharp curve.

Franz remained sitting in his semi-transparent state until I once more accelerated to seventy. Then, quite suddenly, he disappeared.

*How guilty I felt!*

Was it the speed which had despatched him?

Should I have taken a side road and gone more slowly so that he could stay and have more experience of Scotland in the twenty-first century? He had certainly had the good fortune to see a most perfect landscape on an absolutely beautiful day.

But really, what should I have done?

Can you tell me that?

Can you even begin to imagine the inner turmoil that I felt as I hurtled along the motorway?

Perhaps I was not in a fit state to drive at all!

Could I have imagined the whole thing?

But really I felt that I had just wiped him away with my speed.

And I felt so terribly guilty.

But then he had to go, hadn't he? Sometime or other.

Franz could not stay with me, wonderful as it would have been to hear him play his own music. He had to return to wherever he had come from.

I know I have adopted more than my share of lost kittens and unwanted dogs, but a long dead composer... no... not even a genius would be acceptable... no, the family could never have dealt with that.

I want to repeat and assure you that I have never indulged in hallucinogenic substances nor ever had any belief in ghosts, spirits or the afterlife. It may seem strange, but my experience in the car has not changed that long-held attitude.

However, perhaps, just perhaps, my state of joyous exaltation that sunny Spring day, drew back the curtain to another world. If this were the case, I would certainly be discouraged from ever again indulging in such extreme transports of delight, for next time I might find a less congenial shade sitting in my passenger seat.

# ALWAYS IN MY FANTASIES

He was talking with his usual attractive animation about his new idea, however, his wife's attitude was not as receptive as he would have liked it to be. She was baking and seemed busily engaged at the kitchen table. With her back to him and her head only slightly turned, John could just see the tip of Barbara's nose.

He remembered other times when she would have stopped her task immediately and moved closer, smiling happily up at him as he talked.

At forty he felt that he was just beginning to get the real hang of how to live his life properly, but somehow his wife was different. Nowadays her work and the four children seemed to take all her attention and energy. Perhaps a woman was more apt to slow down at that age?

"I've been thinking a lot about this idea recently, darling. How would it be... I mean how would you like it, if I got out of the academic life? Made a fresh start altogether, I mean..."

His boyish enthusiasm blinded him to the expression which passed fleetingly over his wife's face.

"I've been turning it over in my mind, you know, about... umm, well, eh,"

He stopped as he had a sudden inkling that this was going to be harder to explain than he had thought.

"Well let's face it..."

He gave a quiet chuckle and paused for perhaps twenty seconds before taking a deep breath and continuing with his sentence. He had recently introduced this method of interrupting the flow of his lectures, considering it added meaning and weight to his delivery.

He did not notice that his wife's shoulders gave a small impatient shiver.

"... well you know how I like working in wood."

"Mhmhm."

"And I am rather good at it."

"Yes."

It was a qualified 'yes', a 'yes' which expressed agreement without enthusiasm.

"Well," he coughed, "I was *thinking* that it would be great to get *out* of the academic grind and move on... to... Ottawa perhaps, and start a furniture factory. You know, really first class stuff, unique pieces in beautiful unusual wood. And there is a lot of wealth in Ottawa and the sort of client that would appreciate good modern design and originality."

After another studied pause, he added,

"Of course eventually I would employ trained cabinet makers for the practical work, while I concentrated on the design side..."

He watched for Barbara's reaction. He had spoken the last sentence loudly and quickly in order to thwart any interruption that she might make, but she remained silent. She had stopped the energetic mixing and was completely still.

He frowned slightly, for she seemed so negative these days.

As she did not reply, he moved over to her and, putting his arm across her shoulders in a way that he knew she adored, asked,

"How d'you like that idea? I think it could work, darling. Don't ye think?"

"But you've never done much more than put up shelves and make a few coffee-tables."

His brightness faded and he suddenly looked so like their two-year-old Alec when deprived of a toy, that she added quickly, "But of course you always make a great job of it, I know you do. Those shelves in the kitchen at home in Scotland will be up there for ever and I'm delighted with what you do, you're better than a professional joiner I'm sure... but... you are talking about cabinet-making here aren't you. That's something different."

"I made that chair when I was a student and it got top marks."

"Yes, yes it was a wonderful chair and I love it, but it took you *months* to finish it. Anyway that's a long time ago and you had the technology and expertise of the Art College behind you then. Cabinet-makers train for years, you know. And you're talking about a business as well as making the furniture! You know nothing about running a business! That's a skill in itself."

Barbara popped the cake into the oven and brought some carrots and onions to the table. John waited until she was once again busy.

"Oh surely running a business can't be so difficult? For a man with two degrees? I'd soon pick up that side of it, I expect. I think it would be fun!"

He turned away from her smiling broadly again and scrubbing his fingers hard in his thick curly hair.

"Don't you agree, darling? A new start would be so exciting. I probably made a mistake in going into an academic career and not developing my creative side." he turned towards her with his engaging tilt of the head, but her lips were firmly set as she shook her head and continued chopping vegetables with a sharp and violent action.

When they had first met, John's whole-hearted enthusiasm had seemed one of his most attractive qualities. Barbara had been impressed by the thorough research John would invest in any new project. He seemed almost to fall in love with every aspect of a new idea. For instance, gliding had been an early interest. He had read about it, discussed it interminably with experts and, together with other enthusiasts, put a great deal of hard physical work into transforming rough ground into a proper airfield. But John's enthusiasms were not long-lasting and his interest waned before he ever took to the air. There had been several different hobbies since that time, all of them embraced with fervour for some months before the cooling-off period, which was probably instigated by some other fresh idea that attracted his delighted attention. He was certainly not a lazy man but he was difficult to live with, for it seemed that change was the only thing that made him really happy. Although he was clever and hard-working, his achievements seemed to give him no pleasure and dissatisaction was never far away. His prolifertaing enthusiasms were not confined to his hobbies but also to his profession. He had changed his direction and his job several times during their marriag but sadly the optimism and energy which he brought to each new position soon dwindled.

Each time John moved, another house had to be worked on, painted and improved, but decorating was not something Barbara enjoyed. She wondered if she were a really boring person for she was terribly different from her husband. Her interests and hobbies, reading, swimming, sewing and cooking had hardly changed since she was twenty. She had trained as a teacher and looked forward to returning to her profession once the children were older. Change for its own sake held no pleasure for her.

She often felt that dealing with the everyday needs and different personalities of four children, plus John's restlessness had provided her with more change than she was able to cope with.

Now they were in Canada, with another house to deal with and a severe climate which Barbara hated.

Rather late in the day, after thirteen years of marriage, Barbara had realised that more of her energy must go towards protecting her own interests and happiness. It meant changing herself and teaching John that she had changed. It meant reacting with less than the loving approval which she had always tried to give to his constantly renewed plans and shifting goals. Unfortunately by asserting herself, she incurred his anger, which was always so much nearer the surface and so much stormier than her own. She knew only too well the outcome of her lack of enthusiasm and she watched as his face returned to the look of misery and rejection, then quickly darkened to fury and determination.

Bravely and hurriedly she answered him,

"You're talking of a big financial risk, John. You've been used to a regular salary all your life. It wouldn't be like that and you know that you're *slow* with your joinery. You do have a perfect result in the end, but time is so important in business. You have to meet constant deadlines. Besides, doesn't Ottawa have even more snow than Kingston? I couldn't stand more snow, John. I've learned to hate it. I just really look forward to going back to Scotland and the climate I'm used to. I'd really love a *month* of mild rainy days. I find it hard here in both the summer and winter with the kids, you know that. I don't want to make my life in this Canadian climate."

"It was just an idea." His voice was quiet and cold.

"I know, dear."

Though her words were calmly said, she was very uneasy.

She suspected that John was disappointed in this Canadian post. But then he had never seemed to find much pleasure in any of his various jobs. Although he was dedicated and competent and his colleagues spoke warmly of him, he was less complimentary about them. He always spoke to Barbara in general terms of his dissatisfactions at work and she could never make out quite what the problems were.

She had moved to Kingston eleven months ago, much against her will. John had decided that they should come out here at about the same time that Barbara had found she was pregnant with her fourth baby. Barbara was aghast at the idea and for a week, she could not even discuss it with him. However eventually he comforted her with the fact that he would not go out until after the birth. His plan was to go in September for the start of term, get a house ready for the family and come back for her at Christmas. The baby would be four months old and they could all travel out together.

At first, Barbara had considered flatly refusing to go. John had a perfectly good academic job in Glasgow. They had a lovely flat into which a lot of personal and loving labour had gone. For three years she had stripped old wallpaper, scrubbed and painted woodwork, often until one in the morning, as well as adding two babies to the family. Just as the house was almost finished and looking like the home that she thought they had both dreamed about, just as it was ready to live in and be enjoyed as a home without tools and paintpots everywhere, John had noticed the Canadian advertisement and was determined to apply for it. With his unbounded enthusiasm for a new project, he was prepared to abandon this old project of house improvement, almost before it was finished, and start a new life in Canada. With two older daughters of nine and seven, a toddler of two and a half and the new baby, Barbara felt herself not only unwilling, but unable to uproot herself. Her energy was depleted and she wanted to reap some of the benefits of the last three years of hard work. She tried to explain the strength of her feelings to her husband, her dismay at leaving behind the family home that they had worked so hard at, with all its toys and books and paintings. Just as important were her friends, the weekly class she taught, her well-tried domestic help, her friendly mother-in-law and aged grand-mother, not to mention her hopes of returning to her profession in a few years when the baby started school. The sheer amount of work involved in shifting the family from one country to another daunted her.

He appeared to listen to her, but continued with his prepa-rations, flying to Canada for an interview and arranging with an estate agent to rent the flat that they had worked on so lovingly.

When she suggested that she stay in Scotland, he demurred and said that of course he would not leave her. Then he continued with the preparations for departure as though she had not spoken. He was unable to say why he wanted to leave his present job. He refused to discuss it. In fact it was only two months since he had assured her that he was really enjoying this particular work and found a lot of satisfaction dealing with the students.

Now he had changed his mind and wanted to go to Canada.

Reasoned discussion, humour, allegory, tears and anger made no difference to his determination. Because she loved him and the children loved him and a new baby was on the way, she finally accepted the situation. She did not have the energy to stand up to him. She rolled up her sleeves and worked hard towards making it all possible. She worked harder than any pregnant woman in her late thirties might expect to work and she worked with a heavy heart.

It seemed as though this fourth baby and her own health and well-being during pregnancy were of no importance to her husband, just minor incidents in their marriage which must necessarily take a back seat in view of his new venture.

There was still a great deal to be done to the flat if it were to be rented.

Two weeks after the baby was born in August, John left for Canada and Barbara worked harder still. However after six weeks, life suddenly became easier. With the baby in a routine and no last minute changing of plans by John,

Barbara found that she was in control of her life for the first time since she had married. It was wonderful! She led a busy life, but she enjoyed the power to plan and organise her life in her own way. The family was much calmer. John's propensity to procrastinate, coupled with his impulsive decisions and swift temper had often led to last-minute family crises.

Barbara's attitude to her children relaxed and she found herself laughing more. As Christmas approached Barbara was torn between delight at seeing John once again and the horror of leaving her smooth-running life behind. She dreaded to think of starting in some other unknown house and the problems she might encounter as she tried to create a safe and happy environment for the various strands of her family.

The journey had been like a terrible dream. Buffeting winds delayed their flight by hours. It was two am when they arrived in Montreal. The immigration officer was curt and unwelcoming. As she stood holding her baby and swaying with fatigue, answering interminable questions, she wondered if she could fake a fainting spell without hurting the baby.

The heavy automatic car, hired for the final hundred mile drive, added to her sense of unreality, as it skimmed along the snowy roads like an electronic sledge. Once, when they had stopped to rest, the fearful Canadian cold poured threateningly into the car and forced them to continue driving. She had never experienced anything at all like this cold. The sensation was all encompassing and more akin to pain than cold. It reminded her of the Russian stories which she had enjoyed so much as a student, but the reality was terrifying

When they arrived, the house was heated to an unbearable temperature by overly kind neighbours. Their own bedroom proved to be the hottest room in the house while Barbara had always liked a cool bedroom.

The kitchen was unlovely with small windows, a gloomy colour scheme and dark brown counters. Used to a dishwasher, Barbara noted sadly that there was no such luxury and thought longingly of the bright cheerful kitchen at home which had been planned and built with such high hopes and attention to her own wishes.

John clasped her hands and gazing into her eyes, asked imploringly if she thought the house would 'work all right'. Of course she said she was sure that it would. What was the point of telling the truth? She must just make the best of it now they were here.

Although the house was much less spacious than her Glasgow flat, it was more inconvenient, with bedrooms, bathroom and washing machine up a steep flight of fourteen stairs.

The sitting room, with its harsh green walls, was bare of furniture. Bright orange curtains hung at the windows. A depressing nylon carpet in the colour known as 'old gold' covered the floor. Barbara had never come across a nylon carpet before, and she quickly learned that it was a superb generator of static electricity and almost impossible to clean, as the fibres clung malevolently to dirt as well as every small object. Picking up a pin was a struggle. Even worse was the electric shock which passed between her and her children when cuddles or comforting were required. Although the house had many drawbacks, the carpet was to be the chief demon of Barbara's life. She loathed it. The phenomenon of a sharp shock whenever metal was touched was a terribly unpleasant facet of life in a cold climate. And it was fearfully cold. That winter was the worst in Ontario for sixty years. One hundred and forty inches of snow fell and the municipal fathers ran out of money to deal with it.

Because snow is a relatively rare occurrence in Glasgow, Barbara had always enjoyed the beauty and novelty of a walk in fresh snow. But five solid months of living with Canadian snow in its many different forms, taught her to hate the stuff. Walking was always difficult and often impossible with snow that was soft and deep and exhausting, or ice-encrusted and impossibly dangerous, or coldest of all, melted into thick freezing liquid. The cold was so very much more extreme than the worst of British winters that she felt imprisoned with the younger children and although the older girls loved the snow at first, eventually they became bored and irritated by the nuisance and discomfort of it.

Barbara had a morbid dread of falling and breaking an arm and wondered who would look after the children if she were incapacitated.

The house had an ancient and inadequate central heating system and when the baby wakened at five-forty-five each morning, the kitchen thermometer hovered at freezing-point.

In the first few months, the baby and the toddler suffered a series of normal childhood ailments and Barbara worked unbelievably hard, never quite making up for the lost sleep of the transatlantic journey. It seemed as though a wicked fairy had waved a malevolent wand over her pleasantly busy life in Glasgow and substituted a sort of servitude in an ugly inconvenient environment filled with various handicaps and absolutely no treats.

Barbara would often try to shake herself from her depression by thinking of the extreme hardships of the early Canadian pioneers. How very much worse it must have been for them with no corner shop, no fridge or electric cooker, no washing machine, no central heating, no supermarket. What a hell on earth it must have been for them. She could not imagine the hardship they must have suffered. There was no hope for them of returning home. Many did not even survive. Surely she should not complain. Surely her life was vastly more comfortable than that of those first intrepid settlers.

But even comparing her life to those harsh days of old did not help.

Neither did it help that John seemed very dissatisfied with his new job.

Day after day he returned with petulant stories of long useless meetings at which he did little but produce pages of doodles.

Barbara felt she might have been happy to exchange her physically demanding day for a few hours of doodling.

It was at bed-time, two weeks after his carpentry suggestion that, with the look of deep sincerity that she knew so well, he said seriously,

"*You know, you are always in my fantasies.*"

Barbara raised her eyebrows and continued to brush her hair.

"Always a part of them. You are. I mean that."

He came across the room and looking down at her with a gentle and sensitive smile, placed his hands lightly on her shoulders. Barbara's head was bowed to hide her tears, but several dampened her nightgown. She knew his next move so well. He wanted her to raise her head and their eyes would lock in a long meaning look. Far too long. He had always liked that deep gaze to happen between them. When they had first met and there was so much love and emotion, she had accepted the rather theatrical eye contact, but with reservations. She had felt that he extended it far too long and she would always be the first to break it. Sometimes it was hard to stop herself giggling, because honestly the whole exercise was a bit meaningless. He would just look and look and look, until it was embarrassing rather than romantic, awkward rather than reaffirming. Nowadays, after thirteen years of marriage and turmoil, it was stupid and she would not play the game.

His hands dropped to his sides and he repeated,

"You have always been in every one of my fantasies, right up there beside me taking part. Honestly, you have. Always so important."

"What was I? In your fantasies, I mean."

"What d'ye mean, what were you? I suppose you were something different each time. It depended on the fantasy, but *you were always there beside me.*"

"*I* know what I was. I was an adjunct. Just as I am in real life."

"What do you mean, an adjunct?"

His tone was disapproving and superior.

"You know what an adjunct is as well as I do. You were the hero and I was an adjunct. I was the pin in your tie. I was the feather in your hat. I was the parsley on top of the boiled ham... I was... nothing important... I was just an extra in the scenario, I was an adjunct and I'm fed up with being an adjunct."

"I wish you'd stop using that word. You were my mate and of course I was the hero of the fantasy. I expect we are all the heroes of our own fantasies, aren't we. Aren't you the hero, or heroine rather of *your* fantasies? Go on admit it. Of course you are. You must be."

He smiled again, with a paternal encouragement, but her face was not smiling.

"I don't have fantasies any more, John. I don't know

when I last had a fantasy. Life's too busy and too hard, too many little things to do every day and worry about, too many people needing my attention and when I have a moment... I don't... I can't.."

She struggled against the weakness of self-pity, but she was tired and tears filled her eyes.

"Oh, come on now,"

He smiled winningly and gave her a few friendly little taps on the arm, as he would have done to a child.

"Of course you do. Everyone has some little fantasy, I'm sure, just a teeny one even?"

"I DON'T HAVE ANY FUCKING FANTASIES."

She wrenched her arm away and looked straight up into his face with a fierce expression. The tears had dried and only anger was left.

"I've never heard you use that word before" he said quietly, with an echo of reproach in his voice.

"Haven't you? Haven't you?" her voice was getting louder. "I never needed to use it before I came to this bloody house and this fucking climate."

"Sh, sh, the children will hear you!"

"And as for that FUCKING carpet downstairs..." her voice was a fierce whisper.

"Anyway don't you think the kids heard me crying every night those first few months when I was so dead tired? Or perhaps you didn't notice I was crying."

"Of course I noticed"

"And what did you think? What did you feel then? When did I cry before? I hardly ever used to cry."

"I felt sorry for you, of course. I suppose I thought you were having difficulties getting over the birth of the baby... 'baby blues' and that sort of thing. I don't know about those things, do I?"

"Did you notice how hard I had to work every minute of the day? Didn't you see that I was exhausted? You didn't think of trying to do more to help me, physically?"

He walked to the window and stood looking through the thick ice ferns that frosted it, biting his lip.

"Did you? Ever think of helping me, I mean?"

He shrugged in a fatalistic sort of way.

"Adapting to the new department at the University wasn't too easy for me, I suppose."

"Yes, it must have been tough. I remember all those pages of doodles that you produced during conferences with your colleagues."

His face darkened.

"You always seemed to manage fine in Glasgow."

"Yes, with an established house and friends and family and a daily help and a reasonable climate! Yes, I had a wonderful life, but it's not like that here. We were never hard up then either. Buying and furnishing another house was a very big decision to make without my approval and coopera- tion. After a year, we're still living out of cardboard boxes. It's horrible and why don't you help me more now? You're so careless. I hate living in this mess."

She looked around the room where his socks, shirt and sweater lay scattered on the floor,

"Why can't you manage just to throw those things into the dirty clothes basket? My back aches with lifting and picking. Why do you throw everything on the floor always? Please, you just have to throw them in that basket there. You don't have to do anything else. I'll wash and iron them and put them back in drawers, but please just don't treat me like some sort of slave. Don't you think that I have enough picking up to do with four children? I don't know why we came here when you knew I was so much against it, when I felt that it was so difficult. How could you have insisted we come away from our home when we had spent so much energy on it and I had a new baby. I should have been able to enjoy her and I haven't. How could you force me into this situation of overwork, when I was so unwilling and there was no need? And how can you be so bloody fucking untidy all the time?" and the anger gathered again in her stomach and she stood up and kicked the socks and sweater towards the basket.

"I thought you were just fussing because you were preg- nant, I suppose." he mumbled.

She gasped and shook her head, unable to reply.

He took a few deep breaths and moved his neck as though it were uncomfortable.

"And now we're here and I hate it and those damned massive newspapers are piling up in the sitting room on that fucking nylon carpet where you just lay down your apple cores and peach stones, lay them down on the *carpet*. My God, how can you keep doing that? When there is a wastebin there just beside you! When I ask you, when I plead with you... rage at you... I don't know how you can keep *doing* it. Don't you think it stains the carpet? Don't you know it *smells*? and the children follow your example. I'm just an adjunct in your fantasies and in your life, though I'm a bloody hard working and useful adjunct."

She burst into tears and her next words were muffled.

"I don't know what you're saying." His voice was expressionless.

"But I've said it all before and it makes no difference. What's the point in saying it again, John."

"These are all trivialities that you're making such a fuss about. How did they get into a conversation about fantasies. Strikes me a few fantasies would do you good. *Be the best thing for you.*"

Six months later Barbara had recovered some of her normal balance. The second winter had been less severe than the first. Baby Molly was sleeping through the night and Alec had left his tantrums behind. There had been no more talk of a carpentry business in Ottawa. A dishwasher was installed and a neighbouring teenager gave a hand with the housework sometimes. Barbara had met an interesting girl from New York and went swimming with her twice a week, while John seemed delighted to babysit. True, the four children were generally still not in bed when she returned at ten and were possibly watching some highly unsuitable TV, but it was marvellous for Barbara to visit the swimming-pool unencumbered by family. Twice a week she would plough up and down for an hour, renewing her sense of self.

But Barbara still saw her stay in Canada as a limited one. She had stipulated three years and that remained her goal. The deadline of a return to Scotland shimmered like a distant reward and she vowed never to complain about kindly damp weather again.

When their second summer approached, John suggested taking a cabin on Lake Ontario again and Barbara acquiesced, suppressing memories of the previous summer's disasters which had exhausted her for weeks after the holiday... the cleaning of the filthy cabin with a thousand gorging spiders clinging to the ceiling, the stench of dead fish piled on the nearby beach. (These were alewives that died after spawning each year. A natural phenomenon rather than pollution, they were assured by the proprietor, but the smell was terrible). Then there had been the dash to the hospital after Susan's accident with the pony and of course none of it was John's fault, but his reaction of anger and swearing was unhelpful. As for John's obsession with the barbecue, that was as ridiculous as it was ineffectual. When Alec developed an ear infection and it seemed safest to come home, Barbara was ashamed to note that, mixed with her maternal anxiety there was a distinct relief at leaving the awkward cooking arrangements, sagging beds and general discomfort of the summer shack.

Nevertheless, for the sake of the children, she girded her loins and agreed to another holiday on the lake in a different resort and at a different time of year to the suicidal alewife fish.

Two weeks before leaving, they had another argument which though short and quickly resolved, represented a big and enjoyable step for Barbara. For the first time in her life she threw something in anger.

It was a Saturday morning and John was out running, which was a new hobby and happily seemed to help him control his temper.

After finding the weekend papers with their many supplements strewn over the sitting room carpet and picking up fifteen apple cores and five peach stones from the area around the TV where John and the children had been watching cartoons, Barbara went upstairs. There she found their bedroom floor awash with John's clothes, shoes, books and papers. It had the aspect of a room which wished to hide its floor and just at first she was tempted to laugh at the successful and complete coverage of every square inch of wooden boards. However she was trying to prepare for the dubious 'holiday', her back was aching and it really was the last straw.

When John returned, pink, damp and breathless, he was most contrite and assured her that he would tidy up as soon as he had a shower. Barbara busied herself in other parts of the house and baked some scones and a cake. Baking was an occupation which always calmed her.

As she headed upstairs again, she noticed that John was chuckling over the 'funnies' in the sitting room.

The bedroom floor was unchanged, with John's sweaty running togs added to the general melee. Barbara felt weary. It was all so petty and she was so tired. What was the point?

"Those scones smell good. Is lunch nearly ready, darling?"

John's voice sounded from downstairs. How could one love and hate a voice so intensely at the same time, she wondered.

"Can you come up here for a moment John, please"

John bounded up the stairs like a large eager dog.

As the bedside reading-light, the nearest object to hand at the time, soared through the air and crashed to smithereens against the wall, she realised how satisfyingly symbolic it was. Not once in two years had she had the energy or the desire to read at bed-time, while John on the other hand always read for a short time, insisting that he could not sleep without it. Each night, ten minutes after Barbara had fallen into an exhausted sleep, John's book would be dropped on the hard floor with a resounding bang, awakening her to wild heart-thudding, resentful fury. It was his nightly ritual and as with the apple cores on the carpet and the soiled clothes scattered on the floor, no remonstrance, pleading or cross words seemed capable of convincing him of its unnacceptability.

The reading-light was the first of many objects that Barbara enjoyed throwing that summer, and her aim improved considerably, but the marriage was finished before the third winter arrived.

# PARTY CONVERSATION

While holding her gaze, Richard turned his head slightly away from her, smiled a small subtle smile and raised one of his well-marked eyebrows.

It was an expression which he had assumed with considerable success with other women on other occasions and it seemed most effectual when he towered over the female. He was certainly considerably taller than this petite lady. As she looked up at him, he felt satisfied that he had made a good impression.

Richard had not really wanted to come to this house tonight. It had too many memories, some of them pleasant, but others quite horrible.

He had known his host since student days. Their wives, too, were friends, had gone to school together. The two couples had married around the same time and for eleven years, the four of them had been very friendly. Their children were much the same age and there had been shared meals, picnics and barbecues in each other's homes.

Then the break-up with Greta came. He could hardly remember now why it had happened. It just seemed to him that the marriage was finished. It had all been awkward and confused. He felt that Jack and Lily blamed him unfairly for the whole mess. Lily sympathised with Greta and refused to speak to him and he hardly saw Jack for three years. But now that marriage had failed, too, in almost as disastrous and recriminatory a way. As two unattached males, he and Jack had renewed their friendship.

Richard felt faintly self-righteous for he had handed the family home over to Greta with comparatively few squabbles, while Jack had claimed his house as necessary to his business and there were still unpleasant problems to sort out. Of course the fact that Greta's brother was a divorce lawyer had left Richard at a disadvantage.

"Ah, you should have thought of that before!" Jack would say mischievously and rather too often.

At forty-six, Richard knew that he still looked energetic and commanding, if he put his mind to it. His figure was slim and his hair thick. But after a day at the office he would have preferred reading the newspaper or watching television to going to a party where he would drink too much boxed wine and eat predictable and over-salted food from Marks and Spencers. Most of the folk there would be acquaintances that he would just as soon not meet.

However, determined to avoid that looming abyss of middle-age, Richard had gritted his teeth, showered, changed into expensive casual gear and presented himself at Jack's door with a bottle of decent wine and a hearty smile.

He saw the small woman as soon as he entered.

He noticed her partly because she was dressed in a long-sleeved voluminous garment of floating grey fabric. It was a strange dress, but he liked it for that reason. Every other woman present was clad in a black skimpy uniform. To Richard these minimal garments looked exactly like the under-skirt that his mother had worn in the sixties, when he was a small boy. She had called it a petticoat and, long before he learned about Oedipus, he had taken great and terrifying pleasure in watching the smooth creamy skin on her arms and shoulders, as she drifted around the house each morning.

Unfortunately these women lacked that remembered allure. They were mostly too bony, though a few had unsightly fleshy lumps where none should have been. He realised with a strong sense of depression that these women were several years older than that seductive mother that he half-guiltily remembered. Their skin had lost its youthful brightness and elasticity. Richard considered how much better they would look if they had covered themselves up like the little woman in grey. She was certainly attractive and looked younger than the others. Her hair was elegant without the hard sculptured hairdresser look and if she were wearing make-up, it was so skilfully applied as to be invisible. She appeared alert and intelligent and Richard made his way towards her as directly as polite-ness and greetings to friends would allow.

Without introduction or other preliminary, they started to chat like old friends. It was as though she had been awaiting his arrival.

She was even nicer when seen close to. Possibly in her late thirties or early forties, she had soft brown hair, delicate features and perfect teeth, as white as a girl's. She wore a necklace of green stones which seemed close to the colour of her eyes. What he could see of her skin was smooth and slightly tanned as though she had just returned from holiday. Her voice was soft with a trace of accent which he found fascinating though difficult to place. Her name was Amelia.

She was a beautiful woman and Richard was dazzled.

They spoke for more than an hour and Richard was delighted to find her such a great listener. He did most of the speaking, but he could tell that she was enjoying the conversation. She listened with absolute attention. She hung on his every word. She chuckled at amusing anecdotes, she smiled admiringly or tut-tutted when required, she tilted her head and made a sympathetic moue when he spoke of the divorce and his feelings of injustice. She frowned and shook her head when he spoke of the terrible strain of running a successful architectural practice and her eyes sparkled when he spoke of his new and impressive car and its capabilities. Richard was delighted that he had come along tonight. He still had not found out much about Amelia, but it seemed certain that she was a free agent. Any possessive partner would have claimed her much sooner from such an obviously successful rencontre. She was utterly delightful and she obviously found him fascinating too.

Could there be future for them? Even a few weeks of a pleasant affair? Richard felt a sudden wave of self-pity engulf him. His life was terribly lonely and pointless.

Aware of the advantage which his height gave him, he edged nearer to her, forcing her to look up at him more exaggeratedly, then still holding her gaze he turned his head slightly away from her, smiled a small subtle smile and raised a well-shaped eyebrow.

Amelia sneezed loudly and violently.

It was the loudest sneeze that Richard had ever heard.

Then incredibly she sneezed another seven times in quick succession, each explosion an immense shout of noise. As people moved away it gave the impression that the fury of the sneezes was displacing the packed guests.

Richard produced his handkerchief. He was horribly

embarrassed but Amelia was smiling.

"Oh dear!" was all that she said.

"Are you all right? Would you like to go into the garden to recover?"

Richard would have liked to remove himself from the smirks and giggles that he could see on every face. He had always dreaded being the centre of attention.

"No, no. I'm fine. Really. But I should like to sit down somewhere. I hate standing at the best of times but these shoes are fearfully uncomfortable and you're so terribly tall that I have the most awful stiff neck.."

"Oh, I'm so sorry..." Richard was unpleasantly discomfited. The bloom was wiped from their fascinating conversation if she had she been suffering physical discomfort throughout their entire time together.

Richard found an undiscovered sofa in the small study. For years too many children had jumped on it, but at least they were alone. Richard still hoped to regain that first magic atmosphere.

"Are you over your sneezing? Would you like something to eat?"

"No thank you! I try to avoid that prepared rubbish as much as possible... poisonous!"

She sounded snappish and cross.

"I saw fruit there. Some grapes perhaps?"

"No, I really don't want *anything.*"

"Wine?"

She shook her head irritably.

"*No!*"

Richard was confused. He felt that their earlier pleasurable encounter might never have happened. Had he inadvertently said something to offend her? Had those sneezes banished every ounce of romance?

He sat silent, unsure what to say next and it was Amelia who spoke first.

"Have you ever tried shop-lifting?"

"Shop-fitting? Only once or..."

"No, I said shop-*lifting.*"

"Shop-lifting..." Richard was at a complete loss.

"You know what I mean, don't you? Picking up things in shops. Without paying."

"Yes... I know what you mean... but..." Richard's voice was faint and his expression puzzled.

"Have you ever done any shop-lifting?"

"Good Heavens! No, of course I haven't. Well, maybe when I was a kid, sweets and things but never since... of course I haven't. It's stealing. It's illegal."

"What about robbing banks. Have you ever robbed a bank?"

"No," he giggled in a puzzled way, " of course not."

He moved slightly further away from her.

"Are you sure?"

"Of course I'm sure... absolutely never!"

"Or embezzlement? Or Visa cards, I believe there are all sorts of scams with credit card numbers. Have you ever tried that sort of thing?"

There was a faint smile on Amelia's face as she asked these questions and she gazed relentlessly at Richard as she spoke. All the small signs of admiration that she had previously given were no longer visible. Their eyes were now almost on a level and Richard felt his masculine power drain away.

"Never! I would never do anything like that. I don't know what you're getting at. I'm horribly honest. I would never do anything unlawful."

Richard's mind stumbled uneasily over some of his income tax statements, but dismissed them quickly.

Amelia turned her head away and looked out at the garden. She was breathing quickly and she no longer smiled. Her face had a hard quality which Richard could not believe.

He was dumbfounded and truthfully pretty nervous. Was this woman that he had thought so attractive about to propose some criminal activity that they might share? What had he said that would have encouraged her to think such a thing? Nothing. All his talk had pointed in quite another direction, towards his integrity, his kindness and interest in the human condition and his honest success in his profession.

Perhaps she was unstable or even mad?

Amelia suddenly turned fiercely towards him and spoke in a louder voice than he had yet heard her use.

"You were talking before about your illegal activities. You were boasting about them."

"No, no, that's nonsense. You must surely have misunderstood me. I never have been, never would be involved in... anything illegal... or any sort of crime at all."

"Yes, you have. You told me distinctly about driving from London in your new car. You were hardly ever under eighty-five miles an hour, you said. You boasted about it! You touched a hundred several times. You said that, didn't you?"

"Well, of course I said that. Is that what you were meaning by illegal activities? Speeding?"

Richard's release of tension at finding out what she was talking about made him laugh out loud. He smiled widely and shook his head, as he stroked her shoulder paternalistically in his relief at solving the puzzle.

With a violent action, Amelia knocked his hand from her shoulder.

"Don't dare touch me."

She glared at him with such venom that he shrank back from her and measured the distance to the door. It seemed very possible that if the poor woman were mad, he might have to make an undignified but necessary escape. Perhaps she had a weapon concealed in those flowing sleeves?

"Exceeding the speed limit is illegal. Just as illegal as shop-lifting. Isn't it?"

"Oh, I can't agree there, I'm afraid." Richard tried to make his voice airy and amusing but he knew that he was pressed as far away from her on the couch as possible.

"Why not? What's the difference? Explain it to me!"

"Well... I mean for a start, everybody does it, don't they. With a... with a car like mine, for instance, the police *expect* you to add ten miles on or so... to the limit... I'm sure... I mean they're not really surprised if you do. Why, I should say shop-lifting is *entirely* different to a bit of speeding on the motorway. Pretty innocent really... a different kettle of fish altogether, you could say."

He knew his phrases were ill-chosen, but there was a trembling sensation in his hands and he was at pains to hide it from this flushed aggressive woman who had seemed so tender and desirable less than half an hour ago. She seemed to have grown in size, too as she sat there on the couch.

"*There is a difference.*"

"Oh. I'm glad you agree... Amelia."

Richard smiled nervously.

"There's more than one difference. It's very much easier to get away with speeding. Police are not as vigilant at putting a stop to speeding as shopkeepers are at protecting their stock."

"I had never thought of that. I suppose those little tabs that set off electronic alarms at the shop door are quite effective and video cameras too, of course. Those must help. And store detectives, lots of them too... watching people. Yes I must say you have a point... Amelia. You're absolutely spot on there... I would say... ."

Richard smiled again. He was babbling and it was a weak smile, but surely if he were agreeing with her they might finish this night with a semblance of dignity.

"But there is a much bigger difference. Can you guess what it is?"

"No, I... I don't think I can..." With the thought of a concealed weapon in her sleeve, Richard had lost any sense of logic in the conversation.

"Shop-lifting is not life-threatening. That's a big difference, isn't it! It's not even slightly dangerous. You can pocket all sorts of expensive articles and nobody gets killed or even maimed. You could put a two hundred pound cashmere sweater on in the changing room, then hide it under your shirt and walk out of the store and there's no blood or broken bones. There are no screams or moans of agony. There are no terrible fires to burn and disfigure innocent people who were driving at the proper speed. There are no screaming ambulances and flashing lights. There's no blood or entrails or body parts spread across the tarmac. The worst that can happen will happen to the shoplifter himself. He might be marched to the manager's office. Such ignominy! But no pain! Not for him or for law-abiding citizens who happen to be near. Nobody needs to be cut out of a demolished car, while they suffer excruciating pain or feel their life's blood draining away. The shoplifter destroys nothing but his own reputation and he might go to jail, but that is not like being killed outright or sentenced to a wheelchair for the rest of your life, unable to speak. The only person that is hurt in shoplifting is the store owner and he is only hurt in his pocket. It isn't his wife or his child or his independence that he has lost... only his profits."

The last words were whispered and tears were on her cheeks and on Richard's too. In spite of her tears, Amelia's voice had never faltered, had in fact grown stronger until the last phrase. Now it became quiet, yet more insistent.

"Richard, you should not look so shocked at the suggestion that you might indulge in shop-lifting or credit card fraud, fine upstanding citizen and exemplary architect that you consider yourself. Compared to speeding in your beastly powerful car with its possible fatal consequences, Richard, shop-lifting is a minor crime. Though you may be as witty, urbane, sexually irresistible and in your own mind, honest, as you would like to paint yourself, you should remember that it is the results of the crime which determine its importance. Remember, remember that."

She now rose and left the room but Richard had no strength to stand. He slouched across the couch, physically and emotionally numb until the last guest had left.

Jack found him as he put out the lights.

"My God, Richard what have you been drinking? You look terrible, ol' man. Can I help you? I think you should stay here tonight."

But Richard felt that he would be happier in his own flat.

"I'll just wash my face and go, but I'll leave the car."

"Yes, I think that would be wise."

As Richard left the house, he asked,

"By the way, Jack, who was that woman in grey that I was speaking to?"

But Jack could not remember any woman in grey.

"She was attractive, small, fortyish, you must know who I mean. It seemed to me that she had perhaps had some... problems in her life... maybe a tragedy... she was very unhappy. She was in a floating sort of dress and she was... disturbed, I'm sure. Her name was Amelia but I didn't catch her surname. You must know who I mean."

But Jack could not place Amelia and could only remember that 'the birds were all in black and half-naked at that.'

Richard walked home and his Mercedes stood outside Jack's house for a week before it was driven to the dealer's and sold.

# THE BRILLIANT MOMENT

When I was a little girl living in Pittenweem in the war years, I had only a very vague idea of hotels. This ephemeral and idealised perception of what it was like to live in a hotel was probably entirely based on Hollywood musicals. I thought of magnificent foyers, fountain-bedecked and furnished with many couches and potted plants, where a deferential receptionist greeted each guest and asked them to go through the ritual of 'signing the register'. What on earth did that mean? The only register that I knew was the one that the teacher called each morning for the pupils to answer "Here, miss" individually, or, collectively, roar "Absent". But that was just another one of the many unanswered puzzles of childhood. After the signing, the receptionist would summon a smart little uniformed Buttons to carry the many pieces of matching luggage to an elaborate lift, which carried them upwards to a series of splendid rooms, known as a suite. In many of these musicals, Fred Astaire would be tapping his elegant shoes on the polished floor of a magnificent suite, while Ginger Rodgers, in a fur-trimmed negligee, preened in front of enormous mirrors. In the background, generally on a raised platform, rich velvet curtains sheltered a vast bed with sheets, pillows and quilted coverlets, all of glittering satin. Sooner or later a smiling waiter would knock at the door and wheel in a trolley to deliver champagne in a bucket. Of course in spite of their delightful surroundings, there were many complications and quarrels between the couple before the inevitable happy ending and I seldom understood exactly what was happening, but it certainly seemed to me that a holiday in a hotel would be the epitome of luxury and greatly to be desired.

It was an idealised environment which, needless to say, I have never experienced in real life. In fact I have stayed in only a few hotels and most of those have been bland, cramped and unpleasantly redolent of food and nicotine. I generally prefer a holiday apartment but of course then one does not meet the variety of people that are gathered together in a hotel dining room. There is a fascination about such a group which I cannot resist.

It was in the early eighties that I stayed in a small hotel in Yugoslavia.

Poor Yugoslavia! How it has been ravaged and ruined since that time.

My sixteen year old daughter, Sarah and I had decided to take a little adventure abroad and we were staying in a small fishing village on the island of Krk in the north Adriatic. Normally we spent the summer in the family holiday house in Pittenweem and it struck me as amusing that our package holiday should have brought us to a destination which so closely resembled the small villages of the East Neuk. True, there were immense and luxurious hotels on the outskirts of Malente which would have sat uncomfortably on the Fife coast, but the church on the hill, the harbour, the daily catch, the auctioneer and the market were all familiar sights to us. Sadly the night's fishing was meagre compared to the brimming boxes of Pittenweem. The small fish shop near the quay displayed a poor window which was empty by eleven thirty and shuttered for the rest of the day. It was very sad. The one or two fruit shops had half empty boxes and the quality was poor. The town had a general atmosphere of poverty and struggle and I was reminded of my war-time childhood. It was a little depressing. However we had a pleasant room at the top of the hotel. It was the only room with a balcony and we considered ourselves very lucky.

The meals were less fortunate. I am blessed with a tall, energetic daughter who, at sixteen, required regular and adequate nourishment. Each morning we were first in the dining room, often before the staff, and the meals were, like the harvest of the sea, sparse. Sarah would demolish her boiled egg and small piece of toast and look for the next course but there was none. How I longed for a kitchen to boil a pot of porridge or bake some scones to satisfy my poor hungry teenager.

I think that we were the first British tourists to come to that area for some time and they were unsure how to feed our island race. The evening meal was an approximation of soup, meat and two veg. and pudding, but each course was strangely flavoured and insufficient. Probably the poverty of the area had much to do with the imperfections of the meal.

The staff were young and inexperienced and had almost no English and we, the typical monolingual British tourists, were such a mixture of accents that we might have puzzled someone with a much stronger command of the language.

Perhaps it was for the best. Neither staff nor guests could understand a word of what the other said and as the staff kept smiling under a barrage of complaints, the guests were eventually forced into a wry, philosophic acceptance of things as they were.

The holidaymakers certainly were a mixed bag. We came from all corners of the British Isles.

At our first meal, two middle-aged ladies from Manchester sat at our table. They were touring and would stay in our hotel for only three days. They were very talkative about their travels and experiences, describing scenery and architecture with relish and explaining small adventures in great detail. Their shopping excursions must certainly have swelled the economy of many different countries. I thoroughly enjoyed their enthusiasm as it gave me the opportunity to concentrate silently on the excessive bones which mar the fish of Yugoslavia. I could see from Sarah's face that she found their volubility a terrible trial, but her level of tolerance was particularity low at that time.

When the Mancunians left we were alone for a day and silence shrouded our table. I felt quite bereft, as though old friends had departed forever. Against all odds and almost miraculously, I would meet those two ladies again, four years later in a car park in Lyme Regis, when simultaneously we parked side by side in the last two spaces available. I can take no credit for our reunion. They were just two elderly ladies with grey perms and fashionable spectacles who, like myself, were visiting the seaside. The recognition took place because I called my dog to me and one of the ladies recognised my voice! She must have had a wonderfully sharp ear, because as far as I could remember those three days in Yugoslavia, seldom was I given the opportunity to exercise my vocal chords, although, yes, I do remember asking for the salt once.

On our fourth day in Malente, our dinner table was again full when we were joined by a young couple from Ireland.

She was very attractive and wore brightly coloured low-cut dresses, a different dress at each meal. I was impressed and intrigued. Her husband did not always come to the table. He had a 'wake stoamick' she informed me. On her first day on the beach I saw her in a swimsuit and she was turning very pink. I offered her some sunscreen lotion but she waved it away graciously, explaining that she did not believe in such things. By the second evening, her skin was an angry red and the fact that a great deal of it was on view did not help my appetite, though Sarah was unaffected. I offered some cooling cream that I had, but was again spurned.

"Isn't it very painful and tender?" I inquired.

"Sure, it's a little bit fiery but t'will be grand tomorrow when it starts to peel."

It may have felt better next day but it certainly looked much worse. Over her ample shoulders, chest and well-developed arms, the skin was peeling off in long strips. She looked raw. Although these were the days before we knew about the hole in the ozone layer, I was brought up to treat the sun with a great deal of respect and to sunbathe with care. I was aghast that anyone should so abuse their body. Day after day for ten days she worshipped the sun throughout its hottest hours and the various layers of her poor epidermis went through several different stages of horrific disintegration, each one open to our inspection at every meal time.

In answer to my concern she assured me,

"Sure it glows a little bit at night-time, but this skin will all come away an' I'll have jist a lovely tan whin I'm goin' home, you wait an' see."

It was the 'coming away' which I found hard to bear and in order to broaden my horizons and remove my eyes from the nightmare skin, I turned my attention to the neighbouring table. I was surprised to find that both couples were Scottish, though with very different accents. The younger ones, early forties, were from Edinburgh and spoke in the correct, strangulated tones generally attributed to the residents of Morningside.

They were obviously determined Bohemians. The lady's volu-minous attire and generous cascade of beads attested to their unconventionality and in case I was still in any doubt, they almost immediately drew my attention to the fact that they kept an antique shop near the Mound and that they were not married. They rather insisted on the latter fact, however they were charming in their own way. They were obviously very fond of each other and determined to have a good time on holiday. They took advantage of all the organised excursions, boat trips to other islands, walking tours of local beauty spots and even a bus trip to Venice which left at five thirty in the morning and returned at midnight. Their energy was impres-sive though even they found the last a taxing ordeal. They drank wine at lunchtime as well as dinner and often at night went dancing in one of the larger hotels. I admired their energy and their devotion to each other.

The contrast with the other couple was very obvious. They were fifteen or twenty years older and there was a palpable coldness between husband and wife. It was difficult to imagine that they had ever had much in common. Their appearance was almost shockingly different. While she was quiet, small, slim and neat, and dressed each evening in a different, fresh, pretty dress, he was loud, dogmatic, opinion-ated, and shapelessly fat with a shirt-stretching belly. For me, the worst thing was that he seemed to have mislaid his upper dentures. Not only that but as he spoke, and he spoke a great deal, a small inexplicable lump of flesh hung from his toothless upper gum. It was smaller than, but similar to the uvula which no doubt serves an important purpose while it dangles so unattractively above the entrance to the throat. This pink morsel, this pseudo uvula waggled as he spoke and was fascinating in a revolting way. Its very mystery was hypnotising. No doubt its presence was the reason that he did not wear an upper set of teeth.

I wondered how this dainty, fastidious, little woman could stand to be married to such a visually unacceptable bore?

As at breakfast, Sarah and I were always first at table for dinner, on the stroke of seven. And we usually finished first, as Sarah made very short work of her three courses and I was scarcely less business-like with mine. As I had the choice of peeling shoulders or toothless talkers for companions, we would quit the dining room by seven twenty and stroll around the strangely reminiscent harbour. Usually too, we fed some stray cats and kittens in a nearby park, with dry bread and the salty sausage which even Sarah refused. The starving cats refused nothing and when the scraps were demolished their delight in being petted seemed to assuage their hunger pangs.

At eight o'clock Sarah would go dancing and I would seat myself in front of the hotel to watch the nightly promenade. This scene also took me back to Pittenweem, to the days of the Glasgow Fair when a thousand holiday makers doubled the population of the small town for a fortnight. Each night saw a constant parade of all age groups strolling up and down the High Street and the wynds. As long as the weather was clement, crowds would march along the windy cliffs to the swimming pool and then return by way of the 'wee roadie', down the long flight of steps leading to the shore and the harbour. Some would make their way along the quiet seaside path to St Monance or perhaps choose the other direction, past the golf course and the Billowness swimming pool to the bright lights of Anstruther. Some were putting off time until a dance in the town hall started or perhaps the second house of the cinema. Others were waiting for their tea to digest and a fish supper or a poke of chips might be enjoyed. All were dressed in their best and all were there to see and to be seen, with each group keenly observing other groups. There was a constant passing and re-passing of the same groups, groups which would break up, reform and change direction like some laboratory experiment. I found it fascinating.

Those crowded days of my youth were long gone in Scotland but here in Malente, they were recreated and I watched from the hotel terrace, an observer and quite content to be one. Now I was able to analyse and watch the small ruses and conquests, the meaning glance, the loud demanding laugh, the subtle long-continued chase of the shy, the adroit evasion of unwanted attention and, most satisfying to my previously unacknowledged voyeuristic side, the successful pick-up.

As I sat each night, I drank several cups of tea with lemon. There were no pots of tea available and it seemed unfair that my small cup of tea was the same price as a generous glass of brandy or whisky, neither of which beverage has any appeal for me. I could always see and hear the loud toothless man from the dining room at a distant table. He was there every night and showed only too much appreciation of the bargain alcohol. His voice grew louder and more aggressive with each brandy and as the hue of his face and neck deepened, his appearance did not improve. On the fourth night I realised from the accent that his companion, who said little but matched him drink for drink, was the husband of my over-burned Irish friend. His 'wake stoamick' was evidently able to deal with whisky better than food.

Neither wife ever came to the terrace in the evening.

It may seem that I lived a rather lonely life in the evening and I will not deny it, but I was not unhappy. I had three good books to read and the passing parade to watch.

The Bohemian couple asked me to join them one evening in one of the large hotels where there was dancing. Although I was very fond of dancing in my youth, I accepted with some misgivings for in maturity one gets fussier about whose arms are clasped about you.

My goodness! It was an absolutely splendid hotel, quite able to match those luxurious Hollywood dreams that had nourished my youth. I could hardly believe my eyes at the vast staircase, the soaring stained glass windows, marble, stainless steel, beautiful wood! The architect had spared no expense. Elaborate flower arrangements were everywhere. It could not have been more different from our modest and shabby little hotel. To think that it was on the outskirts of such an impoverished fishing village was incredible. I decided that if I returned to Malente, this would certainly be the hotel that I would choose next time. No more bargain package deals for me.

In the foyer a kitsch fountain nervously changed colour every thirty seconds. The hotel guests standing around in groups were preponderantly masculine and many were still in their pristine daytime leisure-wear. As I passed them they

laughed and talked loudly in German. I remembered my
courier saying that many male clubs and professional groups
came from Germany to Malente. It looked as though they
were determined to have a good time when no longer under
the eagle eyes of a hausfrau.

The dancing lounge was less impressive. A small dance
floor was surrounded on three sides by long tables with
benches to sit on, making me think of Sunday school picnics
held indoors because of the rain. It is so inelegant and
awkward to seat yourself in the middle of a bench at a table
that I nearly returned to my hotel at that moment.

When the four musicians started to play, I was again
transported back to my youthful holidays in the East Neuk.
The instruments and the melodies were the same as those
played long-ago in Anstruther town hall at those summer
dances where boys stood sullenly slumped against the wall
on one side, while girls adjusted their hairstyles and giggled
nervously on the other. The wailing electric guitar in this
splendid hotel was just as loud, just as mournful and just as
badly played as the remembered instrument of my youth and
I was amazed to hear so many of the same tunes.

After an hour, no one had asked me to dance. I think I
was almost glad about that although I did think my
Bohemian friend might have danced with me once or even
twice, but perhaps he feared his wife's jealousy. More probably he felt that he had better not start in case I expected an
evening of his attention.

It was stuffy and very loud and I decided that in future a
book on the hotel terrace was infinitely preferable.

At dinner on the sixth day of our holiday I noticed that
the pretty little wife at the next table was alone. I asked
about her husband and she explained, with a sad and meaningful shake of the head, that he was indisposed, which did
not surprise me. I learned that her name was Betty. I sent
Sarah to feed the cats by herself and after the others had left
us, Betty and I stayed in the dining room chatting. In her
husband's absence, she was vivacious and amusing in a way
that I would never have guessed possible. For the first time I
heard her voice properly and was sure that the pleasant
'song' of her accent was that of the East Neuk.

"Yes, I grew up in Anstruther." she replied to my question, "And we lived in Crail until ten years ago. That's a bonny spot. We're on the other side of the Forth now. In North Berwick. It's caulder there and I miss the sun on the beach. I'm often lookin' over and thinkin' of the auld places." The lilt of the Fife coast in her speech was unmistakable.

"Your husband isn't from Fife, is he?"

"Aye, he's from Cellardyke but you'd never guess, would you, he's worked hard at losin' his accent. He's in local government, you know."

She stated this last fact without any emphasis or pride, only as an explanation of his need to change his accent. I thought how much better if he had acquired proper false teeth and improved his image rather than his accent.

I was happy to dismiss him from further conversation. We talked of various subjects and eventually I complimented her on her dresses.

"They are all such pretty colour combinations!"

"Oh I'm glad you like them. I love choosing the fabric. They're all home-made y'know, but I buy quite expensive material and good patterns and I take a lot of trouble to make them as neat as I can. "

"I can see that. They are beautifully made. I thought they were dresses from a very expensive shop."

She laughed loudly and I noticed that, unlike her husband she still had very good teeth.

"I hope your husband appreciates how lucky he is to have a wife that can dress so well and not spend a fortune."

Her face changed immediately and she was silent for nearly two minutes. I wondered if she were trying to control tears and was unsure what to say. Eventually she broke out.

"He doesn't appreciate it one bit and I'm no' sure why he brings me on these holidays. All he wants is drinkin', drinkin'. He's lyin' up there like a pig, sick and miserable. It's aye the same. Why does he no' come away himself if all he wants is drink? We never do the things I'd like to do. We never go for walks or bus runs an' he won't go near the shops. An' he'll never take me dancing. I *love* dancing and he was quite a braw dancer when we were courtin'. There's nothing for me here. I'd be better at hame! I'd be faur happier! But he'll no' let me stay at hame! He's just like a pig up there in his bed. Fu' o' cheap brandy and sick as a pig. An' I've goat tae look efter him!"

She had become quite impassioned and more of her childhood vowels were recognisable in her speech. Suddenly realising that her voice was raised she became embarrassed, although the dining room was by now deserted. She stood and mumbled apologetically.

"I'd better go and see how he's feelin' now."

In the first week Sarah and I explored the town, immediately discovering that there were no sandy beaches. That was rather a disappointment, though neither of us wanted to lie around for long lazy hours. The purchase of a small folding mattress enabled us to have an hour or so of comparatively comfortable sun-bathing each day.

A pleasant path, shaded by large trees wound its way along the edge of the sea with concrete jetties and stony beaches at intervals. It looked as though the stones had been brought to the seaside to create a beach and I thought that they might have found smaller and prettier stones. When I asked the courier where one should swim, she replied, "Oh, just anywhere."

I hesitated for though there was plenty of sea, it seemed difficult to make an arbitrary judgement of the best place to enter the water, for no one else was swimming.

Eventually I took the plunge and was surprised to find the water very cold. Pittenweem has trained me to cold water of course, but this had something extra sharp about it. It almost seemed that there was a stinging on my neck and the underside of my arms where the skin is fine. 'Imagination' I told myself.

However when Sarah joined me in the water she was in no doubt about what was happening. "What the hell is that stinging me? I'm going to get out!"

The courier assured me that she had no idea what could have been stinging us. She had never heard of any such problem before. However, I would learn later that swarms of tiny jellyfish, newly hatched and invisible to the naked eye, were probably the culprits. I continued to brave their miniature attack each day with no more than a slight reddening of the skin to show for it, but Sarah did not swim again.

In the morning we walked along the seaside path, discussing our plans for the day. Where would we eat lunch? This was soon decided as every menu in every hotel or restaurant was exactly the same. We often ate in our own hotel and usually had the same dish of delicious small squid.

On one of our walks we met a snake, five foot long and thicker than a man's wrist. It seemed more afraid of us than we were of it, for it quickly disappeared across the path and into the shrubbery. Sarah at that time, kept a small snake at home and our familiarity with her eight-inch long pet banished, possibly unjustifiably, any fears we might have had of an encounter with the larger creature.

Sarah had made friends with a young man who looked after his uncle's jewellery shop and she was delighted to help him polish and arrange the stock each afternoon, while I was very lazy and read on our balcony or more probably slept.

One day we took a bus journey to Rijeka which was the nearest city. It was very old and strangely reminiscent of Edinburgh with narrow passages, long steep flights of stairs and high retaining walls. I felt quite at home. The shops were more opulent than Malente and we bought delicious strawberries, more than we could eat.

There were many shoe shops in Rijeka and Sarah had been keen to buy a pair of the high-heeled canvas boots which were the favoured footgear of every waitress, though they looked uncomfortable to me, as well as abominably ugly. Fortunately Sarah decided that they were too expensive.

It was a very pleasant day that we spent in the city, but it will be forever marred in our memories by the stressful journey home. For the first ten miles, the bus drove along the edge of a precipice. On the road a thin yellow line was painted ten inches from the cliff-edge presumably to warn drivers of the danger and to keep a reasonable distance from the edge. Our driver however had an old and beloved friend sitting on his left, a friend that he had obviously not seen in many years. Not only had he a lot to tell his friend but he liked to gaze into the other's eyes as he talked. Sarah, who

was seated at the window, watched with pale fascination as
the wheels constantly dipped over the yellow line and came
close to the absolute edge of the tarmac beyond which was a
sheer drop of many hundreds of feet. I was luckier in not
being able to see the veering of the bus, but as I watched
how little attention the driver was paying to the road in
front of him, I too was disturbed and fearful. How glad and
how lucky we felt to descend safely from that bus. Our legs
were almost too weak to carry us back to the hotel.

Sarah and I took two boat trips the following week.

The first excursion was on a small ship and as we joined
the milling crowd to embark, an organ played 'Roll out the
Barrel!', with little rhythm but much cheery power.
Unfortunately this tune is indelibly associated in my mind
with the war years and the unpleasant sing-songs which were
encouraged whenever a crowd of people were gathered
together. The next song would inevitably be "Pack up your
troubles in your old kit bag", or perhaps the maudlin "If you
were the only girl in the world." Then we would move to more
modem ones, "We're going to hang out the washing on the
Siegfried line" or some such other anti-German song, perhaps
one with a more personal and insulting reference to Hitler.
Without a doubt 'Roll out the Barrel!' takes me back more
insistently than any other possible aide-memoire, to those sad
years when Germany was the enemy. So it seemed ironic to
hear that evocative tune when jostling in a crowd of which
eighty per cent was German. Such handsome, polite and good-
natured Germans, each impeccably dressed in sharply pressed
shorts or slacks, their teeth and shirts and fluffy socks so
much whiter than those belonging to other countries, their
beautifully tanned and muscular calves bulging above shining
sandals of leather, leather thicker than the sandals of any
other nation. How ironic and how incredible to be reminded
that these were once the enemy and I waited nervously to see
which tune the unseen organist would play next.

That was a pleasant outing with good food and interesting medieval sights.

The following day we set off in a much smaller boat.
There were around twenty-five passengers and crew. We
were to visit three islands.

The proportion of Germans on board was even higher than the previous day. They were all male and obviously set to enjoy themselves. There was much laughter and beer drinking. One fellow borrowed my scarf and jacket and performed an amusing drag act. Very German.

The first island we visited was mountainous and had at one time been used as a look-out and a fortress to guard the nearby mainland from approaching enemies or pirates. Sarah and I climbed the steep winding pathway to the summit and explored the quaint town that was built there. Then we strolled down, had a swim and dutifully returned to the boat at the proper time arranged for departure.

We waited for fifty minutes because other members of the party had not been so time-conscious. Meanwhile some of the Germans bathed from the boat and I felt rather jealous as the water was blue and inviting. Some even swam right under the boat. I considered that foolhardy in view of the beer that had been consumed. I had vaguely anxious feelings. Something seemed to be not quite right. Why were we so delayed?

We waited patiently and we waited until it was too late to visit the other islands.

Next day the police came to our hotel to interview us. One of the young German passengers had fallen to his death from a cliff on the island!

Had he fallen near that steep pathway that we had climbed? Or in some other more remote corner of the island? Was he pushed? Was it murder? Or just too much beer and foolish horseplay? We will never know.

My courier, an intelligent girl who spoke perfect English, explained to me that because it was the end of the holiday fortnight and everyone was about to go home, there would be no available witnesses. Because the fragile economy was so dependent on the tourist industry, the incident would be hushed up by the police and the media and hurriedly swept under the carpet. Everyone would be glad to have the whole affair stamped 'accidental death'. I could not help thinking about that mourning wife or mother far away in Hamburg or Frankfurt who would never find out exactly what had happened to her darling.

It was sad and sudden and so very unsatisfactory.

A policeman interviewed Sarah and myself. His only questions to me were,

"Was coffee being served on the boat?"

"Yes. "

"What price was a cup of coffee?"

"I'm sorry I can't say, we didn't have coffee."

"What age are you?"

"Fifty-two."

"What does your father do for a living?"

"He's retired."

My father at that time was eighty three.

The shops in Malente had little to offer tourists at that time except postcards and the quaintly carved wooden plates and jugs of that area. We bought some gifts to bring home to friends but for myself I prefer a small natural memento, a piece of driftwood or a pretty stone, but as I have said the beaches were barren and uninteresting. However, on our second last morning, something wonderful, almost miraculous happened. I was swimming about thirty yards offshore. The water was deep and slightly choppy and I was heading for a jutting point of land where I would turn and swim back to the jetty where Sarah was sun-bathing. As far as I could judge this distance equalled half a mile, the length of my normal swim. No one was in the water and no boats were in sight. I was alone and in that delicious communion with the sea and the sky which I enjoy so much. The water was too cold to put my face under the surface and I was ploughing along with an energetic breast stroke when suddenly, a few yards directly ahead of me, I saw a small object floating like a tiny ship in the water. It was an empty shell, a very pretty one and quite large, about two and a half inches in length. It was gaily bobbing on the waves and for its size and vulnerability very far from shore. I grabbed it and felt astonishment and delight in equal measure, but my strongest feelings were of gratitude... gratitude and that quiet awe which a spiritual experience inspires. Surely some sea god or spirit had placed this shell, the only shell that I saw in Yugoslavia, on the surface of the water just where I would find it on my journey towards the point. It must be a special present just for me, for it was so small that if my direction had been altered to the right or the left by a couple of yards, I would have passed it by unnoticed. Where had it come from? And how had it managed to keep afloat on the rough surface of the sea until I secured it?

I swam carefully back to the jetty, using only one arm while I clutched my special gift from Poseidon in my other hand. The jetty stood quite high above the water level and I called Sarah to come over and take my treasure from me before I climbed ashore. In the hand-over, one of us fumbled and the precious shell fell back into the calm water and *immediately filled with water and sank like a stone.* This is not a tragedy, dear reader, the water was very clear and only six or seven feet deep and, though the shell had come to rest amongst a bed of broken glass, I dived down and retrieved it. The fact that I had to face this small dangerous labour only made the shell more precious to me. That whole experience merits the title of this story. My shell now sits beside my bed and I only have to glimpse it to relive and delight in that brilliant moment.

That night after dinner, Betty caught my eye.

"I've got a wee gadget to make tea in my room, would you like a cup?"

I agreed at once and I admit that I hoped to find out more about this ill-assorted couple. I was not disappointed.

We sat on a little couch in the corridor outside their room, while Betty poured us each a cup of tea from a small pot which she had evidently brought with her. All her movements were deft and pleasant to watch and as she worked she told me that Jim was 'sleeping it off ' in their bedroom.

"He's dead to the world in there! I thought last week would have been enough for him but ye see, he never learns. He meets up wi' someone as bad as himself an' the drink's that cheap here an' they just sit an' drink an' blether an' drink an'..."

She sighed deeply and shook ber head. There was nothing I could say.

"And we have to catch the early plane tomorrow!"

"He'll be feeling better by then I'm sure."

"Aye, mebbe. Ye see, it's forty years we've been married

but," she bit her lower lip and paused for several seconds, "But our marriage has never... quite... it's never come right somehow, never..."

Again she hesitated and sighed.

"Jelled?" I suggested.

"Aye, that's just what I mean. Never jelled. No, it's never jelled. I never wanted to marry him, ye know. It was just the way it happened. An' we've never been happy, never really happy."

She sat for a long time looking back into those forty unhappy years and I was unwilling to break the silence. Eventually I spoke.

"Have you children?"

"No, no children."

She smiled wanly.

"How did you meet?"

"Oh, he was aye aboot the hoose, he was my older brither's freend. They were in the same class at the Waid Academy."

I noticed that the accent of her youth had become stronger as she remembered those days.

"Ah niver liked him much then but Ah suppose he liked me."

She described how it had all started in 1941. Her two older brothers were abroad in the forces, her sister was working in England in the Land Army. Betty, the baby of the family, was longing for the day when her calling up papers would arrive and her own adventure would begin. She thought she would like to join the ATS, and imagined herself dressed in the smart, neatly tailored khaki uniform, marching along in perfect step with other young women. She had watched newsreels and films and knew that the rest of the world was waiting to be explored. Anstruther was a boring place that she wanted to leave as soon as possible and her opportunity would arrive with her official summons to do her duty by her country.

"But ye see, when ma papers arrived, ma mither wis awfy upset. Oh, she went an awfy length! She wis greetin' an' greetin' an' she couldnae stop. Ye see Ah wis the youngest and she wis swiert tae lose me an' a'. For oors she sat greetin', greetin'. An' Ah wis greetin' 'cos she wis greetin'.

Then Jim arrived, he wis aye drappin' in for a cup o' tea. He wisnae in the services, he had awfy flat feet and he worked on the railway and that wis supposed to be important work, I think. Anyway, he had niver been called up. Ah don't know if it worried him or no'. He asked us whit wis wrang an' when ma mither explained, he smiled an' said,

"There's nae problem wi' that, Mrs Todd, we'll soon fix that fur ye. I'll just mairry Betty an' she'll no' need tae gang away if she's ma wife!"

He looked that triumphant an' ma mither was that pleased and laughin' an' noddin' her heed an' cuddlin' me an' cuddlin' Jim an' cryin' wi' happiness. Ah jist couldnae say a word. Ah wis jist a lassie in ma teens, remember, and awfy fond o' ma mither. An' Ah wis jist dumb. It wis the last thing on earth that Ah wantit, but Ah couldnae fight it. Ah jist couldnae disappint ma mither, but she did a bad deed that day an' Ah wis foolish to gang along with it. Ah wis weak, Ah suppose, an' awfy young. An' ye see, he wis right determined. He had aye wantit me. An' he goat me. But it wisnae a love marriage, an' as you say, it's never jelled." She sighed, "An' all ma silly wee dreams o' adventure melted clean awa'. Or, at least... Ah hid tae throw them oot the windae. There's another half cup here, if ye'd like it."

This story, so full of pathos and waste, had been told in a stolid unemotional tone and her stoicism impressed me with more pity than tears might have done.

I compared her life to my own which, although it has had its share of vicissitudes, has also a wealth of happy and delightful memories to call to mind, as all lives should have. I longed to ask her if there had been happy moments in the sad colourless life that she had described, but felt the question would be too crass and intrusive and too terrible if the answer were 'no'. My curiosity was again satisfied without asking because, after pouring my tea, she resumed talking with her speech reverting to its previous, more correct pronunciation, though the melodious inflection would always betray her East coast upbringing.

"There *was* one adventure that I had."

She smiled dreamily and I felt a great relief that she had some pleasant memory to recall and to relive.

"It was a few years ago, about nine or ten, maybe. We were in Vienna and by the fourth day, as per usual, Jim had to take to his bed, though, mind you, the drink wasn't as cheap there as it is here.

Anyway I was all on my own wanderin' round the big hotel, when I saw an excursion advertised for that afternoon and I just decided to leave him to suffer, and bought myself a ticket. It was dear, too, really expensive it seemed to me, but I just thought of whit he wis throwin' doon his throat an' bought it an' *that was the best spent money of my life!*"

We both laughed and I urged her to tell me where she had gone.

"Well, there were only eight of us on the excursion, all ladies, and the guide. He was a really handsome big chap, very tall and slim, with thick dark hair and a wee moustache. He spoke perfect English and he was so polite and gallant and oh yes, he had lovely teeth. Really lovely, big and white.

Well, we went in a wee toty bus and we visited three different places. There was a castle and an art gallery an' they were both lovely, but the last place was easily the best. Oh it was *so bonny*, ye've no idea. It was the hall where they used to have the big balls in olden times. Ye went up a great big staircase, all marble and gilt and a thick, thick red carpet and there were flowers everywhere, just everywhere, in big bowls and golden boxes. The flowers were nearly a' pink and white but some red roses too. Just masses of flowers every way you looked and you could smell them, oh, the perfume was lovely. Then we came into this enormous big ballroom with crystal shandyleers and big paintin's on the walls and *more* flowers in big fancy urns and gold everywhere and an orchestra playing. I counted *sixty men* in that orchestra, all in their black and white evening dress. Oh! they were that smart and lovely. So handsome, ivery one. They were playing Strauss waltzes. Och, I can't tell you how grand it all was. There seemed to be an awful lot of violins an' their bows were all goin' up and down at the same time. It was just wonderful. The guide sat us down at a table and ordered wine and we all had a wee glass. It was delicious wine. I've never tasted wine like it before or since, but maybe it was just that everything else was so special. The tablecloth seemed extra white and stiff and there was a big bowl full of pink rosebuds on the table. Oh yes, and we had wee cakes to eat with our wine, just plain wee sponge cakes, like fairy cakes y'know. An' they were delicious. Well next thing, six beautiful ladies in big old-fashioned ball gowns came out of a door at one side... it was like something you'd see in a film y'know... and their six partners came from the other side, they were all in tail coats and they took their partners and waltzed round and round the floor. And the dresses were swingin' out and the tail coats were swingin' out and it was so beautiful and so exciting. I've always loved dancing and specially an old fashioned waltz, if you can get a good partner. Oh and when they all reversed together and started turning the other way, I felt it was me! I felt it was me reversing. I always loved reversing, do you dance yourself? Well, you'll know what I mean without me telling you. But ye didn't meet many that could do it, did ye. Harry would never try. And when they danced past, the perfume of the flowers got stronger and you could hear the sound of the silk dresses rustlin' an' whizzin' through the air and when they whirled close by, you could feel the breeze on your cheek!"

"You're describing it so well that I feel I was there myself!"

"Ah well, but that wasn't the best of it, even!"

Her cheeks were pink and as she laughed delightedly, it was hard to believe that she must be nearly sixty, for she looked as young as a twenty year old.

"The dancers went away out the hall, they'd be needin' a rest I think, but the orchestra played on. Then our guide stood up, and I never found out his name and I'm awful sorry about that, and he said, "Would any of you ladies care to dance?" and he looked straight at me! An' though I'm usually shy, I just stood up right away. Quick as a wink! An' the next thing, there we were, just him and me, there were others later too, but to begin with it was just him and me on that enormous floor waltzing to that great big orchestra. An' I was wearing just the right kind of dress, too, with a big full skirt. An' we went whirlin' round and round and round from one end to the other, with the lights sparkling and the gold glittering. It was so exciting I can't tell you. I can't describe it. Oh he was a lovely dancer, too, so smooth and so strong... and when he reversed, that was just – oh, it was just *perfection*."

   She closed her eyes and sighed happily and I felt a great joy that she had that wonderful memory to treasure, for every lifetime should have at least one moment of brilliance.

# PICASSO OF THE WESTERN ISLES

You must read a page or two before you meet the epony-mous hero, for I wish to set the scene properly and it would be a shame to miss out any one of the eccentric personalities who helped bring this amazing tale to my notice.

Picture a large and fine stone-built house on a hill, looking southwards over the sea. It dates perhaps from the early eighteen hundreds and was built for the minister of this lonely parish. The windows sparkle and the paintwork on doors and windows glistens. A large smooth lawn with care-fully chosen shrubs and roses lies in front of the house. Window boxes hold vivid geraniums and a few pieces of the better type of wooden garden furniture are tastefully assem-bled for those who love to sit in the fresh air. Nowadays it is a Country House Hotel and its quiet conventional chintzy elegance might feature in any House and Garden magazine. The host and hostess are from the South and welcome their guests with cultivated diphthongs.

A narrow road, edged on either side with tall beech trees, leads gently up hill to the house. The surrounding fields are filled with somnolent sheep and playful lambs.

A fascinating tale lurks behind this conventional, civilised comfort, for after the time of the respectable though austere manse, there were many years of neglect and ruin before the house became, for a short period, the scene of passions worthy of the Greek drama.

The peninsula of Ardnamurchan is a thinly populated and in places almost barren area on the extreme west of Scotland. It can have, at times, the softest of warm climates because of the Gulf Stream which caresses its entire coastline, but it can also experience the wildest Atlantic storms, with blasting winds of hurricane force. The soil is poor over much of the peninsula and only in certain areas will you find the sort of rich agriculture that we are used to in other parts of Scotland.

However the wild vegetation is magnificent. The narrow twisting roads are lined with massy banks of ferns, purple rhododendrons and trees sculptured and tortured into fascinating shapes by the wind. Great slashes of yellow broom bombard the eye with colour as you drive along and in May when I have often visited, the beauty is incredible. Any direction will provide a picture for those intent on capturing this beauty in paint or film, the only problem is which view to choose. May is also a desirable time as that terrible West coast scourge, the midge, has not yet arrived on the scene.

The first time that I visited the house described above, I was with an old school friend, Elizabeth, a rather solitary lady in her fifties, with no close family around her. She had discovered this charming hotel some years previously, had made friends with the Browns, the English couple who now owned it and had returned several times to holiday here.

The journey from Glasgow to Ardnamurchan is long and requires several changes, including a ferry ride. As Elizabeth had not been very well, I offered to drive her there and she in turn invited me to stay in this very luxurious nest for a night or two. It was quite an experience and much more like being a guest in a private home than in a hotel. My tiny bedroom was absolutely charming with fragrant toiletries, lace curtains, embroidered pillowslips and an exquisitely padded patchwork bedspread. I learned that this last artefact was an example of our hostess's employment in the long, dark, windy hours of winter when the hotel closed. We were invited to visit her special room, where shelves were piled with pastel tinted fabric, fat bales of padding and all the accoutrements for patching and puffing. Personalised bedspreads were her speciality and Elizabeth had ordered one to match her bedroom. She later complained to me that it was far more expensive than she had thought it would be, but then Elizabeth is an academic who assures me she 'cannot sew on a button' and so is unaware of the hours of skilled patience required for any craft.

There were seven other guests and that evening we met in the sitting room for sherry at seven o'clock. How very civilised it all was! It was like an old fashioned stage set. A fire burned in the hearth and a well-behaved cat lay sleeping on the rug. We chatted to each other like old friends and I could see how important this sort of holiday was to Elizabeth. I knew that she had once holidayed at a hotel for a week without speaking to anyone at all except the waiter.

It was an interesting group. An American couple, who were completely in love with Scotland and had visited many times before, were 'island hopping'. The harbour for the Kilchoan ferry from Mull was within walking distance. Two young couples were driving through the Highlands, celebrating their first year of marriage, the wives outrageously glamorous and the husbands energetic and self confident. A quiet scholarly gentleman had left his yacht moored in some harbour and spent some days exploring the mainland by bus. Tomorrow he would return to Mull by ferry.

Mr Brown, mein host, entered with an air of importance, carrying the evening menu. As he looked us all over severely, he gave the impression of a headmaster taking school assembly. Somewhat peremptorily he called for silence. Everyone stopped talking and sat up rather straighter, holding their sherry glasses carefully. We were all obviously well brought up.

He started to go through the menu, offering and explaining choices in didactic detail. Humorous questions were not well received. At one point the man on my right interrupted with a slightly jocular comment. There was a prolonged silence while Mr Brown frowned then regained his composure and found his place in the menu. It was rather boring and we exchanged meaningful glances with each other and there was at least one suppressed giggle.

At last he invited us to follow him to the dining room. I expected that we might have to go in single file with 'no talking'.

The dining room was Georgian and charming. The decor was perfect for the room, rich yet subdued. Polished mahogany, fresh flowers and shining silver each glittered in its own individual way. A fire burned in the large fireplace at one end of the room. An ornate mirror stood above the mantelpiece, reflecting the table with its snowy cloth and silver cutlery.

"This room is where the marriages were held when it was the manse, just here in front of the fireplace." Mr Brown informed us.

I could picture the simple Highland ceremony. It would be conducted in Gaelic and in most cases there would be little in the way of marriage finery, because this was never a wealthy area. Perhaps a finely knitted shoulder shawl would be the only enhancement of the workaday dress of some crofter's daughter on her wedding day.

I had to admit that they had provided a splendid abode for their minister. But of course the minister was then a very important person in the community. I wondered how many parishioners had travelled miles over the primitive roads each Sunday to attend the service and I also marvelled at where the money had come from to adorn the house with such excellent woodwork and elaborate plasterwork. It was a puzzle. My imaginings added to the pleasure of the evening.

It was certainly a lovely room. We all sat at one large table and while Mrs Brown worked culinary wonders in the kitchen, Mr Brown served the various courses. It seemed very like a private house party.

From the starter of local prawns, through the perfectly roasted Spring lamb and new potatoes, to the rich dessert of raspberry cake and cream, it was a delicious meal. Elizabeth bloomed as the young husbands flirted with the older ladies. The Americans could not find enough good things to say about all aspects of our country. The conversation was amusing and intelligent, or certainly seemed so at the time. Perhaps the accompanying wines helped to sharpen our wit.

Throughout the evening I was aware of those other meals of long ago, when the minister and his wife and family were no doubt served more simple fare by a young Highland lass. How different it must have been. I felt their disapproving shades were perhaps hovering near this modern self-indulgent group with their several bottles of wine, loud laughter and decadent discussion of books and plays.

The next night we had an entirely different group of people for dinner, This seems to be the way with the Country House Hotel which caters for the restless and the wealthy, those who are always on the move.

Just at first I was disappointed. The previous night had been so successful, I would have been happy for an encore.

However this group, although mostly elderly, was just as much fun and as it turned out, highly informative.

The reading of the menu in the sitting room was accomplished with as much serious purpose and lack of humour as before and we moved into the dining room.

The aspect of the dining room seemed changed by the older faces around the table.

The meal was again excellent, but the conversation was more subdued and less general.

I was fortunate enough to sit next to a wonderful conversationalist. He was a local man, husband of the postmistress and driver of the school bus. He had been very kind to Elizabeth the previous year driving her to the ferry on several occasions and she had invited the couple to dinner that night. I shall call him Alec and his wife, Mary.

Alec was the thread that bound together the small villages and lonely cottages of the sparsely populated Ardnamurchan peninsula. He was a compendium of the ancient history and the modern gossip of Ardnamurchan. In driving back and forth along the twenty six miles of twisting and often single track roads between the Corran Ferry and Sanna Bay, Alec learned of all the important happenings, births, marriages, deaths, weddings and possibly many other darker deeds in the area. I expect he knew every scattered inhabitant of Ardnamurchan. He was able to give me news of friends in Salen with whom I had lost touch for thirty years, now sadly dead. He was familiar with another friend of mine who had a holiday house at Sanna Bay, the wonderful sandy stretch at the extreme point of Ardnamurchan and the most western point of Scotland. This friend lives mostly on the East coast, where he is respectfully known as Sir Kenneth.

"Oh yes, yes! That will be Kenny." said Alec.

It was from Alec that I learned the colourful story of John Cochrane, the previous and very different tenant of the manse.

For many years, since Alec had come over from Mull as a boy, the manse had lain empty. A bungalow in the village of Kilchoan housed the minister more conveniently and comfortably. In the large old house on the hill, the windows were dirty, some were broken, slates were blown from the roof, the garden was overgrown and it seemed as though it must lie derelict until it fell down.

"It was a shame, indeed," said Alec in his soft accent, "It got a bad name too. Ghosts, you know. Well, I never saw any myself, but there were stories of strange lights flitting around the rooms at night. I don't really believe in that sort of thing at all, but you know it was so lonely up here on the hill. Well, people stopped coming near it, or even walking by."

"It's difficult to imagine this luxurious house in such a state of disrepair. My goodness! The Browns must have had a lot of work to do when they took it over" I exclaimed.

"Well, certainly they have worked very hard, the two of them, very, very hard. I'll give them that, but it wasn't due to the Browns that the house was saved. Oh no, it was nearly a ruin at one time, you know, and it was another man altogether, John Cochrane, who saved it from disintegration. He worked hard, indeed he did. And his wife. And his wife's mother, too. They were the ones that saw the potential of the house and rescued it. They were just in time, too, for it was very far gone indeed, when they moved in. I don't know what they paid for it, very little, I expect. John never had much money that I could see. But he was a character, was John. He was determined too. I don't even know where he came from, and that's unusual around here! It would certainly be one of the islands, the smaller ones. He was a true West Coast fellow." Alec smiled and winked.

"The people here always like to be sure of where your grandparents and your great grandparents were born. Anyway, John was from the islands somewhere. He and the two women got off the ferry one day and walked up the hill and went all around the big house peering in the windows. And the next thing was, they had moved in. My goodness, those women were wonderful workers! How hard the two of them worked. I don't know what hold he had over them, but he used them like two slaves. They were scrubbing and washing and painting the whole long day. Nor was he idle, himself. He was up on the roof replacing slates and he was mending windows and cutting the front lawn, which was like a hayfield. Mind you, he was a wee bit eccentric and it was said, although I did not see it myself, but when he was up on the roof, he was only wearing his underdrawers. Perhaps the weather was very warm that summer. Certainly people spoke plenty *about* him without being very friendly *towards* him, if you understand what I mean. It was even said that when he cut the grass he was not even wearing his underdrawers, only his Wellington boots. But then the road is quite far away and they might not have seen him too clearly."

Alec took an appreciative swig of the excellent malt whisky, then continued,

"I must say that people took to walking along that road much more often than previously, and they weren't looking at the seaview either... oh yes, there was plenty of talk about them up there on the hill. The house slowly got smartened up but the Cochranes did not mix very much with the rest of us. They were too busy... and he had an ancient Vauxhall car that rattled back and forth to Fort William for food and the many, many gallons of paint. I don't know where he got the money for the paint, but I expect he hoped to do quite well with bed and breakfast, for he had his two slaves there... unfortunately the tourist season was past by the time the house was presentable. Then word got about that he was painting pictures. He was an artist! Now we had never guessed that at all. But he was seen down on the shore putting very thick paint in very bright colours on a board. Thon canvas kind that the real artists use. Not that I'm saying he wasn't a real artist, but we had never known that he was an artist, until he started painting pictures with these bright colours. The lady that saw him painting, old Annie McPhee, said she had never in all her born days seen a picture like that. But then she has lived in her wee croft all her life and I don't suppose she has seen many pictures at all.

The next thing was, John Cochrane put an advertisement in the Post Office window,

'ARTIST'S MODEL WANTED,
YOUNG WOMAN WHO IS NOT THIN PREFERRED'

Mary, that's my wife sitting at the other end of the table there, was reluctant for she did not know quite what he wanted. She had heard that artists' models are often sitting

without their clothes on and she said she did not want to be
involved in anything like that. However, I said that if he paid
his fifty pence for the week's advertisement, his money was
as good as anyone else's. And right enough, within the week,
he had a model! Young Jack McLean's wife, Jenny applied to
be the artist's model. And certainly no one could call Jenny
McLean thin, for she's a very well-padded lass and always
has been. You can easy see she enjoys her food. You know,
she came to the Post Office first and asked Mary if Mr
Cochrane expected her to take her clothes off and Mary was
very embarrassed and had no idea what to say to the girl.
And Mary blamed me greatly for allowing the advertisement
to be put in the window in the first place. Of course Mary
usually does blame me, when things go wrong. I expect that
is what husbands are for. However, Jenny answered the
advertisement and went to the old manse and sat for her
picture and it seemed that he was quite happy for her to
remain clothed. To begin with, anyway. And it must have
been a rest for her, just sitting there, for Jack's farm has never
thrived and I'm sure it would break the heart of the strongest
woman. Anyway, everyone was anxious to see the pictures he
was painting of Jenny, but we never got a chance, and week
after week she spent days at the manse. It seems that perhaps
he got tired of painting her with her clothes on, for I believe
that eventually she started to take them off. Whether she took
them all off at once, or only an item here and there, I don't
know. But after a few months, I am afraid she was spending
her nights at the old manse, as well her days and poor Jack
was left alone in his failing farm. And I doubt that Jenny was
doing much housework up at the manse because there were
two hard working women already there to do it. But then,
quite soon, Mrs Cochrane and her old mother packed up and
moved out the manse and left the district altogether.

And you could not blame them really could you, for it
was a bit much to expect them to stay and work so hard,
when he was painting all day long and had a different lady in
his bed at night?"

Alec finished his whisky and graciously accepted another
dram.

"So what happened then?" I asked.

"Well, quite soon John and Jenny left too. I think perhaps the people were all talking too much. And looking at them in a funny way when they went out, you know. So the pair of them went off to one of the smaller islands and took over the post office there. A very, very wee post office it is, too.

Ah! But when he had gone away! *That* is when we saw what his painting was like! If you will believe me, he had *covered* the walls with paintings. All over the house, *in every room*, there were these pictures painted on the walls."

"What were they like? Were they good?" I wondered. I was fascinated.

"They were like *nothing* I have ever seen in my whole long life! They were *very bright* colours... and very... *well not just what you might want to be looking at every day.* This room now for example..."

He cast his eye round the sedate Georgian dining room and his eyes grew larger and his eyebrows lifted almost to his hairline.

"If you will believe me, there were dancing figures, men and women, all around these walls, near as big as real life and waving their long arms about and kickin' their long legs up and *not a stitch of clothing amongst them!* And some of the faces were very queer like, with funny eyes and noses all away to the side. I'm thinking they were a wee bit like the pictures thon Picasso man paints. Not natural looking at all. Oh no. Not a bit natural. No, no. Never.

I was speechless and looked around the room trying to visualise those wild, colourful dancers, naked and erotic. It took an almost impossible leap of the imagination to picture this sedate room so transformed.

"Yes and there were painted scenes in other rooms that I won't describe to a decent young lady like yourself."

I was in my fifties at the time.

"But what happened to them all?" I asked. "Were they just painted over? Did nobody photograph them?"

As an artist, it seemed appalling to me that perhaps a hidden genius had bloomed unseen, a Scottish answer to Picasso, Matisse or Chagall. How sad that his work, his magnum opus had been wiped away before he could find recognition. The man must certainly have had a great artistic urge. Whether he had talent or not we would now never know.

"Yes, I think someone took some photos, but I don't know. It wasn't me certainly. Those pictures could never have stayed in the house, oh no, no. Not those pictures. And I wouldn't even like to have those photos myself, no, not even wrapped in brown paper and hidden in a drawer, in my own home. No I wouldn't".

I tried to hide my smile at his righteous horror and asked,

"And what happened to John Cochrane? Did you ever hear any more about him? Did he still paint in the very small post office?"

"Well there was a wee bit of a scandal about that too, I heard. Nearly two years later, Jenny was calling herself Mrs Cochrane, whether legally or not I wouldn't like to say. And she was upset by a very large telephone bill that came in from BT. And when she came to look at it, she found that there were telephone calls, long, long-lasting calls and many of them, from their post office to several different ladies on different islands up and down the West Coast... Inner and Outer Hebrides! You must understand John Cochrane was a ladies' man and he had his boat, and one lady at a time was never enough for him, I suppose. Well, when Jenny got to the root of it, she was *so angry*, she pulled the whole telephone mechanism right off the wall! Then she packed her bags and left. I don't know where she went. The problem was that that was the only telephone on the island and so it caused a lot of inconvenience and the islanders weren't pleased and you can't blame them. I think John left pretty soon after she did.

"And what happened to him then?"

"Well I know for sure he came to Edinburgh for a while and he was reciting Burns at evening dinners, special dinners for tourists you know. And I heard he was dressed up to the nines in the full Highland rigout. Then after that was stopped, for he was always a man that liked his whisky and often took a drop too much, I believe he moved on to the medieval banquets, I think you call them, where he was dressed up like a bard of olden days, with ragged clothes and long flowing hair. And a real beard, too. And he was singing and perhaps he was dancing as well, I don't rightly know, but I wouldn't be surprised. But that was some years ago now and what has happened to him since, I cannot tell you.

Alec paused and shaking his head, gazed sadly into his empty glass. Then he looked up with a bright smile and added, "But, never fear! John will be all right, I think, for he can turn his hand to anything."